the Last Minute

NISSA HARLOW

NIMBLE HOPE
PUBLISHING

ISBN: 978-1-7777446-4-9

Published in Canada by Nimble Hope Publishing

Cover and book design by Nissa Harlow

To those who came before me.
Thank you for your lives . . .
and your names.

1

A New (Old) House

I HADN'T WANTED TO MOVE IN THE FIRST PLACE. BUT, BEING the kid in the family, I hadn't had much of a say in the matter. Sure, my parents had asked me, but I could tell they'd wanted me to say, "Yes, get me out of here, away from these memories." I quite liked the memories, thanks, and had wanted to stay put, but I'd felt kind of outnumbered and I hadn't wanted to add another layer of stress to what had already been an awful summer by refusing to go.

"You'll love it," they kept saying, though I think they were really trying to convince themselves. "You can have your own room." They said that like it was a good thing. Like I'd always secretly wanted my own room and had never gotten my way because I'd deferred to Jade. But that was just their assumption and not really the truth. Sure, our styles had clashed, and I'd gotten annoyed by having to pick up her clothes all the time because she'd apparently been incapable of putting them in the hamper that was in the closet literally two steps away from her bed, but I'd never really thought much about having my own space. We'd shared a room. If you went back far enough, we'd even shared a womb. I wasn't going to suddenly say, after seventeen years, that I wanted to go solo.

Now, though, I had no choice. So, as I stood in the doorway to the third-floor bedroom, I tried to imagine how I wanted the space to look. That vision was a long way off from what I saw in front of me.

My bed had been brought up, but it was still in pieces, the headboard and base leaning against the wall; the mattress sat on the floor. It was only a single bed—there hadn't been room for two of anything bigger before—but it was comfortable. The bare wood floors were clean and smooth, belying the age of the rest of the house; they'd apparently only been put in recently. Through the window opposite the door, I could see part of the sloping lawn that led down to the trees at the edge of the property. There was a small stream down there, or so Mom had said. Even from where I stood, I could tell the grass needed mowing.

The house had been empty for a few years after the last owners had moved away. My parents had gotten some kind of great deal, which had made me wonder—aloud—if we were going to find a nasty surprise in the basement: a drug lab, equipment for printing money, or even a few bodies. I'd been informed, with some carefully measured looks of exasperated disdain, that there was nothing in the basement except for a furnace, a hot water tank, and a washer and dryer. I'd managed to turn that into a complaint, too, when I found out I would have to lug my clothes down three flights of stairs every time I wanted to do laundry. Dad had just said that I would end up with really strong legs.

As I heard steps on the landing behind me, I shuffled out of the way so the movers could bring in the dresser. It was huge, taking two sweaty (smelly) guys to manoeuvre it through the doorway. When they asked me where I wanted it, I pointed at the wall to the right, where it would face the bed. They set it down gently, mindful of the floorboards, and pulled off the protective blankets. Then they shuffled back out again in their little paper booties. I walked over to the dresser and ran my fingers over the edges. On the right was the scratch that Jade had made when she'd slammed down her laptop during an argument with me over Christmas break. (Luckily, the computer had fared better than the dresser.) On the left, I could just make out the discolouration of the wood where I'd left a sweaty glass of lemonade when we were ten. It was more than a ring . . . but I'd compensated by covering it up with a decorative scarf. Mom hadn't even noticed until years later, and by then we were able to get away with saying we couldn't remember how it had happened. Jade had never tattled on me, even though she knew. Mom knew who'd done it, too, since that was my side of the dresser and, back then, Jade and I had been *really* serious about keeping to our own sides. When you live in such close proximity for so long, you really do need to have some ground rules.

But the entire dresser was mine now. I doubted I'd be able to fill it, especially since my new room also had a decent-sized closet. Abandoning the dresser, I walked over there and pulled open the door with its glass knob. The little hidey-hole was tucked under the sloping roof so that one side angled down toward the floor, but there was still enough space beside where the clothes would hang for me to store some of my stuff. At least my snowshoes.

"Ivy!" Mom shouted. "Are you up there?"

"Yeah." *Where else would I be?* I wondered as I slipped back out into the hallway. A glance into the bathroom showed me that it was still empty. The box with all my toiletries and hair stuff hadn't been brought up yet. I hurried down the stairs, my sock feet padding against the runner, and sort of skidded down the hallway on the second floor. Our old house had had carpet pretty much everywhere; the hard floors were going to take some getting used to.

By the time I made it down to the first floor, Mom was stepping out of the kitchen and taking a big breath. I realized she'd been about to yell for me again when she smiled and swallowed the shout. Her blond hair was pulled back in a messy ponytail. I rarely ever saw her like this, in jeans and a t-shirt; she looked almost as awkward as a cat wearing a jumpsuit. Linley Ross was impeccable . . . or, at least, she looked that way as she smiled out at the world from benches and bus-stop ads: not a hair out of place, not a wrinkle in her clothes, and not a hint of yellow in her glittering smile. At that moment, though, dishevelled by a moving day, she just looked like my mom. I could almost imagine her baking cookies with me and Jade, the way she'd done every year just before Christmas, her cheeks smeared with flour, her fingers with chocolate. Although, we'd never gotten to sample many of the results; they'd tended to end up at open houses for the potential buyers.

"Well?" she asked. "How do you like it?"

"It's fine," I said, peering past her into the kitchen. I'd yet to really explore the house, and had pretty much just run upstairs to check out my room as soon as we'd stepped in the door and slipped off our shoes. I could see Dad, also in jeans, leaning on the island, his phone pressed to his ear as he sipped at a cup of coffee. "Priorities," I muttered.

"What?"

"You got the coffeemaker working already."

"I hope that's not a complaint. You do use it, too." She tucked some escaped wisps of hair behind her ears as she walked past me toward the front of the house. The door was open, letting in the warm, late-summer air. Boxes were stacked around the foyer, not quite in the way, but certainly not in places that you'd want to leave them permanently. Out at the street, I could see and hear the guys struggling to bring something else out of the truck. Probably the dining room table. For as long as I could remember, my parents had always joked about it. It was large enough to seat twelve. The most we'd ever had sitting there at once was seven, including three grandparents. Now . . . the number of diners was down to three.

"Find your stuff and take it up," Mom said, prying open one of the boxes labelled KITCHEN.

"Right now?"

"I don't want this stuff sitting here for days. Let's go."

With a sigh, I approached the boxes and tried to find the ones that I'd labelled when I'd packed up all my things. There were six, mostly clothes and shoes, but one had some of my picture frames and participation ribbons and other stuff I used for decorating my room. And, of course, most of my boxes had other boxes stacked on top of them. By the time I'd unearthed them all and brought them to the foot of the stairs, my arms were aching. I let out a groan as I stared up toward the second level.

"They're just stairs," Mom said. "Your old bedroom was on the second floor."

"Yeah, but I didn't have to lug up a million boxes every time."

"Six boxes," she pointed out. "And you only have to do it once. It'll take a few trips, but you can do it."

"Can't Dad help me?"

"No, because he's going to be helping me."

"If he ever gets off the phone."

"He's working, Ivy. You know that."

I didn't say anything. Instead, I picked up the first box—a fairly light one that held my bathroom stuff—and started up the stairs. Slowly. If I wanted to make it, I needed to pace myself.

On the second floor, I peered into the two bedrooms. One already had Mom and Dad's bed inside, set up and everything. The bedding was folded in a neat pile at the foot. Past the main bathroom—which was shared by both bedrooms—was a second, slightly smaller space that they would be using as an office. It was still pretty empty; the huge, two-person desk they'd had before definitely wouldn't have fit, so they were going to be getting something else. A couple of file cabinets crouched just inside the door. A printer sat idle on top of one of them. The rest of the room was bare.

I adjusted my grip on the box and began my ascent to the third floor. When I got there, I was tempted to just dump the box on the toilet lid and go back for the rest. But I needed a bit of a break. So I opened up the box and started transferring my stuff to its new home. The bathroom was a decent size, and I had a feeling that the third floor was probably intended to be the master suite. Mom had insisted I take it for myself, though. That meant I got a newly renovated bathroom with a large, step-in shower and plenty of counter space. Below the sink were a number of drawers and cupboards, into which I put my stuff: makeup, hair dryer, straightener, products, and accessories. I stuck the bottles of body wash and shampoo into the built-in caddy in the shower, and when that was done, I took the empty box back out into the hall. Something flickered out of the corner of my eye, and I quickly turned toward my bedroom. But whatever it was—if it had been any-thing at all—was gone. *Probably a bird*, I told myself, and, sure enough, just as I was about to turn away, I saw the flicker of shadow again as something—possibly a crow—swooped just outside my bedroom window. A moment later, I heard the scrabble of bird talons on the gutter.

Empty box dangling from one hand, I made my way back down the stairs, ready to continue my unwanted workout.

DAD ORDERED CHINESE FOR DINNER AND WENT TO PICK IT up, leaving me and Mom to lie on the floor in the empty foyer, exhausted. My legs had started shaking after taking up the fourth box, and after the fifth, my hands had started to do the same thing. Now my arms were burning, and I knew that wasn't even the worst of it; I would probably wake up in agony the next day.

"I think I'm too tired to hold chopsticks," I said.

"So use a fork." Mom's eyes were closed. A shaft of light from the setting sun cut through the glass panel in the front door, casting its glow over her face.

"I can't. It's Chinese food. Jade will tease—" The words were out before I could stop them. "Sorry."

"Don't apologize," she said, her voice overly measured and soft, and that just made me want to apologize all over again. "You're allowed to talk about her. You *should* talk about her."

"I'm not going to, if it makes you sad."

She opened her eyes and turned her head to frown at me. "Ivy, it would make me even sadder if you felt you couldn't talk about your own twin."

I shrugged my shoulders, hearing them slide on the smooth floor, and stared up at the ceiling. "Dad better remember to get extra soy sauce packets."

"We've never ordered from this place before. You might not need them."

"I probably will." With a sigh, I laced my fingers together over my stomach. "We should've just ordered from Garden Palace. At least we know what we're getting from them."

"Your father doesn't want to drive twenty-five minutes out of his way when there's a perfectly good restaurant just a few blocks down the street."

"You don't know it's perfectly good. It might be perfectly awful."

"Well, if it is, you have my permission to complain. But we won't know until we try it." She sat up and smoothed back her hair. She'd been doing that all day, and it hadn't really helped; so much of her hair had escaped its elastic that it looked like she'd styled it days ago. As she reached back to grab the ponytail for tweaking, she frowned . . . and then froze. With a shake of her head, she stood up. "That's him," she said.

"I didn't hear anything."

"I saw his headlights." She tilted her head at the door, then nodded at me. "Up you get. Go wash your hands and—"

"Mom. I don't need to be told."

She was still frowning as I stood up, and as she looked into my face, the expression only deepened. "I know," she said quietly.

Then why did you say it? I wanted to ask. I stopped myself just in time, knowing how rude that would sound. Besides, I already kind of knew the answer. She'd been in super-parent mode for the last few months. I wasn't sure if it was some compensation thing, a way of proving that she was, in fact, a good mother. Not that I had any doubt about that. My therapist, Jean, had said that Mom might've been feeling guilty, even though there was really no reason for her to feel that way. These things happened. You couldn't predict them. And if you couldn't predict them, you couldn't logically blame yourself, either.

Our dishes had been unpacked, but they were still sitting on the counter, waiting to be washed and put away. Mom busied herself cleaning three plates and three forks (even though I knew I'd want to use the cheap wooden chopsticks that would come with the food, no matter how tired I was). I set the table in the cozy little breakfast nook that looked out over the backyard. From that angle, I could see how bad the lawn really was.

"Vaughan will be wanting to get to that tomorrow," Mom said when she saw where I was looking. She set down a glass of water at each of the places, then paused beside me as I continued to stare out into the yard. The wooden fences that marked the edges of the property curved down toward the trees at the bottom of the hill.

"How big is this stream?" I asked.

She shook her head. "Not very. It's mostly a trickle. We had a look the first time we viewed this place, and it wasn't that impressive. You might soak your ankles if you tried to wade across."

"Any fish?"

She turned to me, and, when I glanced at her, I saw that she was giving me a strange look. "You don't fish."

"Yeah, Mom, I know. I'm just asking. I barely know anything about this place. Or this neighbourhood."

As she slid onto the far side of the banquette, she snorted. "You make it sound like we've taken you to another planet."

"Different school district. So, basically . . ."

She looked so sad then that I knew I'd crossed a line. I quickly sat down and reached for my glass.

"Never mind. This'll be good. Nobody here knows about Jade, so . . ."

She tilted her head with a frown. "Are you going to tell them?"

"If they ask." I took a long swallow of water and set the glass back down. "If I make any friends at all."

She sighed and reached across the table to gently touch my hand. She could've admonished me for not trying to make more friends in recent years. But that would've just been rubbing salt in the wound, and she knew it. I hadn't needed anyone but Jade. As it had turned out, my sister hadn't felt quite the same way. There was a reason I hadn't been there when—

"Let's eat!" Dad said, appearing in the kitchen with a couple of plastic bags. "The smell has been driving me nuts all the way home."

"Is that good or bad?" Mom asked, which made him laugh.

"Good. Really good."

"What took you so long? I saw you drive up a few minutes ago."

He plopped the bags on the island and began to pull out the white cardboard boxes and tubs. "I couldn't get the garage door to open. I'll have to get someone to take a look at it."

"So where's the car?"

He tilted his head. "In front of the garage."

"There are crows around," I said. "It might get pooped on."

"Great." He shook his head, and his hair didn't move a millimetre. Unlike Mom, he still looked like he'd just stepped out of one of their ads. From the neck up, anyway. He transferred all the containers to the table, then slid onto the seat next to Mom.

We spent the next few minutes in near silence as we filled our plates with the fragrant food. There was fried rice, deep-fried eggplant, spring rolls, broccoli in black bean sauce, sweet-and-sour tofu, and mixed-vegetable chow mein. I could see the soy sauce packets where Dad had left them on the counter, but it turned out I didn't need them. The food was plenty flavourful as it was.

"So," he said, "are you all moved in?"

"Yeah, right. I don't even have a place to sleep tonight."

"Your mattress is fine," Mom said. "It won't kill you to have it on the floor for one night."

Dad shook his head. "We'll put the frame together after dinner."

"We?" I asked, the word coming out on an exhausted groan. "On second thought, the mattress is fine."

"Lord, will the to-do list ever end?" Mom asked as she stabbed at a saucy piece of broccoli with a splintery-looking chopstick.

"We knew there would be a few things to do," Dad said. "This place has been sitting empty for three years."

"Why didn't it sell?" I asked. Both of them looked at me in surprise. "It's a reasonable question," I said. "Is there something wrong with it?"

"It's been *empty* for three years," Mom said. "It hasn't been on the market for three years."

"Oh." Frowning, I pulled up a tangle of noodles with my chopsticks. "Why not?"

"The sellers weren't ready, I guess."

"That's weird, right?"

Dad chuckled. "Yes, it's a little weird. But you'd be surprised how much weirder things can get in the world of real estate."

"Remember the buyer who wouldn't look at anything except properties that faced west?" Mom asked.

"Or the couple who refused to buy that house that was otherwise perfect because the gable had an acute angle?"

"Don't forget the guy who wanted the bathroom to have an exterior door."

"Is that even a thing?" I asked.

"I've seen it a few times," Mom said. "Usually when the property has a pool. This guy just wanted to . . ." She trailed off, frowning.

Dad shook his head. "We're still not sure," he admitted. He'd almost finished his food and was staring wistfully at the half-empty containers. "Are you two going to want any more chow mein?"

"I will," I said quickly, because I knew well enough that if we let him have free rein, we'd go without. He took another small serving for himself and proceeded to eat it in two forkfuls.

"Have you got everything ready for Tuesday?" Mom asked. I shrugged.

"I guess."

"A new school," Dad said. "Exciting."

"Yeah. A brand-new school for my last year of high school. Fun."

"You know Dana offered to let you live at her place during the week if you wanted to stay at your old school," Mom said, referring to our old next-door neighbour.

"Mom, she's like eighty."

"So?"

"So, I'd probably cramp her style."

Mom smiled and shook her head.

"And what if the school checks?" I went on. "It's totally obvious we're not related."

"Why do you have to be related?"

I rolled my eyes. "Forget it, okay? I don't need to go live with the cat lady. I don't want to spend the next year with allergies from—" Shaking my head, I stared down at the remains of my dinner and studiously picked at the grains of rice with my chopsticks.

"Ivy . . ." Mom began, but I reached for my water and downed half the glass so I'd have something to do. And so I wouldn't have to look at her.

"Can I be excused?" I asked when I'd finished with my transparent charade. "I at least want to get some sheets on the mattress."

"You don't want any more chow mein?" Dad asked, looking really worried. I shook my head.

"You can have it." I slid out from the banquette and grabbed my plate.

"I'll do that," Mom said, her voice gentler than it needed to be. I dropped the plate back on the table and scurried for the door. "Do you want your fortune cookie?"

I almost said no, but then all I could think about was how Jade and I had eaten ours, snapping each one open together—like a wishbone—with the fortune going to the person holding the biggest piece of cookie. Jade had probably saved every single little strip of paper she'd ever gotten; I'd found them after the memorial when I'd gone through some of the stuff under her bed. She'd had quite a collection, since she'd won most of the fortunes.

I turned on the ball of my foot and headed back to the island, then reached into the bag and grabbed one of the cookies from the white paper sack. Then I practically ran for my room. All the way up two flights of stairs. When I reached my destination, I closed the door behind me and went to sit on the edge of the mattress. If I squinted and looked at my hands just right, I could imagine that one of them was Jade's. The cookie broke easily, crumbling under my touch, and a smattering of crumbs dusted the floor. I grabbed a larger piece that had broken off and popped it into my mouth as I pulled the little strip of paper from the cookie half in my right hand.

You will soon help someone in need.

"Yeah," I muttered. "I'll probably be washing crow poop off Dad's car tomorrow. Thanks for stating the obvious."

I stood up, placed the fortune on the dresser, and proceeded to eat the rest of the cookie. Then I went in search of my bedding.

2

In the Cafeteria

BY LUNCHTIME ON THE SECOND DAY OF SCHOOL, I'D COME to the conclusion that Mom and Dad had either not done their research about the area (which was unlikely), or they just hadn't thought living in such an affluent area would be an issue. It wasn't like we were poor, but it was hard not to notice the way people were dressed and the kinds of cars so many of the students were driving. My style tended more toward a retro-vintage look, which didn't exactly fall in line with the sleek, chic, and flashy fashions that the others (especially the girls) were wearing. On Wednesday, as I sat by myself in the cafeteria and ate leftover pizza from the night before (Mom and Dad had been in takeout mode for much of the summer; I wasn't sure why I'd thought that would suddenly change), I quietly watched the other students, trying to determine which ones looked approachable.

If Jade had been there, she would've just rolled her eyes and dragged me over to the nearest group of kids, introduced herself, and had a handful of new contacts in her phone within minutes. She probably also would've been a lot less judgemental. I realized I was discounting an awful lot of the people who walked past based on the type of bag they were carrying or the shoes they were wearing. Somewhat ashamed of my snap judgements, I took a closer look at the pair of girls at the next table. Groups of two were always risky. I'd found that out the hard way at summer camp when we were thirteen. Gemma and Stanleigh had been nice enough, but I'd soon learned that when you were dealing with best friends, you were always going to be the odd one out. Despite the fact that we'd shared a cabin and they'd tried to include me, it had just never worked; I hadn't shared their history, and I couldn't understand even a fraction of their inside jokes.

Beyond the two girls who seemed to be having a lunch of energy drinks and French fries (which, let's face it, was pretty fearless; they were a definite "maybe") was a table full of boys who were playing some sort of game that involved aiming bits of food at each other's open mouths. They were probably my age, since I recognized a couple of them from my classes, but they sure didn't look it.

Swivelling casually in my seat, I glanced at the table behind me, which was an interesting mix of guys and girls (and one kid that I wasn't sure about, but who had their hair dyed an awesome shade of lemon yellow); some had books open in front of them, others were playing with their phones, and a seemingly passionate couple was busy with their tongues. One boy on the end looked either bored or tired; he sat with his head propped on one hand, his eyes closed. A half-eaten salad rested on the table in front of him.

Wake up, I thought, simply for my own amusement. So it startled me when his eyes popped open and he saw me staring. I quickly turned back around and refocused on my slice of pizza.

"You're new, aren't you?" a voice asked. I looked up to find the two energy-drink girls looking at me. I wasn't sure which one had spoken, but I nodded anyway. The taller one—a pretty girl with smooth, almost-black hair—waved her hand, beckoning me over.

"Come and sit with us," she said, and based on her pronounced accent, I realized that her friend had been the one to speak before. Since there was really no reason to refuse, I gathered up my plastic container with my half-eaten pizza slice and walked over to their table. The other girl slid aside on the bench to make room for me. She was shorter and heavier than her friend, with overly curled blond hair and mascara so heavy that it looked like she had spiders crawling around her vibrant blue eyes. She smiled as I sat down.

"I'm Marissa," she said. "But you can call me Rissa."

"Okay. Hi."

She laughed. "And you are?"

"Ivy," I said quickly, hoping these girls didn't already think I was a bit slow.

"I'm Bo," the dark-haired girl said. "But you can call me Eunice."

"Why?" I asked, which made Rissa laugh again, and I realized I was not making the best impression. "I mean, what's wrong with Bo?"

"That's what I keep asking her," Rissa said.

Eunice smoothed her hair back over her shoulders with both hands. "My family chose new Canadian names when we came here."

I wasn't sure I would've called "Eunice" a particularly new name, Canadian or not. It sounded like someone's great-great-grandma to me. But I was named after a creeping vine that had a reputation for destroying masonry; I really wasn't one to talk.

"So, Ivy," Rissa said, "are you new to the area? Or just to the school?"

"Just the school," I said. "We lived in Cedar Valley before."

"Why would you come here?"

"What's wrong with here?"

"Nothing," Eunice said, giving Rissa an annoyed look. "It's nice."

"It's snob-central, is what it is," Rissa said, turning back to me. "I'm sure you've noticed."

"Is it?"

"Well, you were sitting all by yourself, surrounded by dozens of kids who couldn't be bothered to talk to you." She paused to glance at her phone, which was vibrating on the table in front of her. With a frown, she swiped her finger across the screen before turning back to me. "So. Need some friends?"

I laughed nervously. "Is it that obvious?"

"Well, it is to me. But I notice things." She suddenly reached across the table and grabbed Eunice's phone out of her hands.

"Rissa!"

"Where's your schedule?"

With a sigh, Eunice took back her phone and found the requested item, while Rissa did the same.

"Get yours out, Ivy. Let's see if we have any classes together."

I found the schedule I'd been e-mailed and the three of us huddled together over the table so we could see all the phones at once. It turned out that I had only one class with Eunice (Biology) but I had four with Rissa, including the two that afternoon: French and Canadian History.

"Good!" Rissa cried when she saw the overlap. "Now I have someone to fall asleep with when Mr. Sharma starts droning about prime ministers and Parliament. I had him last year. He really has a knack for putting students to sleep."

"Great," I muttered.

"It is. Just do the reading, and you'll be fine. And you can catch up on your sleep during class."

Eunice sniffed and shook her head as she put her phone back down on the table.

"Have you two known each other for a long time?" I asked.

"Two years," she said.

"Yeah, we're not BFFs or anything, if that's what you're worried about." Rissa tugged at one of her stiff curls. "I mean, we are, but not the exclusionary kind."

"What does that mean?" Eunice asked, her brow creasing over her dark eyes.

"Just that we're open to having other friends," Rissa said. "Aren't we?"

Eunice nodded and smiled in my direction. "Yes."

"I love your hair colour," Rissa said, changing the subject with dizzying speed. "Is it natural?"

"Yeah . . ." I said. "Why? Isn't yours?"

She shook her head. "Not exactly. It's blond, but not *this* blond." She pulled a curl forward and waggled it up and down. "Last year, I tried a new brand of dye, and I ended up looking like Sailor."

"Who?"

She pointed over toward the crowded table. I figured she meant the kid with the lemon-yellow hair. "Last year, it was orange. Like, orange-orange. Not like yours." She dropped her own hair so she could slide a strand of mine through her fingers. "I always wished I was a redhead."

"We're no fun in the sun."

She laughed and gave my hair a gentle tug. "Yeah, but you don't have to spend tons to get your hair looking like this. It's already awesome."

"So, was Sailor's hair tomato red the year before?" I asked. Rissa blinked, then smiled.

"No. Bright pink. But, yeah. You figured out the pattern. I think they're working their way through the whole rainbow." She turned to better see the table with its eclectic mix of kids and edged a little closer to me so she could keep her voice down. "They're non-binary. They-them."

"Okay."

"As for the rest of them, they're all cis and mostly straight . . . except for Tim. He's gay." She pointed to the boy sitting between the couple—who were still making out—and Sailor. His brown hair, which was shaved on the sides and fairly long on top, was defying gravity with so much product that I wondered how long it took him to rinse it all out when he showered. "Lucie and Josh are *not* gay, but that's pretty obvious. I swear, one of these days, they're going to swallow each other's tongues." She spent the next few seconds attaching names to faces, and I despaired of being able to keep track of them all.

"Who's the guy about to fall asleep in his salad?" I asked when she finally stopped for a breath.

"Oh. That's Kemp," she said, lowering her voice to a whisper for some reason. It certainly wasn't for his benefit; if he could sleep with all the echoing noise of the cafeteria, one more voice wasn't going to make that much of a difference. "Eunice has a thing for him, so—"

"No, I don't," Eunice said, which caused Rissa to twist around in her seat to give her friend a disbelieving look.

"Yeah, sure. Show me your phone."

Eunice grasped the device and brought it to her chest. Rissa just smiled and shook her head as she turned back to me and leaned in close.

"She's got his picture as her lock screen."

"Are they a couple?"

"No, because she's too shy to go talk to him," she said, casting a glance over at Eunice, "and she won't let me break the ice for her."

I looked over at the boy, who appeared to have fallen fast asleep. He wavered a little as his head balanced on his hand. If he wasn't careful, he was going to end up having to blow salad dressing out of his nose. "Does he have narcolepsy?"

"I don't know. Maybe. He probably has PTSD or something.

His brother died a few years ago, and he was supposedly with him at the time. That would mess anybody up."

So would not *being there*, I thought, but I kept it to myself. So there was at least one person at that school who might've been able to relate to what I'd gone through earlier that summer. Not that I was about to walk over there and say something like, "Hey, my sibling died, too. Want to be friends?"

"They never did figure out what happened," Rissa said. Eunice grunted, and I felt the thump as something hit the underside of the bench we were sitting on. Rissa turned with a frown. "What?"

"Kemp didn't do anything."

"So they say." She shook her head and turned to me. "I mean, he doesn't *seem* like the type, but isn't that always how it is? Family and neighbours are always like, 'He seemed like such a nice guy! He wouldn't do anything like that.'"

"He didn't," Eunice said.

"You don't go splashing around in a river in the middle of the night and expect people to think you're innocent."

"What?" I asked. Rissa shook her head.

"I don't know what they were doing. But Austin—that was his name—hit his head and drowned or something. Like, what's a seventeen-year-old guy doing playing in a river at midnight? And what's his little brother doing with him? I mean . . . it's kind of weird."

It did seem weird, although I didn't think it sounded that suspicious. If Kemp and his brother had been anything like me and Jade, they would've done a lot of stuff together. Even stuff they probably shouldn't have been doing.

"I remember Austin," Rissa said, reaching for her energy drink. But as soon as she lifted it, she gave it a woeful shake and set the empty can back on the table. "Kemp and I were in grade eight. Eunice wasn't here yet. If she *had* been," she said, casting a wicked glance in her friend's direction, "she totally would've been crushing on the other brother."

Eunice shook her head. Rissa just grinned.

"Yes, you would have. Austin was *hot*. If you ever get close to Kemp," she said to me, "check out his eyelashes. Then imagine them multiplied by ten. That's what Austin's were like."

Even from where I sat, I could see that Kemp's were pretty impressive. With his head slightly bowed and his eyes closed, he was showing them off to full effect. Rissa giggled a little as we both watched his head make a slow slide off his hand, heading for the table. He jerked and caught himself, just before he could do a face-plant in his salad. Nobody at his table seemed to notice; they were all busy talking to each other or engrossed with their phones. He stood, picked up his plate, and headed for the recycling bins near the door.

"Too bad," Rissa said, swivelling around in her seat to face Eunice again. Her friend's gaze was fixed on the retreating boy; she didn't turn her attention back to us until he'd disappeared through the doors.

"Do you have any classes with him?" I asked her. She nodded, smiling.

"Math."

"Which isn't great," Rissa said, "because Eunice is like the only Asian kid in history who's terrible at it." She leaned closer to my ear. "Which means she finished last year with a B-plus."

Eunice shook her head, as if the reminder were too much to bear.

"I nearly failed it," I admitted. "Maybe you could help me."

She smiled and nodded, but then the warning bell chimed and Rissa let out a huge sigh.

"Back to hell," she said.

"Why?" I asked. "Is the teacher for French bad, too?"

She shook her head as we all stood up. I stuffed the last bit of pizza into my mouth and put the empty container back in my bag while the girls gathered up their garbage. "It's school," she said. "It all sucks."

I smiled a little to myself. Maybe it wouldn't suck as hard as I'd thought it would, now that I'd met a couple of people who might one day become my friends.

3

Two Dead Boys

FRENCH TURNED OUT TO BE OKAY, BUT CANADIAN HISTORY was just as bad as Rissa had implied. I spent much of the first class defacing the edge of one of my new binders, uncharacteristically bored. There was something about the teacher's voice that was almost soporific, and I was surprised that I didn't hear a chorus of thumps behind me as people passed out and their heads hit their desks.

After it was over, Rissa and I exchanged contact info, and I headed outside to wait for Dad. Our house was close enough that I could walk—and I *would* be walking—but he and Mom had offered to drive me to school and pick me up for the first week. I wasn't about to turn them down.

Dad spent the drive as he usually did, talking into the otherwise-silent air in the car as a disembodied voice filtered through the speaker of his phone that was clamped to the dashboard. Work stuff. I pawed through my bag, double-checking to make sure I'd brought all the required books home to do my homework. Seeing everything that I needed, I pulled out my phone and did a quick search on the names Rissa had mentioned. I also added "accident" and "death" as keywords. The findings were sparse; other than a short blurb on one of those memorial sites, there was just one small article from what looked like the local paper.

Austin Hayes, age seventeen, had been taken off life support about a week after drowning in Smokefish Creek . . . wherever that was. The article didn't say, so I assumed that meant the location would've been familiar to locals. I was about to look it up, when Dad pulled into our driveway and up to the garage door. I slid my phone back into my bag and unbuckled my seatbelt.

"Going somewhere?" Dad asked. For a moment, I thought he was still talking to his phone. When I realized he wasn't, I paused, my hand already on the door handle.

"Yeah . . . Into the house?"

"I'm putting the car in the garage."

"Looks like it."

He frowned and jabbed the button on the automatic opener clipped to the visor.

"Is that supposed to do something?"

"I paid nearly two-hundred bucks to make sure it would." With a grunt, he shook his head, grabbed the opener as he shut off the car, and pulled his keys from the ignition. I left him to wrestle his phone from the dashboard as I slid out of the car and headed for the front door.

The house was quiet when I got inside, and Mom's favourite pair of shoes—the ones she claimed were lucky, so she wore them to every showing—weren't by the front door. I stopped in the kitchen to deposit my empty pizza container in the dishwasher, then grabbed a bowl of cereal before I headed upstairs. Dad followed and left me on the second floor as he disappeared into their office. There was still no desk, so I saw him settle himself on the floor with his laptop just as I began the final climb.

My room was at least starting to look like a bedroom and not so much like a storage locker. Dad had helped me put my bed together the day after we moved in, and it looked a lot better as a piece of furniture than it had in pieces. My fake stained-glass lamp (which was actually just plastic) sat on my bedside table. I dug my phone out of my bag, plugged it in, and set it down beside the lamp. Then I pulled out all my books and tossed them on the bed before grabbing my laptop from where it was charging on the dresser and settling down on top of the chenille bedspread.

I always liked to get my homework out of the way. Even if it took hours. But, as I opened up my laptop and reached for the battered-looking Chemistry text, I found that I was distracted. My curiosity had been piqued, and I just had to know more.

So I procrastinated, feeling guilty the whole time. Jade would've rolled her eyes and told me to live a little. That would have been easy for her to say; everything had come so easily to my sister. Her grades had always been better than mine. She hadn't needed to study as long or as hard as me to get a similar grade. That ease with which she'd glided through school had made me envious since we were little. We were identical twins, after all. What had come easily for her should have come just as easily for me.

As my laptop started up, I was suddenly confronted with the photograph of the both of us that I'd chosen as my background screen. *Have I really not used this since June?* I wondered.

I supposed not, because I didn't recall feeling my heart squeeze the way it was at that moment as I looked at the two of us. Yes, we were identical twins . . . but you wouldn't have known it from the way we presented ourselves. While I looked much the same as I had since we were little—with my red hair cut into a long bob with bangs, and the thick-rimmed glasses that Dad said reminded him of a pair his father had had when he was young—Jade had gone for another look altogether. Her hair had been cut into a short pixie style, dyed blue-black. The glasses had been replaced by coloured contacts, which meant that even our eyes looked different: Mine were our natural light brown, hers a vibrant blue. She'd spent hours every few months getting her eyebrows and eyelashes tinted, as if she'd somehow been ashamed of her natural complexion . . . and, I'd sometimes felt, the twin who'd reminded her of how she'd used to look.

Before I did anything else, I changed the background screen, swapping out the picture of us for a photo of a brilliant pink flower we'd spotted on the way to the library. It still reminded me of her, but then, almost all of the photos I'd taken would have. I hadn't taken any over the summer, though those probably would've been tainted by a different kind of memory.

I brought up a search engine and, armed with Austin's full name and the name of the place he'd had the accident, did a more thorough search. The results yielded little more than before, but I did find a picture of the guy. He didn't look that much like Kemp (although, I hadn't gotten a great look in the cafeteria). The eyelashes were pretty impressive, though. Aside from that, he had black hair and dark blue eyes, as well as heavy eyebrows that seemed to hint at a Mediterranean or Middle Eastern background.

Having exhausted those results, I did another search, this time on the creek itself. Smokefish was just one of many that ran through the local area. Nothing special. I found a basic map showing the local creeks, but there was nothing else on it, so there wasn't really any context or any way to tell where, exactly, Smokefish Creek was.

With a sigh, I closed the browser and brought up a note-taking app, then grabbed the Chemistry book and settled down to do some homework.

THAT NIGHT, MY MOUTH TINGLING WITH MINTY FRESHNESS from my toothpaste, I lay in bed and stared up at the ceiling. There was no overhead light, so the only thing illuminating the space was the lamp beside me, and that provided more colour than light. I was definitely going to have to talk to Mom and Dad about that. Either I'd need to get a different lamp, or we'd have to figure out a way to suspend a chandelier or something. It would be a long, dark winter up there if we didn't do anything at all.

There was a tall space beside the dresser that had been bugging me ever since we'd moved in. The wall was bare, and it looked like the perfect place to put a mural or something. It was just too bad I wasn't an artist like my sister. Our old room had been decorated in a crazy style, with her mural work gracing almost every vertical surface. Even though it wasn't *her* style, she'd incorporated some of my favourite Art Nouveau figures into the mix: women in flowing dresses with crowns of flowers. She'd even painted one of them half naked, but since we were only fourteen at the time, Mom had made her clothe the model. It wasn't that she was bothered by it, either; she just didn't want to have to hear from our friends' parents when they found out about my sister's nudes.

The blank piece of wall would've fit that half-naked woman perfectly. But she'd been painted over, along with all the rest of Jade's work, when Mom and Dad had put the house on the market. Mom had taken pictures, but I had grabbed a paint roller and scrubbed away all of my sister's hard work. When I was done, and the walls were a dull, neutral grey, I'd burst into tears of relief. I hadn't cried before or since.

Beside me, the lamp flickered, and the blobs of colour that were being cast upward shifted a little. I rolled my head to the side, just as a slight movement caught my attention. My body startled before my mind could catch up, and it took a moment before I registered the figure sprawled across the hard floor near the foot of my bed.

I scrambled up to a sitting position, and my first instinct was to scream. But, for some reason, the sound wouldn't come out. My diaphragm seemed to be locked, and I couldn't even breathe as I stared down at the boy who was pulling himself silently across the floor.

His skin was dark and he wore little except what might have been some sort of loincloth, but I couldn't see it because it was under him, leaving his mostly bare butt exposed. He made no sound, but I could see him struggling to breathe, his ribs straining at his skin. As he lifted his head, I could see that his eyes—couched under a heavy brow and as dark as ink—were wide, almost bulging. His tongue protruded a little, and he seemed to gulp at the air, as if he couldn't pull it in fast enough.

I shook my head and pulled the bedspread up around my neck, watching in horror. A part of me wondered if I was asleep and dreaming. Was this the result of something I'd eaten? A takeout-induced nightmare? Food poisoning, maybe? Or was it something worse than that? Jean had told me to let her know if I started to experience any weird symptoms, and I had a feeling that seeing a half-naked dying boy on my bedroom floor definitely counted.

The kid began to claw at the ground, raking his fingers over my floor with such desperation that I expected to hear the scrape of fingernails on the floorboards. But the whole scene was strangely silent. I watched, my own eyes bulging, as the boy's mouth moved. He was trying to say something. Or maybe scream. But he couldn't. His eyes were bloodshot. His lips, which had at first been a dark pink, grew dusky. As his head fell forward, smashing his nose against the floor, he continued to struggle, his torso hitching. And then, suddenly, he went still. I waited, my heart pounding, my head feeling like it was going to explode. After a few more seconds, I blinked . . . and the floor was empty. I drew in a noisy breath as my diaphragm unlocked and I was able to breathe again.

"What the hell?" I gasped, reaching for my glasses on the nightstand. I put them on and peered at the floor, even though what I'd just seen was so big that glasses weren't going to make much of a difference. Pushing my bedspread and sheet away, I stumbled out of bed and over to the spot where the boy had lain. I knelt down and hesitantly reached out to brush my fingers over the floor. I wasn't sure what I was expecting to feel. An icy cold, maybe? But I didn't feel anything except the tingle in my own fingertips, and I was pretty sure that was just because I'd held my breath for way too long.

No. I hadn't held it. I simply hadn't been able to breathe. Just like the boy. Just like . . .

Pulling off my glasses, I closed my eyes and sat there for a moment, listening to the settling pops of the house after the warmth of the day.

And I wondered if Mom and Dad would be open to letting me move down to the second floor. I wasn't sure if I wanted that bedroom after all.

4

Basketball

"WELL, YOU LOOK AWFUL," MOM SAID WHEN I APPEARED IN the kitchen the next morning. She looked great (as usual), which was annoying as hell, given the night I'd just had. No amount of makeup seemed to be helping, either. The dark circles under my eyes were proving to be no match for my concealer (which I rarely used anyway, since I didn't like covering up my freckles).

"Thanks a lot."

"Rough night?" Dad asked.

"You could say that." I grabbed a mug from the cupboard and poured myself a cup of coffee. I added two heaping spoonfuls of sugar, but no milk, which made Mom frown like she was about to scold me. "You guys could've told me you bought a haunted house."

Dad snorted into his coffee cup. "A what, now?"

"Well, this place is either haunted, or I'm losing my mind. Take your pick." I slumped onto the banquette and took a long swig of my coffee, even though it was still a little too hot and hurt my throat going down.

"Bad dream?" Mom asked. "You know Jean said—"

"Yeah, I know." I sighed. That was probably all it was, really. Grief—combined with the stress of starting at a new school, exhaustion, and too much takeout—was making me loopy. It probably didn't help that I'd been looking up a dead boy a few hours before bedtime.

"Make sure you eat something," Mom said as she grabbed her keys from the counter. Her travel mug was already in her hand. "I'm showing the place over on Larkspur at nine," she said to Dad. "Meet me there after you've dropped Ivy off?"

He nodded, so she left. I blinked at my cup on the table. My eyelids felt like they were made of sandpaper. I hadn't felt so awful since Jade had brought home that bottle of peppermint schnapps. We'd sampled way too much of it, and Jade's excuses for our breath ("We've been eating candy canes!") hadn't flown with Mom. We'd both gotten grounded for a month, even though Jade had obviously had a bigger hand in the debacle; I never did find out where she'd gotten the bottle.

"Maybe you should take the day off," Dad suggested.

"Somehow, I don't think that would go over very well," I said, taking off my glasses and pushing my cup aside so I could put my cheek down on the table. Dad immediately pressed the back of his hand against my forehead. "I don't have a fever. And I'm not ditching school on the third day. That's ridiculous."

"If you're sick, you're sick."

"I'm not sick."

"You're not *not* sick."

I blew out a breath and sat back up. Dad was frowning at me. "Did you ever meet the previous owners of this place?" I asked.

He shook his head. "No. It was all handled through their realtor. Why?"

"Just wondering." Slipping my glasses back on, I reached for my coffee. "Are you *sure* nobody died in here? Like . . . in my bedroom?"

"I think that would've been disclosed."

"Yeah, well, you know perfectly well that people don't always disclose things, even if they should." I took a few gulps of my coffee, trying to ignore the burning.

Dad shrugged. "I don't know what to tell you, Ivy. There's nothing like that that I'm aware of."

He didn't ask why I would be asking a question like that. He was as skeptical as they came. He didn't believe in any god, and he didn't think anything happened after death. He and Mom had argued about that just before Jade's memorial service; he'd said he didn't want it to be full of "fairy-tale references" or religious platitudes. Not that he could've controlled what other people said. I'd felt him tense up beside me when her boyfriend had started talking about heaven, and how they would one day be reunited.

So if Dad didn't believe in the continuation of his own daughter's soul, he definitely wouldn't believe in ghosts. I wasn't even sure *I* believed in ghosts, despite what I'd seen writhing on my bedroom floor.

"I had a pretty bad dream," I said, hoping to steer Dad's thoughts away from the paranormal. The last thing he needed was to be worrying about his remaining kid becoming obsessed with the dead.

"About what?"

"A boy. Dying. I mean . . . it had to be a dream. It's just . . . when it happened, it felt so real. Like I wasn't asleep." I shook my head and took another sip. The slightly burnt flavour of the coffee beans seemed to be waking me up a little and giving me some much-needed oomph. "I didn't sleep much after that, and I thought maybe I'd seen a ghost. But it wasn't," I said quickly. "He didn't look like he was from around here."

Dad raised his eyebrows. "What does *that* look like? This is a pretty diverse area, Ivy."

"Jeez, Dad. Way to make me sound racist. I'm just saying, I don't see many of the guys at school running around in loincloths."

He shook his head with a chuckle. "No, I guess you wouldn't. But that pretty much rules out a ghost, wouldn't you say?"

I nodded. The boy's appearance was one thing that went against the ghost theory. The other thing was the way he'd died. Choking, gasping, unable to take a breath. It seemed that even my subconscious mind wasn't very creative when it came to killing off the characters in my dreams.

Dad nodded toward the fridge. "You want to grab something? We need to get going."

"I don't need anything."

"Just take some fruit with you. You don't want *me* to get in trouble, do you?"

"Mom knows I'm old enough to take responsibility for my own bad habits," I said, but I dragged myself up from the banquette and grabbed an orange from the bowl on the counter anyway.

OF COURSE, MY FIRST PE CLASS OF THE YEAR HAD TO LAND on a day when I was feeling like a zombie. It was a co-ed class, too, and I was afraid I was going to set women's lib back a few decades, the way I was tripping and klutzing my way through the class. I was paired up with a girl named Evanie (in the echoes of the gym, I thought she'd said Stephanie at first), and we were doing basketball drills. Or trying to, anyway. I was *awful* at basketball, and always had been. As we approached the basket, Evanie took her shot, which swooshed into the net easily. She tossed the ball to me, and I held it in both hands as I looked up. Then I took my shot. The ball didn't get anywhere near the net. Worse, it came straight back down and hit me on the head, even though I tried to duck out of the way. Half the class must've seen that, because it was followed by an awful lot of laughter. I ran to retrieve the ball from where it had rolled over by the retractable bleachers, my cheeks burning.

"Heads up!" someone shouted. I'd just looked up when something big and orange slammed into my nose. I heard a crunch, and everything went blurry. Staggering back, I hit the bleachers. A whistle echoed in the cavernous gym.

"Ross! You all right?"

It took a moment before I realized the voice was talking to me. I looked up to see what appeared to be a blurry version of my PE teacher hurrying over. Something trickled over my lip, and I instinctively probed at it with my tongue. Blood. *Great*, I thought. *As if I haven't already made a spectacular impression today.*

Ms. Kelski took the ball I was still holding and tossed it away. "You all right?" she asked again.

"I don't know." I reached up and swiped at my lip. My fingers came back smeared with red. They were shaking, too.

"Head down to the nurse's office. He should be able to find some ice for you."

"Do I need ice?"

"I'd be surprised if you didn't." She bent over and swept something off the floor. With a cluck of her tongue, she held it—no . . . them—out to me. I took the two pieces of my glasses and looked down at them with a sigh. They'd snapped, right at the bridge.

"Where's the nurse's office?" I asked.

"Just past the vice-principal's . . ." She trailed off. I must've been giving her a pretty blank look. "You're new, aren't you?"

"Kind of."

"Hayes," she said, waving her hand at someone behind me. "Could you show her the way to the nurse's office?"

I turned around, only to find Kemp approaching. He sort of pulled up when he saw my face, and, for a moment, I thought he might've been about to run in the opposite direction. *Is it that bad?* I wondered.

But he recovered from his shock (or disgust or whatever it was) and nodded, then held out his hand to guide me toward the door. I noticed he didn't touch me, though, and when I glanced down, I could see why. My nose was dripping blood all over my shirt . . . and the floor. Transferring the two pieces of my glasses to one hand, I cupped the other hand under my nose and nodded at Kemp to lead the way. Before we were even out of the gym, the activity started back up again.

"Evanie doesn't have a partner," I mumbled. My voice was starting to sound weird. Nasally. Kemp just shook his head.

"She can pair up with mine."

I pulled my hand out a little so I could see how the bleeding was going. There was an impressive puddle in my palm. I quickly slid it back under my nose. "If they wanted me to duck, they should've said that," I muttered.

"What?"

"They yelled, 'Heads up!' So I looked up."

"Wouldn't you still have looked up if someone had told you to duck?"

I pondered that for a moment, then shrugged. "I don't know. Maybe. But at least it wouldn't have seemed like they were trying to get a better target."

He grunted. "I'll keep that in mind for next time."

I turned to him with wide eyes, keeping my hand carefully under my nose. "It was *you?*"

"Sorry." He folded his arms across his chest like he was cold. "I'm *really* sorry," he added, and winced as he glanced at my face. "I'm a terrible shot. Basketball's not my game. I'm more of a hockey sort of guy."

"You play?"

"I watch." He let out a little grunt. "Let's just say I'm not much of a jock."

"Neither am I," I said. "But you probably already figured that out."

"We should pair up next time," he said. "Then we wouldn't have to inflict our . . . um . . . talents on any of the kids who are half decent at sports."

"I don't know. That might end in a bloodbath."

"I think you're halfway there."

"To the nurse's office?"

He shook his head. "No, to a bloodbath. The nurse's office is right there." He pointed. We'd reached the administration area; if I followed the line of his finger, I could see the open door tucked near the back of the space. There were no signs that I could see, but through the doorway I saw a paper-covered table.

"Oh. Thanks."

"Yeah. You're welcome, Ivy."

I blinked. "You know my name?"

"Yeah . . . Don't you know mine?"

I did, of course, but only because I'd been gossiping. With a frown, I stared at him for a moment. He glanced away sheepishly, then looked down at his feet. His arms were folded again, creating a shield.

"I saw you in the cafeteria yesterday," he said. "You looked kind of familiar, so I . . ."

"You what?"

"I'm sorry about your sister."

I swallowed hard, not sure whether to play dumb or simply accept his condolences. Instead, I managed to get out, "How do you know about my sister?"

"Heard about her from my parents. It . . . kind of upset my mom."

"Yeah, well, it kind of upset mine, too."

He winced and shook his head. "No, I mean . . . My brother died a few years ago. So this sort of thing . . . It catches my parents' attention. Anyway, that's how I heard about it. I wasn't stalking you or anything."

"I didn't think you were."

"Okay. Well . . . I guess you can make it to the nurse's office from here."

I raised my eyebrows at him and was rewarded with a dull ache. "I should hope so."

He unfolded his arms and went to shove his hands into his pockets, perhaps forgetting that his gym shorts didn't have any. His hands skidded uselessly against his thighs. He salvaged the move by pretending to rub the sweat from his palms. "I'll see you around, then?"

"Probably."

"What do you have next?"

"Art."

"Really?" he asked, sounding skeptical.

"Yeah. Why?"

"Guess I'll see you there, then." He shrugged and started to walk backward. "If you can keep that nosebleed going, you might have a new medium to work with."

I narrowed my eyes at his stupid joke, and his cheeks reddened a little.

"Sorry," he said.

"I'm sorry my face got in the way of your shot."

He cracked a tiny smile. "If that was my shot, what the hell was I aiming for?"

"You tell me."

His smile grew. It actually made him look kind of cute, though he still wasn't in the same league as his brother. "I'll have to think about that," he said.

"Well, be sure to figure it out so you can avoid aiming at whatever it was next time." I sniffed hard as something tickled my nose from the inside. The slurpy sound almost made me gag.

"Go before your nose falls off," he said. "I'll see you in Art." He paused and grinned. "I'll even let you tell everyone about my terrible aim if they ask what happened to your face."

"They're going to ask, aren't they?" Already, I could tell that my nose was a little bigger than it usually was. I probably had bruising to look forward to, as well.

"Yeah." He laughed and shook his head. "I'm sorry, Ivy. But don't worry. I'm sure you'll repay the favour before the year is over." He whirled around and jogged off before I could think of a witty comeback. I supposed it didn't matter, though. With my skill—or lack thereof—he was probably right.

5

The Artist

By the time the bleeding had stopped and I'd gotten some ice on my face, the bell had already chimed. I ended up changing out of my gym strip in an empty locker room. After a quick check in the mirror—which was unnerving, but not quite as bad as I'd feared—I headed to the art room. Of course, everybody was already working on something. And they all had to look up as I walked in. I still had the cold pack pressed against my nose, and that—along with what was under it—was a pretty good excuse for why I was late.

"Kemp said you'd had a little accident," the teacher, Ms. London, said. I shrugged. She was a young woman, probably not much older than us, and a total stereotype of an artist: dreadlocks in her blond hair, too many piercings to count, a dress that brushed the tops of her bare feet, and so many bracelets on her wrists that she made this sort of clicking sound with every movement. As she approached, I detected a distinctive skunky scent. Given the amount of swelling in my nose, I wondered how strong the odour actually was. "I think he saved you a seat," she said, waving a clicking arm toward the back of the room where Kemp was sitting at one of the large tables. A backpack sat on the surface next to his paper, but as I made my way over there, he quickly swept the bag to the floor. I slid onto the stool, still clutching the cold pack to my nose and pretending not to care that everyone was staring. "Unless you plan on drawing her, eyes on your work," Ms. London said. She slipped a piece of paper in front of me and pointed at the container full of various pens and pencils that was sitting on the table between me and Kemp. "First day," she said. "So I just want to get to know you." She tapped the paper with her finger. "Show me who you are."

"Okay," I said, rather uneasily, and she swept away in a fog of funk. I turned to Kemp, who was staring, looking rather amused. "What?"

He shook his head and ran his fingers back through his thick hair. Out of his gym strip, he looked a little more relaxed. His navy polo and slim-fitting jeans hugged his body in all the right places, and I thought I might've been starting to understand why Eunice had such a crush. Unfortunately, there was that: Eunice had a crush. I wasn't sure what was going to happen when I told her that, not only had Kemp walked me to the nurse's office, he'd also saved the spot next to him in Art.

"You didn't break it," I said.

He raised his eyebrows. "Break what?"

"My nose."

"Oh. Right. Good." He shook his head again. "I'm still sorry."

"I know." My gaze drifted over to his paper, where he'd

already sketched out the beginnings of some sort of scene. "Wow. That's amazing."

He snorted and turned to regard his work. "Not really. But thanks." He leaned his left forearm on the edge of the paper as he went back to sketching. His fingers were sure and nimble. The tip of his pencil scratched over the surface as he marked out the reaching branches of spindly trees. After a few seconds, he paused and turned back to me. I took that as my cue to set down the cold pack and reach for something to draw with.

"You work in ink?" he asked as I pulled a pen from the container and slipped off the cap. With a shrug, I brought the tip to the paper and started to draw some lines. My hand shook, and I was certain everyone in that room knew I wasn't really supposed to be there. It wasn't like I hadn't taken the prerequisites. Jade and I had signed up for Art as soon as we'd been able to pick our first elective. She'd continued with the aim of one day going to art school and turning her skills into a career. I'd continued because I hadn't had much of a choice; I hadn't wanted to have to start all over with Drama or Sewing or Woodworking. Besides, I'd loved watching my sister work. She'd always seemed so sure of herself, with whatever she'd had in her hand: a paintbrush, a pencil, or even a lump of clay. Her ease reminded me of Kemp's, and as I continued to add more lines to the page in front of me, I snuck a sideways glance. He was watching my hand with a frown. I stopped.

"What's wrong?"

"Nothing," he said. "I just didn't expect . . ." He shook his head and turned back to his own page. "Never mind."

"What?"

His shoulders shrugged a little, though it didn't disrupt the flow of his pencil strokes. "I just got the impression that your sister was the artist. Not you."

"What did you think I was, then?" I asked, for some reason annoyed that he'd been able to see through me so quickly.

"An artist," he said. "Just not this sort."

"What sort, then?"

He shrugged again. "Fashion designer, maybe? You have that look about you."

"What look?"

Dropping his pencil, he sighed. As he ran his fingers through his hair again, he turned to me with a frown. "Sorry. Never mind. I'm just assuming too much. And I should know better."

"Meaning . . . ?"

"Have you noticed that people think they know you? After . . . I mean . . ."

"Yeah," I said quickly, so he didn't have to explain.

"One little article somewhere—which isn't even *about* you—and people assume they know everything. Even if they should know better because we've all been at the same school for years."

"What do people assume about you?" I asked. For some reason, that made him smile a little.

"Depends on how childish and shallow they are. You would not believe how many people assume I'm a stoner."

"Why?" Frowning, I looked him over. He didn't fit the stereotype, and I hadn't detected the same smell lingering around him that I had from our teacher. He laughed softly and began to trace out some letters on the table between us.

"My name," he said, just as he finished. I leaned a little closer so I could make out the faint block capitals. HEMP HAZE. "The guys have been teasing me about that since grade eight."

"Oh."

"There's a reason I don't use the stuff. I don't need to reinforce that idea." He found an eraser and quickly scrubbed out the letters, then brushed away the rubber leavings.

"Ivy and Hemp," I muttered to myself, realizing a moment too late that I'd said it out loud. He laughed and shook his head.

"Sounds like a dynamic duo. Or a company that sells handmade bedsheets."

I felt my cheeks rush with a violent heat. Weirdly, some of it seemed to go to my nose, and it felt like it began to pulse. When I glanced up at Kemp, he was looking kind of alarmed. I quickly grabbed the cold pack and slammed it—not quite gently enough—over my face.

"Sorry," he said. "I didn't mean—"

"Is it that bad?"

He frowned. "Is what that bad?"

"My nose. You looked worried."

Shaking his head, he sighed. "I didn't mean . . . About the duo thing . . ."

"Oh. It's okay. Never mind."

"I mean, you could have a boyfriend for all I know." He turned back to his paper and began to frantically sketch. "Or a girlfriend."

I thought about telling him I didn't, but wasn't quite sure how to proceed. It seemed like he was flirting a little, but I couldn't be certain. And I didn't even know if that was what I wanted. After all, I'd only met Eunice the day before. Was I really going to blow that potential friendship by starting something with her longtime crush?

We worked on our drawings for the rest of the class, mostly in silence. The cold pack kept letting out little crinkling noises since I kept it pressed against my nose the whole time. It was starting to feel more like a room-temperature pack, but at least it offered a sort of mask for my expressions. The image on Kemp's paper slowly took shape, a wintry scene of a stream bordered by bare trees. The lines on my paper, on the other hand, stayed mostly as lines. *It's abstract*, I told myself, but even that felt like a bullshit excuse. My drawing skills had always been subpar; even if I had wanted to pursue something like fashion design, my lack of sketching skill would've put the kibosh on that career track pretty quick.

Everyone was so engrossed in their work that nobody seemed to notice the time until the bell actually chimed. And then there was a mad scramble to put away the drawing implements and hand the papers in. As I returned the pen to the container, I regarded my work with a sigh. Fearing that abstract lines might not have been enough, I'd tried to draw a simple self-portrait, but the proportions were all wrong, and the result looked like something Jade would've done in kindergarten. With a shake of my head, I slid off the stool, clutched the not-so-cold pack in my hand, and picked up my terrible drawing.

"Ivy, wait."

I paused, the page fluttering between my trembling fingers, as I turned back to Kemp. He leaned down to grab his backpack before swiping his drawing from the table and joining me in the aisle.

"Want to go grab some lunch? There's this café down at the centre that makes awesome grilled-cheese sandwiches."

My eyes went wide. Seeming to realize he'd said something wrong—but probably not sure what—he quickly shook his head.

"Or we could just grab something in the cafeteria if you don't want . . ."

"I kind of told Rissa and Eunice I'd meet them there." I looked down at my drawing, and then back up at him, only to find that he was staring at it. I whipped the ugly thing behind my back, which made him smile.

"Cubism?"

"It wasn't supposed to be." With a sigh, I headed for the front of the room. He kept pace, though, and I didn't feel like I could just leave things like that. "Do you want to join us? I mean . . . I don't know if you know Rissa and Eunice, but they're pretty nice."

"I know them," he said. "Not well, but I know them." He smiled as he slid his paper onto the pile on Ms. London's desk. She glanced at it, then nodded to herself.

"May I have yours, too?" she asked, obviously spying the paper I still had tucked behind me. Mortified, I pulled it out and flipped it over, placing it face down on the pile. Of course, she just picked it up and examined it. I braced myself for a lecture.

"I think it's a statement about innocence," Kemp said, which just earned him a raised eyebrow from our teacher.

"Innocence? Perhaps." She looked at me steadily, her gaze kind of burrowing into my brain, as if she wanted to pluck out each and every secret. I swallowed hard.

"Maybe I'm just not that good at drawing," I said.

Her lips twitched, and she set the paper down on top of all the others. "'Good' is an entirely subjective term. Besides, I'm more interested in meaning. What does that"—she pointed to my drawing—"mean to you?"

Years of trying to give teachers the answers they wanted had made most of us experts at bullshitting our way out of these sorts of situations. But I was too tired to play games. I shrugged. "It means I'm in over my head. I suck at art. My sister's the one you would've loved. I'm just here to honour her."

Ms. London looked down at the drawing, then back at me before nodding sagely. "I don't think you suck at art as much as you think you do."

"I can't draw."

"Everyone can draw. Not everyone can be honest. And not everyone can *feel* their work."

I raised my eyebrows. But that seemed to be all I was going to get out of her. She gathered up the stack of drawings and padded over to the window, presumably to have a better look in the sunlight. I turned to Kemp, who was still hovering at my side, his backpack slung over his shoulder and a bemused smile slung across his mouth.

"Feel my work?" I whispered as we practically tiptoed out of the art room. When we were safely in the bustling hall, he laughed.

"I think she just means your art is coming from the right place."

"But it's not art," I protested. "It was basically a stick figure wearing glasses."

He chewed on his lower lip for a moment. "Why are you really taking that class?"

"Because Jade can't."

"Exactly."

"Did you ever do something stupid like that for your brother?"

He slowed a little, staring off ahead of us. Instantly, I was afraid I'd said something wrong.

"I'm sorry," I said. "That's none of my business. Never mind."

"No. It's okay." He shook his head. "It's just a complicated answer."

"Why?"

"Because I was doing stupid things to try to help him even before he died. And maybe if I hadn't, he would still be here."

I followed him through the halls toward the cafeteria in silence, any other questions I might've wanted to ask frozen in my mouth, trapped behind my numb tongue. I hadn't meant to pry—after all, I knew how annoying those sorts of questions could be—and I felt terrible. As we reached the cafeteria doors, he glanced back and came to a stop.

"You okay?"

"Yeah. You don't have to . . . I mean, if you don't want to sit with us, you don't . . ."

"You don't want me to?" he asked, with a frown that looked kind of hurt. It wasn't that I didn't want him to—

and I was sure Eunice would've been thrilled to have him join us—but I was still feeling bad about what I'd made him admit, and I didn't know how to back things up to before they'd gotten really awkward.

"I think we should make a deal," I said slowly. He raised his eyebrows, so I went on. "No talking about the dead siblings at school."

He stuck out his hand so quickly that it seemed he might've been waiting for me to say that. I grabbed it, and we shook. "Deal," he said. His hand squeezed mine, warm and strong. I wasn't sure why he wasn't letting go, but I actually didn't mind. "Now, can I sit with you or not? If not, I'll have to watch Josh and Lucie go at it again, and I don't think my stomach can handle it."

"I'm surprised you noticed," I said, finally pulling my hand away . . . though not without a twinge of regret. "You looked like you slept through lunch yesterday."

He shrugged. "I don't sleep great at night. Sometimes a cafeteria nap is required."

"Not today, I hope."

With a chuckle, he shook his head and stepped forward to pull open the door. I scurried through as he held it for me, and stepped into the blast of echoing noise.

Rissa and Eunice were already tucked into the same table as the day before, with identical lunches spread in front of them: fries and an energy drink each. I was ravenous from not having anything except a cup of coffee that morning (the orange was probably still sitting in one of the cupholders in Dad's car, untouched), so I dumped my bag on the seat beside Rissa and headed for the lineup. I hoped Kemp would take the hint and sit next to Eunice, and when I glanced back, I was glad to see that he had. I quickly dug in my wallet to see how much cash I had on me. With the couple of toonies that Dad had told me to take out of the car's console that morning, I had just enough for a veggie burger. But when I got up to the case and peered at the food within, I noticed the unappetizing greyish hue of the patty and opted to just get some fries instead. I supposed the other kids had already learned their lesson when it came to the school's veggie burgers, because the things didn't appear to be selling.

When I slipped into my seat at the table, Kemp was nowhere to be seen, Eunice's cheeks were pink, and Rissa was grinning madly. But her smile died when she saw my face.

"What the hell happened to you?"

"Didn't Kemp tell you?"

"Why would he?"

"He did it."

Eunice let out a short, sharp sigh, which made Rissa laugh.

"Are you seriously jealous of getting punched in the face?" she asked.

"He didn't punch me in the face," I said.

"Then what happened?"

I shrugged and bit down on a fry. It was really salty. Without answering, I got up and went to plug my remaining coins into one of the drink machines. When I returned a minute or so later with a bottle of water, Kemp was back. Eunice probably didn't realize it, but she was sort of leaning away from him, as if she needed the distance to get a better view. If he noticed her weird posture, he didn't let it show. He had his own cardboard bowl of fries on the table in front of him, and he'd grabbed a few packets of ketchup from the condiment rack. He pushed them to the middle of the table before grabbing one for himself.

"Help yourselves," he said. Rissa and I obliged. Eunice just kept staring at him.

"You were saying?" Rissa said to me. "How, exactly, did you get a bruised nose?"

I glanced at Kemp, who gave me a sheepish smile. "Basketball."

"Did you elbow her in the face?" she asked him. He blinked and shook his head.

"No. I was trying to take a shot. I just have really bad aim."

"I'll say," she muttered. "Are you sure that's not broken, Ivy?"

"The nurse didn't think it was. But my mom will probably want me to get it checked out, just in case."

"Where are your glasses?" Eunice asked. She frowned at me, as if she were just registering my presence for the first time.

"Broken."

"I'm *really* sorry," Kemp said. "I'll pay to replace them. Just give me your—"

"It was an accident," I said. "Besides, I was almost ready for a new pair, anyway. I think my prescription's changed again."

"You should totally get a pair of cat-eye glasses," Rissa said. I turned to her as I raised my eyebrow.

"Why?"

"It would go with this whole thing you've got going on here." She waved her hand up and down in my direction.

"Are you saying she dresses like your grandma?" Kemp asked, grinning as he chomped down on a ketchup-dipped fry. Rissa quickly shook her head. Her long, blond hair was pulled up in a ponytail; as she moved, the spirals twisted like whirligigs.

"No. Besides, there's nothing wrong with dressing like *my* grandma. She was pretty trendy in her time." She grabbed another ketchup packet and squeezed out the red dollops across her remaining fries. "It's just that Ivy's got this retro vibe. She really should have the glasses to go with it."

"I thought I did," I said. My black, heavy-framed glasses were about as retro as you could get. Or so I'd thought.

"I liked your glasses," Kemp said with a shrug. He delivered another fry to his mouth as Eunice watched in fascination. Her own lunch was getting cold in front of her.

"You guys should see the drawing he just did," I said, hoping to steer the conversation in another direction. My fashion sense was not something I particularly liked to talk about. Especially not now, since it would just make me remember how my style had been so different from my sister's, and then I'd spend the rest of the day lost in memories.

"Yeah?" Rissa said, with a pointed glance at Eunice. "I *told* you he was taking Art."

"It was just a sketch," he said, looking embarrassed. I frowned in confusion.

"Of what?" Rissa asked. When it didn't seem like Kemp was going to answer, I took a deep breath, watching his reaction.

"A stream through some trees. It looked like a winter scene. Really pretty."

The table grew quiet. I looked around to find Rissa staring at me with wide eyes, Eunice frowning at me, and Kemp stabbing a fry so hard against the bottom of his cardboard bowl that it looked like he was trying to put out a cigarette. I knew I'd said *something* wrong, but I didn't know what. Quickly, I racked my brain, trying to think of what it could've been. The only thing I could think of was that it had something to do with his brother's death, but the drawing hadn't been . . .

Oh, god. Had it?

He'd drawn the stream during the day, not at night. And it had looked like a shallow, placid trickle . . . not something someone could've drowned in. It hadn't even occurred to me that what he'd drawn could've been related to where his brother had died. Or . . . where he'd started to die, really, because he'd actually died in the hospital, not—

"It's fine," he said quietly, so quietly that I almost couldn't hear his voice over the echoing din in the cafeteria.

"I'm sorry," I said. "I didn't mean to—"

"That wasn't the spot, anyway." Licking some ketchup off his thumb, he shook his head and reached for his backpack. "I forgot. I told Lucas I'd . . ." But he couldn't think of an excuse—because we all knew that was what it was—so he just grabbed the rest of his fries and stood up. "I'll see you later," he said, in such a generic way that I couldn't tell who he was talking to or if he even meant it at all. We watched as he headed out the door, but not before tossing his uneaten fries and container into the bins.

"Whoa, Ivy," Rissa said.

Across the table, Eunice seemed to relax.

"I thought you liked him," I said. She frowned and tucked her hair behind one ear.

"She does," Rissa said.

"So why does she look so happy to see him go?"

Rissa just raised her eyebrows at me, as if the answer should've been obvious. It took a few seconds of thinking for me to catch on.

I'd just blown it with Kemp. So I was no longer a rival.

"You're welcome to him," I said. "I don't have time to bother with someone who might or might not be offended by what I say."

"You brought up the creek," Rissa pointed out.

"Only because he drew it."

She shook her head and reached for another ketchup-smeared fry. "I've never seen someone crash and burn that fast."

"What's that supposed to mean? I only met the guy a couple of hours ago. It's not like we were in any sort of relationship."

"You seemed to get along pretty well until you brought up that drawing."

"Yeah, well, we have a lot in common."

She let out a short laugh. "You both smoke weed?"

"No!" Eunice and I snapped at the exact same moment. Rissa held up her hands.

"Jeez. Sorry."

"That rumour only got started because of his name," I said.

She shook her head slowly. "Is that what he told you?"

"Yeah." A sudden, sharp wiggle of worry tickled in the middle of my chest. "Why?"

"His brother was a known pothead. He showed up to class stoned the last few months of his life."

"So? What does that have to do with Kemp?"

"Yeah," Eunice said. "Just because his brother smoked—"

"They *both* did," Rissa said. "Trust me. I was there at the time. They both reeked of the stuff, and I know for a fact that Kemp got suspended for like a month. He missed so much school that he had to redo a couple of classes."

"I didn't smell anything," I said, my voice small. It wasn't that I was bothered by the prospect of him experimenting with drugs. After all, Jade hadn't exactly been an angel in that department. What irked me was the fact that he'd lied. And after I'd been nothing but honest with him.

"Are you sure you can smell anything?" Rissa asked. "Try closing your mouth and taking a breath. I bet you can't even do it."

Just to prove her wrong, I clamped my lips shut and inhaled. It was way harder than it should've been, and I had to stop and cough at the halfway point. Letting out a moan, I rubbed my fingers into my eyes.

"This day *sucks*."

"Yeah, well, get used to it," she said. "We've got ten more months to go."

6

Nightmare

After school, I went straight to my room to work on my homework. When I finally came down for dinner, Mom took one look at me and frowned.

"What did you do?"

"I didn't do anything," I said. "Some kid hit me in the face with a basketball during PE."

"On purpose?"

"Yeah, Mom. Totally on purpose. He did it to five other kids, too, just for fun."

Her frown deepened. "I was just asking."

"The nurse said it probably wasn't broken."

"Believe me," Dad said. "You'd know it if it was." He turned to Mom. "She's fine, Linley."

But Mom wouldn't let it go until I promised to slather some arnica cream on the bruises after dinner. I went and did that as soon as I'd finished my pad thai, heading straight for the bathroom because I knew she'd be listening. I locked myself in and stared at my reflection for a few moments. I was going to be bruised for the next few days, but other than that, my nose didn't look that bad. Dad was probably right. He would've known, too, since he'd broken his own nose multiple times playing hockey as a teenager. I was surprised neither of them had brought up my glasses, but I decided to count that as a win . . . and with the way my day had gone, I needed as many of those as I could get.

I brushed and flossed my teeth, then washed my face, being gentle around my nose. After patting it dry, I found the old tube of arnica cream that I'd last used when I'd tripped and fallen into a tree during a snowshoeing excursion the previous winter. (Snowshoeing wasn't exactly the most hazardous of sports, but I'd still found a way to damage myself, much to Jade's amusement.) The cream had worked great on my shoulder, but I wasn't sure if it would be as effective on my nose. I smeared some over the feature in question anyway, then had a quick pee before turning off the light and heading for my room.

Two floors down, I could hear the TV. Mom and Dad were probably curled up together in front of it, binge-watching one of their series. I was kind of glad they were getting back into that, but I was also kind of not. It had never bothered me before, back when I'd had Jade; we'd found plenty of ways to occupy ourselves. We'd watched movies on one of our laptops, sprawled on our stomachs, shoulders pressed together. We'd gone outside so Jade could practice her photography skills in the twilight; I'd often been her model, both for the photos and for the paintings she'd made from them afterward. On a few occasions, we'd even ventured into the kitchen to bake something, which had always resulted in a mess and Mom banning us . . . for a little while, anyway.

But now I was on my own and I was lost. My homework

was done, and I didn't really feel like the friendship level with Rissa or Eunice was high enough yet that I could call them up for a chat.

So I put my old pair of glasses back on and sat cross-legged on my bed in front of my laptop as I went in search of information that could help make my day make sense. First, I searched for Kemp's name. Aside from the few articles I'd found before, there was nothing except his social media accounts. I clicked on one and started scrolling back through the photos. I saw plenty of people I didn't recognize, as well as a few that I did—Tim, Josh, and Sailor were all there, along with some others that I recognized from the cafeteria but couldn't name. I had to go way back—almost six years—before I found a single picture with his brother in it. It appeared to be Austin's birthday, and it was some sort of family affair; I could see a couple of little kids around the edges, and someone was holding a cake with a blur of lit candles in front of him. Kemp wasn't in that photo at all, so I figured he'd probably been the one to take it.

I scrolled forward to the most recent selfie and clicked it, only to find that it was more than three years old. It was just Kemp holding the camera so that the setting sun silhouetted his head and made his brown hair almost glow. The comments, however, were a little disturbing:

LucieClair01 what happend?
Tim_Blake omg I cant beleive it. where r u?
JoshJ:))) is he ok? let me know haze. pls pls let him b ok.
DDORourke_! hunter said your bro's in the hospital
SailinSailinSailor omfg haze! are you dead? you better not be dead cause you totaly still have my shoes

I looked closer at the photo. It was hard to tell, but he did look younger. Something wasn't right, though. The dates didn't line up with what I knew. The comments were from January. Austin hadn't died until March, and he'd only been on life support for a week, so . . .

I did another search, this time looking for events that had happened in the area in January. I didn't come up with much, other than a few random mentions of accidents that I couldn't connect to the brothers at all. There was a shooting, but that didn't seem likely; I doubted I wouldn't have heard *that* piece of gossip. There was a freak accident involving an icy branch, a hot tub, and a couple of naked teens. But, again, I probably would've heard about something like that, at least from Rissa. The other two articles were both about car accidents, but since there'd been no deaths, no names had been mentioned.

I slid the laptop aside, reached for my bag, and pulled out my phone. Rissa's contact info was already there, so all I had to do was dial. She picked up right away. I could hear frantic music in the background.

"Where are you?" I asked.

"At home. Just a sec." There was a shuffling noise, and the music abruptly cut off. "Sorry. I like it loud. It helps me concentrate."

"Really?"

She let out a groan. "Don't tell me I'm outnumbered. Eunice thinks it's weird, too. She has to have, like, complete silence when she's doing her homework. Fair warning, if she ever invites you over to study."

"Thanks. I guess."

She laughed. "What's up?"

"What else do you know about Austin Hayes?"

"Not that much. Why?"

"Was there another incident or something? Besides his death? 'Cause I was looking at one of Kemp's social media accounts, and there was this weird post from January."

"Last January?"

"No. Like, three-years-ago January."

"Oh. Yeah . . . I think that's around when Kemp started smoking pot."

"At thirteen?"

"Yeah, well, his brother was a bad influence. What do you want me to say?"

"So that's all that happened? Because the comments were really weird. It sounded like there was an accident or something."

"There was. Austin was driving and he flipped the car with both of them in it. Couldn't have been too serious, though, because Kemp was back at school after a few days."

"What about Austin?"

"Don't know. He was a lot older than us, Ivy. I didn't really pay attention to what was going on with the grade twelves."

"Did he ever come back to school?"

"Of course. Like I said, he came pretty stoned for a while."

"After the accident?"

"Yeah."

"What about before?"

"I don't know. Jeez, Ivy. What does it matter? He's been dead for years."

So? I wanted to retort. *That doesn't mean they should be forgotten.* But I kept quiet as I reached for the laptop and clicked on the link for the second accident. My phone still pressed to my ear, I skimmed over the article. Two teenage brothers, car flipped into a ditch, road closed, minor injuries. There was nothing that identified the Hayes brothers, but I was pretty sure I had the right accident.

"While I've got you," Rissa said, "can I ask you something?"

"Sure."

"Are you going to date Kemp?"

I snorted. Which hurt. A lot. "Ow."

"Don't hurt yourself," Rissa said. "I just need a 'yes' or 'no' answer."

"I don't know," I said. "I guess it depends on whether he'll ever talk to me again."

"You know Eunice likes him, right?"

"Why do you think I worked it out so he'd sit next to her?"

"That *was* pretty great. I've been trying to get them in close proximity for months. Eunice is like a timid little bird, though, when it comes to him." She paused, then took a deep breath. "I just don't want to see her get hurt. That's all."

"Look, I don't know what's going to happen between us. Probably nothing. I'm not going to try to stop her, if she wants to ask him out."

"That's never going to happen. He'd have to ask *her* out."

"Does he like her?"

"I don't know. You know him better than I do."

"Rissa, I only met him this morning. You know way more about—"

"Yeah, I know *about* him. You know *him*."

I took a deep breath and let it out slowly. "In any case," I said, "I'm not looking for a relationship at the moment."

"Well, if you ever decide you're ready, try to look in a different direction. Kemp is taken."

Does he know that? I wondered. Since I didn't have anything more to say, I just told Rissa I'd see her at school and ended the call. Then I read the article once again, more carefully, searching for any detail I might have missed. But there wasn't really anything. There wasn't even a picture of the accident scene.

I flipped the laptop closed and plugged it in on my dresser to charge. Then I put on my pyjamas, climbed into bed, and pulled up the novel I'd been reading on my phone.

I DIDN'T REALIZE I'D FALLEN ASLEEP UNTIL I JOLTED AWAKE. My phone had turned off and was lying at my side, still in my hand. I couldn't even remember where I'd been in the story. With a yawn, I sat up and started to reach over to plug the phone into the charger. My heart clattered in my chest as my vision flickered and my lungs locked.

Not again, I thought. A part of me was still awake enough to realize that I was aware of my confusion about the last episode and my uncertainty about whether or not it had been a dream. But my dreams had never been this real before, and I'd never continued any dream—or its theme— from one night to the next. And so I knew, with a chilling certainty, that whatever was going on was terrifyingly real.

Instead of the boy I'd seen before, this time a little girl

stood in front of me. She was looking at something, but I couldn't tell what that was because all I could see was her. She stood on her toes as if trying to see over something. She couldn't have been more than six or seven, and she was dressed like a little doll. Her boots had buttons, her stockings were smudged with dirt, and her frilly white pinafore was covered in matching brown marks. Her golden curls reminded me of Rissa's, though they were darker and tighter, long ringlets that hung down over her shoulders. She didn't appear to be dying; in fact, she was quite alive, standing on her toes, jumping up, and pushing her hands forward as if she were trying to move someone out of the way. At one point, she swung her head around and looked right at me, as if I'd called her name, and I caught a glimpse of her excited face.

But no sooner had I relaxed into the seeming placidity of the vision than she reached out and pushed hard. She stumbled forward and, the next instant, her body crumpled as if it had been thrown into a washing machine. Invisible forces pummelled at her, bloodying her limbs. Whatever was happening, it was too fast for her to register. She didn't scream. Her eyes were wide, but she didn't appear to be crying out at all. But I wanted to, as the next instant her head crumpled like it had been crushed by a giant, invisible hand. The bloody, broken body vanished almost at once. And I let out a scream.

The next thing I heard was Mom and Dad thundering up the stairs. They burst into my room where they found me shaking, still holding my phone in one hand. I couldn't even remember what I'd been doing with it.

"What's wrong?" Mom cried. Her hair was mussed and her pyjamas were wrinkled, but her eyes were bright and wide. Dad, on the other hand, still looked half asleep; following Mom up the stairs had probably been more of a reflex than a conscious choice.

I couldn't answer, in any case. I stared at the floor where the little girl had been, almost expecting to see a pool of blood. But, just like when the boy in the loincloth had gasped and died on my floor, the little girl had left nothing behind. I took in a few deep breaths, then threw the phone onto the bed.

"Another nightmare?" Dad asked.

"Another ghost."

"Ivy." He sighed deeply, as if my words had personally offended him. "You know there's no such thing."

Mom sat down on the edge of my bed and picked up my phone. "What were you doing?"

"Sleeping." I drew in a shaky breath. "I was reading, and I fell asleep."

"What were you reading?"

"*The Secret Garden,*" I said, and I slowly began to consider the idea that had obviously already occurred to Mom. The clothes seemed about right for the era. The girl had been a bit young, but . . . Shaking my head, I let out a long exhale. "Mary Lennox doesn't *die,*" I said. "And she certainly wouldn't have died like that. Not in a children's book."

"Our minds are capable of making us believe all sorts of things," Dad said. "You were probably just dreaming the PG-thirteen version."

"More like R," I said, pulling off my old pair of glasses and rubbing the bridge of my nose. I winced as my fingertips touched the forgotten bruises. Mom reached out and smoothed down my hair.

"Get some sleep, Ivy. It's been a stressful week. We all need our rest."

I took the hint and grasped the offered phone. I plugged it in to charge, then set the glasses on the nightstand. But I didn't turn off the lamp.

"Are you all right?" Mom asked. I nodded, even though I wasn't. Just because I wasn't going to be able to sleep didn't mean they had to stay awake, too. She gave me a kiss on the forehead, and I snuggled down under the covers, turning toward the window. As soon as I heard the door close behind them, I lifted up the phone to check the time. It was just before eleven-thirty. I wondered what time it had been when the last ghost had come calling.

Because, as confused as I was about what was going on, I knew one thing for certain: Neither of the horrible deaths I'd seen had been dreams.

7

Chased by a Bear

MOM'S SUGGESTION FOR THE ARNICA CREAM HAD BEEN A good one. I realized that the next morning when I looked in the mirror after my shower and noticed that the bruising was mild (I looked more like I had dark circles under my eyes than anything else) and most of the swelling had gone down. Instead of makeup, I applied another layer of the cream, hoping it would take care of the rest of the mess.

When I stumbled into the kitchen, Mom took notice of my unsteady gait first. Then she fixed her gaze on my face. I was about to tell her the cream had worked when she frowned.

"Why are you wearing those old things to school?"

I reached up to situate the glasses more firmly against my face. The wire-framed pair were subtler, and they made me look totally different. They were also weaker, which meant I'd probably be suffering from a headache by the end of the day. "I got hit in the face with a basketball yesterday," I said. "Why do you think I'm wearing these?"

She sighed. "Jade, glasses are expensive. You need to be more—" Her voice faltered. I was surprised she'd gotten so far into the next sentence before realizing what she'd said.

Frowning, she reached out and pulled me close for a hug. "I'm sorry, Ivy."

"It's okay." Being mistaken for my sister might've bothered me before but, in a weird way, it almost felt like keeping her involved as part of the family now.

"She was the one who went through three pairs in grade five alone," Mom said.

"I know."

"You were always so careful. We never needed to worry."

"And you don't have to worry now," I said, pulling away from her so I could get a cup from the cupboard. "I was going to need a new pair soon, anyway. And I'll pay for the frames."

Dad grunted. "No, you won't."

"Then I'll at least try to pick some inexpensive ones." I poured myself a cup of coffee, added lots of sugar, and took a sip. It was way too hot, as it always was. I never seemed to learn. "Mom," I began, deciding that she would be the least likely to dismiss me if she figured out the real reason I was asking, "is there any way to find out the history of this house? Like, who owned it before us?"

"It's an old house, Ivy. It would've had multiple owners."

I nodded. I didn't say, "And one of them probably had a little girl with blond ringlets who died a horrific death." Although, there was still the matter of the boy in the loincloth, who I was pretty sure had never lived in our house.

"We've got the name of the previous owner," Dad chimed in from his seat at the banquette. "Why?"

"Just curious. But I'm more interested in the older owners. Like . . . from when the house was first built. When was that?"

"The forties," Mom said, and my heart sank.

"That recently?"

She nodded, and I stared down into my cup of coffee with a frown. That made it unlikely that the little girl had ever lived in the house.

"What about the property?" I asked, raising my gaze to hers. "Was there another house here before that?"

"I don't know, Ivy. What's with the sudden interest in the house's history?" she asked, but then her mind provided the answer. I could see the moment when she understood because her eyes widened a bit and her gaze darted in Dad's direction.

"Never mind," I said, because I didn't really want to bring my father into a discussion about ghosts (which he didn't believe in), and because I was fairly certain that I wasn't dealing with localized ghosts, anyway. The boy wouldn't have been from the immediate area. The chances the girl had been were greater, but why would she have been if he hadn't?

Something else was going on. I just wasn't sure what.

My Friday schedule was the same as the Thursday one, which meant I had two classes with Kemp, including Art. I managed to steer clear of him in PE (which wasn't too hard, since we ended up going for a cross-country run, and his legs were a lot longer than mine; I ended up doing the whole thing with Lucie, who actually had some entertaining things to say when she didn't have her tongue lodged in Josh's mouth). But when I got to my next class, the only available seat was next to Kemp, so I didn't have much of a choice but to confront him.

He was a lot sweatier than he'd been the day before, and his hair was kind of plastered to his head around his temples. He was already deep into the sketch in front of him and didn't seem to notice when I sat down. It didn't look like anything for the class; he worked with pencil in a small sketchbook, his sure fingers flicking the tip across the page.

"Hi," I said.

"Hey."

I bit my lip and looked down at the empty table in front of me, then up toward the front of the classroom. Ms. London was pacing back and forth, mumbling to herself. She reminded me of an actor right before showtime doing a last run-through of her lines.

"How's your nose?" Kemp asked, not even looking up from his sketchbook.

"Better."

"Good."

"Look, I'm sorry about—"

"Here," he said, pushing the sketchbook across the table toward me. "What do you think?"

I shook my head. "I wouldn't know." *Yeah, right. Like I'm going to step into that minefield,* I thought.

He glanced at my face and, when he saw that I hadn't even looked, he frowned. "Really, Ivy. I want your opinion."

"Why? So you can get mad at me for it?"

He set down his pencil and swivelled on his stool to face me. "What are you talking about?"

"You're really going to pretend you don't know?"

"I don't have to pretend." He edged the sketchbook a little closer to me and blinked his thick eyelashes. "Have a look?"

Warily, I turned my attention down to the page. When I saw what was there, I had to try really hard not to react. He'd drawn me, probably as he'd seen me the day before, judging by the angle. My hair was tucked behind my ear, and my lips were kind of pinched, the way Jade had always used to tease me about; it was just something I did unconsciously when I was concentrating. She'd done it, too, but pointing that out had just made her roll her eyes. Kemp had drawn me without my glasses, but he'd also left out the bruises and swelling. It was an excellent likeness, and it made me wonder what he'd modelled it after, since most of what he'd seen of me so far had been discoloured and puffy.

"Why would you draw that?" I asked. He blinked, taken aback.

"Why wouldn't I?"

"It's creepy. You have to look at a person for a *long* time to be able to draw them that well."

"Are you accusing me of being a creeper?"

I shrugged. He slammed the sketchbook shut and muttered something under his breath. But I didn't have time to get into it with him because Ms. London finally began her performance. I'd missed it the day before, bleeding in the nurse's office and all. This time, though, I watched in a sort of amused disbelief as she went on some long, rambling spiel about pointillism. After what felt like a full hour—but was only about ten minutes according to the clock on the wall—she finally freed us to work on our assignments. I stared at the blank page in front of me in despair. Drawing something recognizable with lines was hard enough. I had no idea how to even begin.

"In summary," Kemp muttered.

"What?"

"Dots." He poked his pen at his page to emphasize the point.

"Have you done this before?"

"Last year."

"What did you draw?"

He turned away, and I didn't think he was going to answer me. But he was just reaching for his phone. He pulled it out of his backpack, tapped at the screen, and turned it toward me so I could see the drawing of a grotesque man in an ornate frame. I leaned closer, wishing my old glasses were a little more powerful.

"You did that with *dots?*"

"Yeah." He turned the screen, flicked his fingers across it, and angled it back toward me. He'd zoomed in on a portion of it, and I could see that the image was, indeed, made up of thousands of tiny black points.

"Who is that supposed to be?" I asked.

He raised his eyebrow. "Can't you tell?"

"Not really."

He sighed and returned his phone to his backpack. "We were reading *The Picture of Dorian Gray* in English. So I figured I'd draw that. It was easier than trying to come up with something else."

"Oh. I've never read it. Is it good?"

With a shrug, he tapped the cap of his pen against his chin. "It provided inspiration." After tilting his head a little, he braced his free hand against the paper and began to peck the pen at the clean white surface, leaving a series of little dots behind. I watched for a moment, envious of his sureness.

"I don't know how to do this," I said quietly, pressing my pen right in the middle of the page. The solitary dot left behind was centred almost perfectly. I hated to have to spoil the symmetry with more, but I doubted Ms. London would accept such a minimalist piece . . . unless I managed to bull-shit my way to a decent grade. "Do you think she'd believe me that the rest of the dots are invisible? They represent the social isolation and feelings of invisibility that run rampant in our world today."

Kemp snorted. When I glanced at him, I could see his mouth twitching.

"Actually, the one lone dot represents ourselves. We're the only ones we can really see. We're the only ones we *want* to see. Our inherent selfishness—"

"How are you not a straight-A student?" he asked, shaking his head.

"What do you mean?"

"You've got the BS down to an art form."

"Yeah, well, that's probably the only art form I'm good at. And I'm not even *that* great. Everything I learned, I learned from . . ."

When I stopped talking, he looked up. "From?"

"We promised we wouldn't talk about them."

He nodded. But he didn't turn back to his paper. I took a deep breath.

"I'm really sorry," I said. "About yesterday. I didn't mean to bring up—"

"It's okay."

"No, it's not. I upset you."

He shrugged. "If I'm being honest, I was kind of looking for an excuse to leave. It wasn't you," he said quickly, just as my expression fell into what felt like a devastated frown. "And it wasn't anything you said about the drawing. Not really."

"Then why'd you bolt like you were being chased by a bear?"

He winced a little. "Wasn't I? Eunice's feelings aren't exactly . . . um . . . hidden."

"You don't like her?" I asked as a strange mixture of indignation on behalf of my friend and relief on behalf of myself flowed through me like a warm drink.

"I don't *dislike* her," he said. "But I kind of get the impression that she's looking for more than just friendship."

"She likes you."

"Believe me," he said. "I know. And if she'd just tried to talk to me or something, I might've liked her, too. But she's been *staring* at me for two years now, and it's just plain creepy at this point."

"She's harmless."

"Yeah, and she's also too shy. If I have a girlfriend, I'd like for her to at least be able to talk to me. Sitting there staring at each other would get old really fast."

"I'm sure she'd open up once she got to know you," I said. *Why are you doing this?* I wondered. Kemp obviously wasn't interested in Eunice. Why was I so invested in this weird non-relationship they had going?

"You know," he said, "if I didn't know any better, I might think you were trying to pawn me off on your friend so you didn't have to date me yourself."

My mouth went dry. "What?"

"It makes me *very* reluctant to ask you out. Nobody likes being shot down." He tapped a quick series of dots, forming a dense curve that, from a distance, looked almost like a solid line.

Heart pounding, I pressed my pen to my own paper, holding the tip there for so long that I ended up with a rather large dot. I had no idea what to say to that, since he hadn't actually asked me out, and, even if he had, I wasn't sure what the proper etiquette would be. At that point, I felt like I knew Kemp better than Eunice or Rissa, so the question of loyalty was a complicated one. In any case, though, it didn't really matter, since he hadn't actually asked.

Or had he? Had his invitation to lunch the previous day been his first attempt? And then I'd gone and dragged him into a situation that had made him uncomfortable. Not that I'd known; I'd simply been trying to do something nice for Eunice.

"Do you want to see a movie tonight or something?" he asked, keeping his voice low and his head bowed over his paper. Not that that kept the kids around us from hearing. A couple of them turned around, and the girl in front of us smiled knowingly. I felt my cheeks redden and, for some weird reason, my nose began to throb a little. Had I developed some sort of weird Pinocchio syndrome where, instead of my nose growing when I lied, it throbbed when I got embarrassed?

I realized I hadn't said anything for way too long when Kemp leaned down and braced his hand on his temple, sort of hiding his face from my view. Quickly, I ran through the possible scenarios. It sounded like fun, and if I timed things right, the nightly ghost visit—if there was one—would happen while I was out of the house. Mom and Dad would be okay with me going out since it was a Friday night. Plus, I hadn't been to the movies in ages; just the thought of theatre popcorn made my mouth water. It seemed like a no-brainer.

But then, there was Eunice to consider. If news of the date got back to her—and I had no doubt that it would—she would be devastated. And since Rissa would probably take her side, I'd be left with no friends except for Kemp. And if things ultimately didn't work out with *him*, it could end up being a very lonely year.

Still, if I'd learned anything from my twin sister, it was to seize opportunities, especially if they were things you really wanted to do. You didn't always get another chance.

So I glanced at the girl in front of us, then turned to Kemp with an exaggerated expression of disappointment. "I can't," I said, even as I reached down to pull my phone from my bag. "I told my parents I would—"

"Yeah. Okay. Never mind." He slumped a little on his hand and turned his head away from me as he continued to stab his pen at the paper. When, a moment later, his phone chimed, he didn't reach for it. My heart sank.

"Your phone's—"

He sighed, dropped his pen, and got out the device. As he read the DM I'd sent, his eyebrows rose slowly. I could tell he was trying not to smile, trying to keep up the charade. Because, of course, I hadn't rejected him at all. The message I'd sent—*I'd love to. Call me later and we'll work out the details.*—should've been proof enough of that.

THINGS WERE WEIRD AS SOON AS I BUCKLED UP IN THE passenger seat of Kemp's car. He peered at my house for a moment, then shook his head before pulling away from the curb. His car was fairly new, probably with plenty of safety features, though it didn't seem to have things like power windows. It still had that new-car smell, but I could also detect some fast-food odours. An empty plastic sports bottle was wedged into one of the cupholders, and when I glanced in the back seat, I saw that there was a sweatshirt bunched in the corner, as well as a pair of ratty runners on the floor.

"Stop checking out the mess," he said. I turned back to him with a smile.

"Should've cleaned up if you didn't want me to see."

"I didn't have time."

"You didn't have time? Or you just got busy doing something else and forgot there was a mess in here until I noticed it?"

"Like I said. I didn't have time." He wiggled his fingers on the steering wheel and shot me a cheeky smile. "So, I thought we should probably head over to the theatre at the mall."

"There's a mall around here?"

He shook his head. "It's not close, so there's less chance of running into your friends."

I sighed and sank back against the seat. "You know *someone* is going to see us. It'll get back to Eunice somehow."

"You don't know that. But, if you're really worried about it, we can always disguise ourselves."

"Do you have a fake moustache in here or something?"

He laughed. "You'd attract way too much attention if you wore one of those."

"I meant—"

"Yeah, Ivy, I know what you meant." He shoulder-checked and pulled into the left lane as he got ready to turn. "I think one of Austin's hats is still in the trunk. I could wear that."

"Not much of a disguise, is it?"

"I never wear hats. So, yeah, it kind of is." He chewed on his lip for a moment as he glanced in the rearview mirror. "This isn't going to get you in too much trouble with your friends, is it?"

I shrugged. "I don't really know them well enough to know if it will or not."

"We don't have to see a movie. We could hang out at my house instead."

"Oh. I kind of didn't eat much dinner because I was saving room for popcorn."

He laughed and shook his head as the light changed and he pulled onto a rather busy road. "You know we have a fridge, right? We do have food."

"Are your parents home?"

He sighed. "Yeah. You're right. Mom would be all over you. I haven't had a girl over in ages."

"Three years?" I asked hesitantly. He glanced at me out of the corner of his eye. "Sorry. I forgot the rule."

He shook his head. "The rule only applies during school hours, doesn't it?"

"I don't know."

The ride continued in silence for a while. I had no idea what Kemp was thinking about, but I was sitting there, ruminating over every word we'd said. That *I'd* said. I'd gone and brought up his brother's death again, and I suspected that explained the uncomfortable silence in the car. As I watched the headlights of the other vehicles blur past in the gathering shadows, I let my eyes unfocus and tried to think of something to say. Something that wouldn't make the situation any more awkward. Eventually, though, it seemed that saying nothing was making everything worse, so I took a deep breath, only to be immediately interrupted.

"We can talk about them, if you want to," he said quietly. "If you don't, that's fine, too."

I let out my breath in a rush of relief and turned to look at him. His expression was reassuringly neutral. "Do you talk about your brother a lot? With your parents, I mean?"

"Sometimes. Depends on what we're talking about. Good memories, yeah. Bad ones . . . not so much."

"What are some of the good ones?" I asked, just to keep him talking. And to keep me from having to say anything else.

"There are way too many to count." He squinted against the sun, which was right down by the horizon, about to disappear. "Like the Halloween when I was four and he was seven. He got the idea that we'd go as Professor X and Wolverine."

"From the X-Men?"

"Yeah. Dad was totally into it, too. He used the old stroller to make that fancy wheelchair thing for me, and made those adamantium claws out of some gardening gloves and plastic cutlery." He chuckled to himself. "Mom was *not* happy."

"Why not?"

"Because Dad didn't realize how Austin had it all figured out. My brother didn't know Dad had bought a little pink swim cap for me, and Mom had just left it all up to Dad, so she didn't know what Austin had planned."

"Which was?"

"He shaved my head with Dad's hair clippers."

"Oh." I swallowed back a giggle. "Were you upset?"

"Not until Mom saw me. She freaked out, so I freaked out. Austin wasn't allowed to go trick-or-treating that year. And then he blamed me. He wouldn't speak to me until Christmas."

"Aw. But I bet you looked cute."

He snorted. "Mom's got plenty of pictures that show otherwise. She never did let Austin live that down." The road sped by under us, the car's tires humming. "What about you? Got any head-shaving stories?"

"Not quite. Although, when we were three, we did do each other's makeup with Mom's permanent markers. Blue for eyeshadow. Red for blush. The works."

He laughed. "Nice."

"Yeah, not so much. Mom was mortified. Can you imagine

having to drop off a couple of three-year-old tarts at preschool every day? We looked like we'd just escaped from a whorehouse during the Gold Rush."

"I'm guessing there are pictures."

"Of course. Parents always take pictures of stuff like that so they can embarrass us with them later."

"The perfect payback."

"Did you ever get Austin back for shaving your head?"

"I shaved off one of his eyebrows when I was thirteen. But I was kind of under the influence at the time, so . . ."

"Stoned?"

He cleared his throat. "I don't do that anymore."

"You told me you didn't do it at all."

"No, I merely implied it." He let out a deep sigh. "I guess it was too much to hope for that you wouldn't find out."

"I heard you got suspended."

He shook his head. The mall—glowing like a gaudy beacon in the twilight—was coming up, so he pulled into the other lane and slowed a bit. "Nope."

"But you missed a lot of school, didn't you? Rissa said you had to repeat—"

"Austin had just died. The last thing I felt like doing was sitting in a classroom. I didn't get suspended. Nobody had the heart to do that to me after that night." He frowned and gripped the steering wheel. "I just wish their sympathy had extended to my grades."

"You didn't have to repeat the year, did you?"

He shook his head. "Half the classes, though. I never did catch up. I won't be graduating with you guys this year. I won't fulfill enough graduation requirements."

"Next year?"

With a short laugh, he glanced over at me. "Yeah, right. I'm not putting in any more time than I need to. I'll just get my adult diploma and be done with it. Good thing I never planned on being a doctor, eh?"

"What do you want to do?"

"Not sure. I might look into one of the art schools, but I still wouldn't know what to specialize in. Can't exactly make a living as an illustrator these days."

"Why not?"

"I guess I shouldn't say that. You *can*, but you have to be really good."

"You are."

He smiled. "Thanks, but there are plenty of other artists who are just as good."

"You would've liked Jade," I said, leaning my elbow against the window and bracing my knuckles on my temple. "She wanted to study graphic design and get into marketing. But she could draw really well, too. You should've seen the mural in our old bedroom." My last few words sounded a little squeaky. Kemp glanced over at me in alarm.

"You okay?"

"Yeah."

"It's still fresh. I know. I couldn't listen to anyone talk about Austin for the first year. One time, I even told my math teacher to shut up when he tried to compare our skills. And I was the one who was coming out looking like the math whiz."

I nodded, not trusting myself to say anything. He stayed quiet, too, as he wove the car through the traffic, heading for the entrance to the mall. I'd been there plenty of times before with Jade—though not since—and as we got close, I felt my stomach start to tighten. *This was a mistake,* I thought. But what could I do? We'd already driven out there. Even if we abandoned our plans, there would still be the return trip to get through. I bit my lips together to keep them from trembling.

Kemp remained quiet until he found a parking space within sight of the theatre. The lot was crowded, and I could see a lineup out the glowing doors. After he turned off the car and pulled the keys from the ignition, he turned to me. "I'm sorry, Ivy. Maybe our rule should apply outside of school, too."

I shook my head. "It's not that. I don't mind talking about her. Besides, I need to get used to it."

"Give it time. It'll get easier."

I turned to him with a frown. He shook his head quickly.

"Not losing her. Talking about her. Trust me on that, okay?"

Taking a deep breath, I stared out toward the coloured glow of the theatre. "I wasn't there," I said. "I still feel guilty about that. It makes it harder."

"Why?" he asked. His voice was more gentle than it needed to be, but I appreciated the fact that he knew to tread carefully.

"I was her twin. Sometimes I feel like people are judging me because I wasn't there."

"Why weren't you?"

"She was camping with her boyfriend's family."

"And you hated the guy?"

I smiled and shook my head. "No. It was just . . . *their* thing. I would've been a third wheel."

"What happened, exactly?" he asked. "The article I read said something about medical distress, but that could've been anything." He bit his lip. "You don't *have* to say, if you don't want to."

"No, it's okay." I dropped my hands to my lap with a sigh and twisted my fingers together. "It was an allergic reaction."

"Peanuts?"

I shook my head. "No. That would've been better, actually, because then she would've been prepared. It was a bee sting."

"I'm sorry."

"Yeah. Thanks."

He was quiet for a few moments. But then he leaned toward me a little, though his posture was hesitant. "You know you couldn't have done anything, then, right? The outcome would've been the same whether you were there or not."

"Not necessarily."

He didn't ask me what I meant, for which I was grateful. Instead, he turned and looked out the windshield toward the theatre. "Want to go get in line? We probably should, if we want to get decent seats."

I nodded and unbuckled my seatbelt. As we slipped out of the car into the warm autumn evening, my skin broke out in goosebumps anyway. I wasn't sure why until I reached Kemp, who was waiting near one of the spindly trees beside a row of cars. As we walked toward the theatre, he stayed close to my side, and I remembered that I was on a date. He didn't seem to have forgotten. Then again, he was probably used to talking about dead siblings at that point, and it didn't discombobulate him all to hell. Like he'd said, it was still fresh for me. Too fresh.

By the time we got through the lineup, the movie we wanted to see was sold out. Kemp turned to me, looking rather embarrassed.

"Not your fault," I said.

"Want to see something else?"

"Do you?"

He glanced at the offerings and shrugged. "Not really." Turning away from the ticket window, through which I was getting tantalizing whiffs of popcorn, he looked over toward the mall proper. "Want to go get something to eat instead?"

"Like what? The food court will be closing in a few minutes."

"There's a place over there that makes really good wraps," he said, pointing at a smaller strip of mall-adjacent businesses and the brilliant lights that were dazzling through the darkness. "Or . . . I think there's a pizza place across the street."

"Wraps sound good."

"Sorry it's not popcorn."

I laughed. "It's okay. Some other time."

"So this disaster of a date hasn't turned you off me for good?"

"Why is it a disaster?" I asked.

He tilted his head as he stepped away from the theatre, inviting me to join him. "Because I dragged you all the way out here and then we couldn't get tickets. Plus, I upset you with talk about your sister."

"It would take a lot more than that to make this a disaster."

"Like what?"

"Food poisoning. Getting back to your car to find the tires slashed. You getting handsy and me punching you in the face."

He snorted. "Well, I can't make any promises about the first two. But if I do something stupid with my hands, you have my permission to punch me. I'd probably deserve it."

"It'd be payback for that time you hit me in the face with a basketball," I said, but I knew my joke had fallen flat even before the last word exited my mouth. He cleared his throat and looked away. I hugged myself and watched the pavement as we headed across the parking lot.

By the time we reached the wrap place, neither of us had said anything. So I stopped a few feet away from the door. He'd just reached out to grab the handle, but when he saw me, he froze.

"What's wrong?"

"I'm sorry," I said. "I wasn't blaming you."

"I know."

"I was trying to be funny. I wasn't."

"I know." His lips twitched in the hint of a smile. The expression was kind of irresistible, even if he was being a little bit annoying at that moment. I stepped closer and looked up at him.

"If I punch you in the face, it'll only be because you did something really stupid like grab my ass."

"Got it." He glanced down for a moment before returning his gaze to my eyes. "What about your hand?"

I frowned. "What about it?"

"Am I allowed to hold it?"

Since his right hand was grasping the door handle, I reached out and took his left. He pulled away so fast, my heart tumbled into my shoes. But then, after furiously rubbing his palm on his jeans, he slipped his hand back into mine with a smile. It was still a little damp—and very warm—but as he gave my fingers a gentle squeeze, I found myself smiling right back at him, suddenly feeling that this might not have been such a mistake after all.

WE ATE OUR WRAPS IN HIS CAR WITH ALL THE WINDOWS open so the gentle breeze could carry the sounds of the evening to us. We made kind of a mess, culminating in Kemp getting ranch dressing all over his lap. We laughed as we picked shredded lettuce out from between the seats, and then climbed out of the car to brush the escaped rice from our clothes.

"I guess I'll be spending the weekend vacuuming," he said, bending over to examine the greasy stain on the crotch of his jeans. "Shit. I hope Mom does *not* notice that on the way in. I don't need to hear 'the talk' again."

I couldn't help laughing, even as my cheeks got warm. "What?"

He looked up at me with a sheepish grin. "Think she'll believe it's actually ranch dressing and not something else?"

I didn't know what to say to that. Aside from knowing he hadn't had a girl over to his house in a few years, I didn't really know much about his history (or reputation) when it came to dating or sex. He leaned over into the car and began brushing off his seat. I followed his lead, even though I hadn't managed to make quite as much of a mess. The interior light cast the shadows of his eyelashes over his cheeks. I didn't realize I'd stopped moving and was just staring at him until he looked up and raised his eyebrows.

"What? Do I have something on my face, too?"

"Actually, yeah."

Bracing one hand on the seat, he reached up with the other and swiped it over his mouth and chin. When he was done, the tiny piece of lettuce had been dislodged. I nodded.

"Better."

He collapsed into his seat and pulled the door closed. Leaning his head back against the headrest, he crooked his finger at me. I climbed in and shut the door, my heart picking up its pace. I thought he might reach for my hand once we were both safely inside, but he didn't. He just watched me for a few moments, his eyebrows twitching in a contemplative frown.

"Thanks for the wrap," I said. "It was good."

"You're welcome." His voice was distracted. Finally, he swivelled toward me, careful to avoid the gearshift with his knee. "Are you okay? You look . . ."

"Bruised?"

"Besides that. You look kind of tired."

I shrugged and sank back in the seat. "I haven't slept that well since we moved in."

"Yeah. It takes a while to get used to a new house. When

we moved a few years ago, I freaked out every night because the pipes did this weird thing where it sounded like someone was pounding on the front door. Every time Dad got up to pee, I thought someone was going to break in."

"I doubt they'd knock first."

"They would if they wanted to see if anyone was home."

"It's nothing like that," I said. "The pipes are fine. It's just . . ."

"What?"

I wasn't sure if I should tell him. After all, things were going pretty well, and I didn't want to scare him off, thinking that he'd just gone on a date with a crazy person. Especially when I still needed a ride home. Not that I thought he was going to dump me in the parking lot and drive off without me. *Honestly, Ivy. Stop being ridiculous.*

"Got a ghost?" he asked, then let out a short burst of laughter. His smile died a moment later when he saw my face. "Ivy?"

I shook my head. "I don't know what it is. Dad doesn't believe in ghosts. He thinks it's just nightmares. But . . . I've had bad dreams before, and they've never been like this."

"Like what?"

"Real. And awful." I sighed. "At the same time every night."

"What time?" he asked. His voice wavered a little, and he almost sounded scared. Which scared me.

"About half an hour before midnight. I mean, I've only had two so far. So I don't actually know if it's a pattern."

He chewed on his lip for a moment, a deep frown creasing the skin between his eyebrows. "What were the dreams?"

I shook my head. "It's probably nothing. I've been under a lot of stress, between Jade and moving and starting at a new school and—"

"Why don't you want to tell me?"

Turning my head away to face the rapidly cooling night air, I sighed. "Because you'll think I'm really disturbed. Especially if you think I'm just dreaming. Dreams like that probably indicate a hidden psychopath or something."

"You're not a psychopath."

"How do you know?"

"You wouldn't care as much as you do."

"How do you know that's not just an act?" I asked, keeping my head turned. *What are you doing?* I asked myself. *Are you* trying *to push him away?*

Maybe I was. The last thing I really needed was the complication of a romantic relationship. Folding my arms—which were rapidly developing goosebumps in the cooling air—I tried to still my trembling lip. Out of the corner of my eye, I saw him lean forward. A moment later, he tucked my hair behind my ear.

"Because I see what you're doing. I wish I didn't have to understand what you're feeling, but I do. I've been there. I know what it's like to feel guilty for living when they can't. You don't think I've tried to sabotage my own life more than a few times?" The backs of his fingers, still hovering near my face, brushed my cheek. "You're going to learn this for yourself, Ivy, but I'm going to tell you anyway: Screwing up our own lives doesn't help them."

I knew that, logically. But, sometimes, I still felt like I needed to punish myself, as if doing so could somehow diffuse the loss. As if I could share the burden, the broken promise of Jade's unlived life.

"They'd want us to live the lives they can't," Kemp said quietly.

"How do you know what they would want? We can't know. Maybe they're sitting somewhere, blaming us."

He took a deep breath and let it out slowly in an exhale so measured that it reminded me of the ones Mom used to do when Jade and I had done something really naughty and she'd been on the verge of yelling at us. "Maybe I have to believe I know what they want. Maybe that's the only way I can keep functioning." He slumped back in his seat, pulling his fingers away from my face. I missed his touch almost immediately, but the moment had passed.

9

Don't Scream

IF THERE HAD BEEN A VISIT FROM A GHOST ON FRIDAY NIGHT, I must've slept through it. Saturday night passed without incident, too, so by Sunday evening when I climbed into bed, listening to the rain patter on the roof above me, I figured I was in the clear. And that was a relief. I'd slept well for two nights—despite coming home from my date with Kemp feeling awkward and guilty, like I'd done something wrong—and I was looking forward to another decent night of rest. I clicked off the light, checked the time on my phone (11:15), and snuggled down under the covers to let the gentle sound of the rain lull me to sleep.

I woke with a start, not because I'd heard anything, but because I couldn't breathe. In a panic, I kicked off the covers and sat up, struggling against my paralyzed diaphragm. My mind immediately went to the boy in the loincloth who'd silently gasped and died on my floor, because that was exactly what I felt like I was about to do. In the gloomy, raindrop-shadowed room, I saw the ghost.

Unlike the first two, this one was a lot older. The man had stringy grey hair that reached to his shoulders, but his clothes were fine, albeit a bit dirty. He stared straight ahead with his pale eyes for a few moments, and I began to hope that this static vision was all I was going to see. If past encounters were anything to go by, I only had a few more seconds to get through. Just a few more seconds before I could breathe again.

But then the man began to move. His hands were behind his back, and as he got down on his knees, he almost lost his balance. I couldn't see anything else besides him, so when he bent forward, it appeared that he was defying gravity. I didn't understand, not until a moment later, and then it was too late to even close my eyes. His head detached from his body, falling silently to the floor as blood spurted from his neck. For a few awful seconds, his eyes stared. And then he was gone . . . and I was screaming.

"What is going on?" Dad shouted, bursting into the room ahead of Mom, bringing with him a painful shock of illumination from the light in the hallway. I shook my head and took a few gasps of air, trying to make up for the time when I hadn't been able to breathe at all.

"Another nightmare?" Mom asked.

"This is getting ridiculous," Dad said. "She needs to see someone about this and—"

"You can't just fix your kid like your garage-door opener," Mom snapped. She grabbed his arm and pushed him out the door. "Go back to bed."

He went without complaint, though probably because he was still half asleep. Mom shook her head with a sigh.

"I'm sorry," I said miserably. "I'll try not to scream next time."

"You just scared him," she said, sitting down on the edge

of my bed. She absently pulled at the bedspread, even though my legs were sprawled on top. "You scared me."

"Sorry."

"It might not be a bad idea to see Jean."

"She's not going to be able to help."

"How do you know?"

I bit my lip. *Because she's not a ghost whisperer,* I thought. But, instead, all I said was, "She'll just want me to talk about Jade. And this has nothing to do with Jade."

"Are you sure?"

I was pretty sure. After all, the visions—or whatever they were—had only started after we'd moved. If Jade were going to come back and haunt me with horrible visions, or if I were going to dream about these awful, random deaths, why hadn't I done it in our previous home? I was fairly certain that all of this had to do with our new (old) house.

"Just think about it," Mom said. "Talking might help."

Yeah, I thought. *It might.* If I could find the right person to talk to. "Do you have the name of the previous owners?"

She blinked in surprise, but then nodded. "Hayes."

I nearly choked. "*Hayes?*"

"Ivy, I don't want you contacting them."

"I won't," I said, because I certainly had no intention of doing so. Especially not when I could talk to their son any time I wanted.

"Promise? They don't need to be badgered with questions about ghosts."

"Who said anything about ghosts?"

She frowned. "That's what you think it is, isn't it? I promise you, Ivy. The house is not haunted."

"Well, my bedroom certainly seems to be."

Reaching out, she smoothed down my sleep-mussed hair. "I want you to talk to Jean. When you're ready," she added when I opened my mouth to protest. "But I want you to tell her about this. Maybe she has some suggestions."

"You don't believe me."

"I believe you're seeing something. But you've lost your twin sister. Your mind might be handling that trauma in ways we don't understand."

I sighed and turned away as my throat got tight. Mom's seeming indifference was something that had bothered me since the day Jade had died. It was the only thing that got me close to crying, and, even then, the tears that prickled were those of fury, not sadness. I knew my parents loved my sister, but the way they'd both sort of shut down enraged me. I often wondered if their inability to cry was linked to mine, and if one of us could just get through that barrier one day, we would all break down and start to heal.

She rubbed her hand over my arm and got up. The light from the hall slid away as she pulled the door closed, leaving me in the gloom once more. I waited, listening for her footsteps on the stairs, and when I figured it was safe, I reached for my phone.

What the hell? I shot at Kemp, my hands trembling so badly that I could barely hit the right letters on the screen. *When were you going to tell me that we're living in your old house?*

There was no answer. Not that I'd expected there to be. He was probably asleep and wouldn't get the message until morning . . . unless he was one of those people who actually slept with their phones, in which case he was ignoring it.

I took a deep breath and turned off the phone before setting it back on my nightstand. As I curled into a ball under the covers, still shaking from having to witness a beheading on my bedroom floor, a new—and rather unpleasant—thought popped into my mind.

If this house were somehow still connected to the Hayes family, would I soon be getting a visit from Austin?

10

Road Rash

KEMP DIDN'T EVEN LOOK AT ME DURING THE FIRST FEW minutes of PE, so I knew he'd gotten my text. As soon as we'd been released to run through the wilds of suburbia, he took off with some of the other boys and one really tall girl named Brianne who I suspected was on the track team. Annoyed, I jogged along at my own pace, watching them get farther and farther ahead.

I wanted to talk to him, but if he wouldn't answer my texts, I would have to do it in person. I also knew that he would finish his run long before me and disappear into the locker room before I had a chance to catch him. And though we sat next to each other in Art, the openness of the space wasn't exactly private; I didn't need half the class eavesdropping.

Knowing I'd be a sweaty mess for the rest of the day—but not really caring, so desperate was I for answers—I broke into a sprint. It didn't take me long to catch up since they were just jogging with their enviably long legs. Still, by the time I pulled up alongside Kemp, I wasn't sure if I'd be able to talk and run at the same time; it was hard enough just breathing.

He glanced at me and did sort of a double take. Then he slowed a little. I shook my head, causing my ponytail to swing.

"Don't . . . slow down."

"You sure?"

I watched as the other boys and Brianne pulled ahead. When they were safely out of earshot, I sped up a little so he'd take the hint. My runners pounded the pavement, and my side was developing a really painful stitch, but I didn't want to stop or slow down. Somehow, the discomfort distracted me from the awkwardness of what I was about to do.

"Why did you . . . lie to me?" I asked, panting as I pumped my arms.

"About what?" His voice was steady. It didn't seem like he was even trying.

"Your house. You . . . could've told me."

"You already seemed freaked out about your dreams. I didn't want you thinking you lived in a haunted house."

I gasped, half from his words, half from the way my heart was pounding in my chest. "Is it haunted?"

"Depends on what you mean by 'haunted,'" he said, nudging me with his elbow as we peeled around a corner.

"Haunted. As in . . . full of ghosts."

He didn't say anything. I frowned and turned to look at him. "Kemp, spill it. If . . . there's something we . . . should know about our house . . . you need to—" Suddenly, my ankle turned as I hit an uneven patch of ground. I knew I was going to fall, even before it happened. I took two huge leaps forward, trying to compensate, and Kemp reached out to grab me. But it didn't do any good. All that happened was that we both went down with a skidding thud that I felt through my teeth. A few of the runners behind us laughed as they made a detour around our sprawled limbs.

"Shit," Kemp muttered as he rolled over and sat up. "Are you okay?"

My palms stung, and as soon as I turned over and looked down, I noticed the blood beading up from the nasty road rash on both knees. Kemp was staring at a similar sight, although he must've gone down with a little more force; the blood was trickling down from his knee through the hair on his left leg. He lifted up his right arm and craned his neck to see a near-identical wound on his elbow.

"Are *you* all right?" I asked. He nodded and stood up, then looked at my hands.

"I'd help you up, but . . ."

I got to my feet, feeling a little lightheaded. My heart was thumping after my sprint, and my vision was still sparkling around the edges. I took an experimental step forward and was relieved to find that I hadn't actually injured my ankle. I couldn't really say the same for my skin, though.

"Come on," he said, tilting his head after the other runners, who were just disappearing around the next corner.

"I can't run that fast," I said. "Obviously."

"So we'll just walk." He chewed on his lip for a moment. "But only if you promise not to yell at me. If you do, I'm out of here."

"Fine. No yelling." I held up my hands in surrender. He frowned at my palms, and when I turned them toward me to look, I spied the scuffed, reddened skin.

"I haven't had a wipeout like that since I was a little kid," he said, turning and starting to walk. I limped after him, holding my side. The stitch was still there, annoyingly persistent.

"Bike?"

"No. Austin found a shopping cart and sent me down the hill in front of our house."

"That's not much of a hill," I said.

"It is once you get going." He let out a humourless laugh. "I begged him to let me go first. So I was the one who got to find out what happens when you skid ten feet on your front after you get flipped out of a shopping cart with a wonky front wheel."

"What happens?"

"You pretty much sand your nipples off." He rubbed at them with a suffering sigh. I shook my head.

"It's a wonder any boys make it to adulthood. You do some really stupid stuff."

"Yeah. We do." His voice was suddenly cold. I looked up at him with a frown.

"What's the real reason you didn't tell me about the house?" I asked. He shrugged and examined his left palm.

"If I tell you, you'll probably just yell at me."

"I promised I wouldn't."

"You might think I'm crazy."

"I already do. You did ride a shopping cart down a hill and sand your nipples off."

He cracked a smile. "Okay, fine. I'll give you that one."

"Is Austin . . . ?"

Turning to me, he raised his eyebrows. "Is Austin haunting the house?" When I nodded, he shook his head. "Not exactly."

"What does that mean?"

"If I tell you, your opinion of me will go from 'regular crazy' to 'batshit.'"

I grunted. "Try me. After what I've seen, I kind of doubt it."

He glanced at his watch before coming to a stop. My shoes scuffed on the sidewalk as I drew up next to him. Pointing at the edge of a nearby lawn, he went and sat.

"What are you doing?"

"I'm going to tell you what's going on. But I'm not doing it where anyone's going to hear us. There're already enough rumours about me going around. We don't need to add to that."

"What rumours?"

"That I'm a pothead. That I got suspended for trying to sell weed to the shop teacher. That I had something to do with Austin's death." He grabbed a handful of grass and pulled. A few blades popped and snapped. "One of those is true, by the way," he said, brushing the broken grass from his hands. I sat down slowly, close enough to know that the first rumour wasn't true. The second one probably wasn't, either, unless he was lying about the suspension or he was talking about some other incident. The third one I didn't believe at all and wouldn't waste any time worrying about.

"So what rumour would you be starting today?" I asked, folding my legs in front of me. His legs were bent, his soles sitting on the ground. When I leaned forward, I could see that his knee had stopped bleeding. The drying trail of blood reached halfway down his leg.

"That I've completely lost my grip on sanity. And that Austin had, too. I'm not going to let that rumour take hold. His reputation has already taken enough hits."

I waited for him to go on, but he didn't. He went back to tugging at the grass, and I started to get a little worried that whoever owned the house we were sitting in front of was going to come out and start yelling at us to get off their lawn. I plucked at my shoelaces while I waited, shoving the aglets into the grommets, one after the other, just for something to do.

"It started after the car accident," he said at last. I stopped playing with my shoes and turned to face him. He was staring off at the house across the street. "Austin had a concussion. The doctor said it probably wouldn't cause any lasting problems. And it didn't seem like it did, at first. He didn't have any physical symptoms, so we thought he was okay."

"But he wasn't?"

He shook his head. "He kind of changed after that. His personality, I mean. He got really paranoid, and *really* protective of me. Mom and Dad just thought it was because he felt guilty for endangering me. But I was fine. He didn't seem to get that, or . . . I don't know." He tossed away a handful of grass blades and rubbed at the drying blood on his leg. "He started smoking pot to cope. He said it relaxed him. And because I wanted to do everything he did, I smoked it with him."

"I thought you said he got protective of you."

"Yeah, and I was a stubborn little shit. He didn't *want* me to do it, but I wasn't about to miss out. We'd share a joint before school. He couldn't relax enough to make it through his classes without doing that."

"What does this have to do with the house?" I asked.

"Nothing. I'm just explaining why he . . . His state of mind was weird, okay?" The blood didn't seem to want to come off his leg. He picked at it, halfheartedly, then draped his arms around his knees. "After the accident, he started having dreams. At least, that's what he said they were at the time. But they weren't like anything I'd ever experienced, or even heard of. It's got to be some pretty scary shit to drive a seventeen-year-old kid to sleep on the floor of his parents' bedroom."

"Did he ever tell you what he dreamed about?"

"Not really. But I found this journal he'd been keeping. He was writing them all down. They weren't really dreams, though. I mean, not like the kind you usually think of."

"What do you mean?"

"Dreams are often like little stories, right?"

"Yeah."

"Well, these weren't. They were just . . . dark. All deaths. And there was no context. He'd just suddenly see some random person, and a minute later, they'd die."

My heart—which had started to calm down—seemed to quicken once more. "A minute?"

"Yeah. It was always really quick, from what I could tell. He'd catalogued about twenty-five of these things. I found the notebook when he was in the hospital. Dad and I had come home to get some of his things so he could have them around him when . . ." He cleared his throat. "Anyway, I found the notebook and read about all of this stuff. If he had just told someone, maybe they could've helped. As it was, he had to face it all on his own. It must've been torture, going through that every night."

"Do you still have the notebook?" I asked, my voice barely more than a whisper. Kemp turned to me with a frown.

"Yeah. Why?"

"Could I see it?"

He let out a humourless snort. "That's really morbid, Ivy."

I looked down at my lap. A moment later, he swore.

"You're seeing the same thing, aren't you? Is that why you asked about the house?"

"Kind of," I admitted, still staring at my lap. "Doesn't that make *me* batshit?"

"No, but it seriously calls into question the safety of that house."

"Because it's haunted?"

He shook his head. "No. At least . . . I don't think so."

"What do you mean? If those aren't ghosts, what are they?"

"Promise you won't laugh?"

"It's hardly a laughing matter," I said. "It's messing with my sleep, and it might've messed up your brother."

He took a deep breath and let it out really slowly before he said, "Those aren't just random ghosts. I think they were Austin's past lives."

Poor Kemp probably thought he'd scared me off. I didn't say much as we got up and walked slowly back to the school, stopping at the nurse's office for bandages and ointment for our scrapes. I was silent through most of Art, too, and barely looked at Kemp's pointillist piece. My mind was somewhere else. Mainly on the floor of my bedroom.

"Was your parents' room on the third floor?" I asked near the end of class, so surprising him that he turned and looked at me as if I'd just spoken my first words ever.

"Their room? Yeah. Why?"

So the spot where all those ghosts were dying was probably the same spot where Austin had lain when those same deaths had freaked him out and driven him up to his parents' room. I spun the capped pen on the table absently, the page in front of me still only graced with a handful of dots.

"Ivy?"

"Yeah." I blinked and turned to him. He raised his eyebrows. "You okay?"

"Could I see the journal?" I asked.

"It's pretty graphic."

"So's what I'm seeing."

He sighed and nodded. "I'll bring it tomorrow."

"Thanks."

"Do you need some help?" he asked, and I frowned as I tried to figure out what he was talking about.

"With what?"

"That." He waved his pen at my paper.

"I'm supposed to do it myself, aren't I?"

"You're supposed to do *something*. You've barely started, and it's due on Friday."

I looked over at his paper, where a beautiful picture was already taking shape. I could make out the leaves, their veins captured in myriad tiny dots.

"Maple," he said.

"How Canadian."

With a smile, he leaned closer and peered at my paper. "You could turn that into a flag," he said, stroking his finger just above the undulating line of dots that cut through the middle of the otherwise blank white space.

"What kind of flag?"

"Doesn't really matter," he said. "Ms. London will be looking more at the actual technique than the result. I had her last year," he added when I gave him a questioning look. "Or you could try to turn that into a snake, but living subjects are harder to get right."

"I'll take your word for it."

He smiled, looking like he was about to offer some more advice, but then the bell chimed. We gathered up our stuff and handed our half-finished drawings to the teacher for safekeeping.

"Lunch?" I asked. He shook his head.

"Probably not a good idea. I'll see you on Thursday, though, okay?"

I nodded, somewhat disappointed. "Don't forget the journal."

"I won't."

I watched him walk off, probably focusing a little too closely on his butt. Then I headed for my locker so I could grab my lunch.

Rissa and Eunice were waiting for me in the cafeteria. But as I slid onto the bench beside Rissa and opened up my container of leftover chili and rice, I could tell that something was wrong. Immediately, I wondered if Kemp and I had been seen on Friday night. My mind frantically tried to come up with an excuse.

"What is it with you two?" Rissa asked. I frowned and shook my head as I plunged my fork into my lunch.

"What? Who?"

"You and Kemp. First, he sends you to the nurse's office by throwing a basketball at your face. Then you both do a face plant in the middle of the street?"

"Says who?"

"Everybody," Eunice said, giving me a dark look. I sighed.

"Are you seriously jealous of me falling and tearing the skin off my knees? It wasn't like we fell in each other's arms or anything."

"That's not what I heard," Rissa said. She sipped at her energy drink and plucked at her spidery eyelashes.

"What did you hear?"

"That you were about to fall, and he gallantly tried to save you."

I swivelled on the seat so I could pull up my skirt a little. "Does it look like he saved me?"

Eunice stood up so she could see. Her expression fell, and I almost felt bad for destroying the little illusion she had going of Kemp being some sort of knight in shining armour.

"I tripped, and he reached out to try to help," I said, pulling my skirt back down over my scraped and bandaged knees. "But we both ended up on the ground. He actually got the worst of it. His knee was bleeding down his leg."

"Gross." Rissa dipped a fry in ketchup, then glared at it, as if it were the condiment's fault for looking a little too much like blood.

"I'm fine, thanks. Don't worry about me."

"You're obviously fine." She shook her head. "If you're not careful, though, people are going to think you two have something going on."

"Well, we don't. We're just friends." I hated the lie as soon as it was out of my mouth. Did I really owe Eunice anything? If Kemp liked me—and not her—how was that my fault?

"Oh, I was going to ask you," Rissa said. "Have you done the reading for Mr. Sharma's class yet?"

"Chapter three?"

She shrugged. "I don't know. I think it was about the Charter or something."

"Yeah. I did it the night it was assigned."

"Well, good for you," she said, mistaking my simple statement of fact as a judgement of her. "Did you take notes?"

"A few. Why?"

"Think I could borrow them?"

I shook my head. "That chapter is only like six pages long. Why don't you just read it?"

She shrugged and stabbed a fry at a blob of ketchup. "Fine. Be that way. Don't help me."

"That's not fair," I said. They both turned to look at me. My voice *had* been kind of loud. But I was annoyed. "I can't help having two classes with Kemp. I can't help it if he hit me in the face with a basketball. That's hardly a meet-cute, you know. And I certainly can't help it if he likes me."

"Does he like you?" Rissa asked.

"What if he does? Do you two expect me to turn him down so we can all bitch and moan and drool over him in solidarity? We're in grade twelve, not grade five. I'm not going to avoid a potentially great relationship just to make you feel better."

They were both silent for so long that I really thought that was it. *So much for those friendships,* I thought. I slapped the lid back on my chili and stood up.

"You're right," Eunice said. She stared down at her barely touched fries, her hair hanging in sleek curtains on either side of her sad face.

"No, she's not," Rissa said. "She *knew* you liked Kemp, but she still—"

"He doesn't like me," Eunice said. The tone of her voice seemed to be sort of final. It was one of those situations where you kind of wanted to say, "Of course he does!" Even if it was just to make her feel better. But all three of us knew that those words would've just been a comforting lie. The table remained silent.

I was the one who finally had to break the spell, because if any of us wanted to eat something before lunch was over, we needed to start moving again.

"Should I sit somewhere else?" I asked.

Rissa looked like she was contemplating my suggestion, but Eunice quickly shook her head.

"No. Stay here."

I glanced at Rissa, who just shrugged. So I sat back down and opened up my container. We ate in silence for a few minutes, the only sound in our little bubble the slurping of the girls' lips on their cans. I picked out most of the big chunks of tomato in my chili and ate them first, then separated out the onions. Dad always added way too many.

"So," Rissa said hesitantly when my container held little

but a pile of onions and her cardboard bowl was merely smeared with ketchup. "Are the rumours true?"

"Which ones?"

"That he smokes pot."

"Does he smell like he does?"

She shrugged. "I haven't been close enough to him recently to find out."

"He smells like a sweaty boy," I said. "Especially after PE. He doesn't smoke anymore."

"What about his brother?"

"Yeah, he smoked it."

She shook her head. "No, I mean, did Kemp have something to do with . . . ?"

I gave her a withering look. "What do you think?"

"I think," she said, "that you're the only person at this table equipped to answer that question."

"Well, I'm sorry to disappoint you, but I don't know. He hasn't really talked about his brother much." My face flushed with the lie, and I felt my nose throb. Though the bruises had mostly faded, I apparently still had a touch of that Pinocchio syndrome.

"Hunter said he heard Kemp drowned his brother in the creek," Rissa said, watching me carefully for my reaction. I closed up my container and slipped it—and my fork—back into my bag.

"And you believe him?"

"I don't know. Do you?"

I snorted, then glanced at Eunice, who was looking pretty annoyed . . . but not at me. "Based on what I know of him," I said, "I highly doubt it. Besides, Kemp was only like thirteen at the time, wasn't he? How would he have over-powered his older brother like that?"

"He could've knocked him out with something first."

"Why?" I asked. "What possible reason could he have had? He's pretty easy-going. When he gets pissed off, he gets quiet . . . not violent."

"Nobody ever suspects the quiet ones," Rissa said, flipping a blond curl over her shoulder.

I shrugged. "Why bother asking me if you're not going to believe my answers?"

"Maybe I'm trying to protect my friend from a potential murderer."

"Make up your mind," I said. "Kemp's either a great guy that I stole from Eunice, or he's a psycho killer that you need to protect her from. You can't have it both ways, and you're making my brain hurt as I'm trying to figure you out."

Eunice suddenly snorted. Rissa and I both turned to her in surprise.

"What?" Rissa asked.

Eunice looked like she was fighting a smile. She absently gathered up her empty ketchup packets and stacked them in the cardboard bowl. "You don't need to protect me, Rissa."

"So you're just going to let Ivy steal the guy you've been wanting to date for the last two years?"

With a shrug, Eunice pulled her hair back and flipped it over her shoulders. Rissa shook her head in disbelief.

"Suit yourself, then. Keep dreaming about him and never get anywhere."

Eunice just smiled a little, and I was suddenly hit with the understanding that that was exactly what she wanted.

As I remembered her physical reaction to sitting right next to Kemp, the pieces of the puzzle clicked into place. She wasn't in love with Kemp; she was in love with the *idea* of him. She was satisfied with admiring him from afar. Whether that was due to fear or shyness or something else, I wasn't sure. What I did know, however, was that she was okay with the way things were. Rissa was the one who wasn't, and the girl was doing everything in her power to make sure Eunice came around to her way of thinking.

I couldn't really blame Eunice for her stance. Dreaming about something was much less messy than living it. At least, that was what I told myself. Knowing that I would have to vicariously live through another death—at least twenty more, if Kemp was right about the number—was bad enough; at the very least, I could console myself with the fact that those deaths weren't something I would ever have to experience firsthand.

11

Smokefish Creek

THE NEXT COUPLE OF DAYS PASSED SLOWLY. SLOWER STILL, it seemed, because of the nocturnal visitors. On Monday night, it was a naked boy who appeared to be running from something. He barely moved as he ran, and his feet sort of slid across my bedroom floor. Something—I couldn't see what, as was always the case—tackled him and brought him to the ground, and I watched as a huge bloody wound tore itself through the side of his neck. Blood squirted out with a violence that would've had me gasping in horror, had I been able to breathe at all. That invisible something then seemed to grab him by the back of the neck and drag him away. The vision only lasted for a few more seconds before disappearing. I managed to keep my wits about me and not scream, and I was pretty pleased with myself until the next night . . . when I saw the worst one yet.

The problem with the visions was that there was no context. I couldn't see anything but the person, which often led to weird sights that seemed to defy the laws of physics . . . like the old man whose head had fallen off, but not before he'd leaned forward at an impossible angle.

Tuesday night's vision was no different. It began with a young man, probably only a few years older than me, running and reaching up to grab something. He must have caught it, because his feet seemed to dangle as he kicked and tried to pull himself up. But then his hands slipped, and he tumbled to the ground. The next instant, he was in two pieces, cut right through the middle. He stared at his legs lying a few feet away, and screamed silently as the massive wound, gaping with entrails, released his blood in a terrifying rush. It only took a few seconds for him to stop moving. Only a couple more before the vision disappeared. I only just managed to get the pillow in front of my face before I screamed.

I slept fitfully the rest of the night and was a wreck by Wednesday morning. I dragged myself through my classes. Rissa told me how terrible I looked at the beginning of English. I was too tired to argue. I draped myself over my desk and listened to the teacher talk. I got called on once, and I managed to drag myself to a sitting position and answer the question to her satisfaction, so when I went back to my catnap, she didn't bother chewing me out for it.

By lunch, I just wanted to go home. I'd felt tired before, but this was something different. It didn't seem like the fatigue was just a result of a few bad nights of sleep. The problem seemed to go deeper. But I was too tired to figure it out. Instead of my usual bottle of water, I bought an energy drink and gulped half of it before Rissa and Eunice had even gotten back to the table with their fries.

Of course, then I ended up in hummingbird mode for the rest of the day . . . which sucked, because I had Canadian

History that afternoon, and Mr. Sharma was in fine boring form. I could barely keep my legs still, and it didn't help that the massive can of sugary-sweet oomph had filled my bladder. I held it as long as I could, which turned out to be almost the whole class, before finally asking if I could go to the bathroom.

Mr. Sharma looked at the clock. "You've only got five more minutes. Hold it."

"I *can't*," I said, my face flushing with embarrassment and indignation. A few of the boys at the back of the class snickered. Mr. Sharma just rolled his eyes and waved his hand. I gathered up my stuff and ran out of there, while the teacher gestured frantically at the homework assignment on the whiteboard. I glanced at it, but couldn't stop. I knew I'd have to call Rissa about that later. Hopefully, she wouldn't give me a hard time.

The final bell chimed just as I was washing my hands. My bladder was almost aching with relief. I watched my reflection as I rinsed off the soap, noticing the slight tremor in my head. As a coffee drinker, I wasn't used to getting such a buzz out of caffeine. It got me going in the morning, but that was about it. At that moment, it felt like I'd stepped on a live wire or something, and I didn't like the feeling at all. I quickly dried my hands and left, heading for my locker to grab my jacket and the books I needed to bring home with me.

"Ivy."

I turned at the sound of the familiar voice, only to see Kemp walking in the other direction, his head turned to look back at me. I'd already passed him without even noticing. He frowned when he saw my face.

"You all right?"

"Not really."

He walked closer and pulled me against the wall, out of the flow of traffic as the classrooms around us continued to empty and more kids got ready to head home. "Is it still happening?"

I didn't have to ask what he meant. I just nodded. "I had to watch some poor guy get cut in half last night." Drawing my hand across my stomach, I looked up at him with a shudder. "Try sleeping after *that*."

His expression deepened into a frown. "Cut in half? Did you see how?"

"No," I said, rubbing my fingers up under my glasses. "I can't see anything around the person, so I don't know where they are or what they're doing." I blinked and resettled the glasses on my nose. "I think he fell. But that's all I could see."

He blew out a breath and tugged his backpack around to his front. After unzipping it, he pulled out a small notebook with a worn, green cover. "I put it in here on Monday night. I didn't want to forget." He pushed the notebook at me, but I didn't take it. I was suddenly—inexplicably—afraid.

"Are you sure?" I asked.

He frowned. "What do you mean?"

"It was your brother's, right? Are you sure you trust me with it?"

"Why? Are you going to go run it through a shredder or something?"

"No." My hand shook as I reached out to take the notebook. "Thank you."

"Maybe you'll find some answers in there."

"I sure hope so."

He zipped up his backpack and slung it over his shoulder. But then he just stood there, gripping the strap of his bag and frowning at me. "If you want to talk about any of this . . ."

I nodded. But I doubted I would. For some reason, this felt like something I had to do myself. Whatever it was, it was connected to Austin, not his brother. And until I knew more, I didn't want to say too much.

We spent another few awkward moments just standing there before he finally gave me a quick smile and walked down the hallway, opposite the direction I needed to go. I turned and hurried to get my stuff, eager to get home so I could crack open the notebook I held pressed against my chest and maybe, just maybe, figure out what was going on.

DAD DIDN'T SHOW UP, SO I CHECKED MY PHONE, ONLY TO find a message from him saying he had a showing and I'd need to walk. I sighed as I tucked my phone back in my bag and set off, though I wasn't that annoyed about it. I knew the way by then, and it wasn't all that far. Still, I was a bit impatient because I wanted to get home, open Austin's notebook, and finally start to make sense of what I was seeing.

The house was quiet when I stepped inside, and my questioning call was met with more silence. So, after kicking off my shoes by the front door, I padded into the kitchen, grabbed an apple and a snack-size bag of chips, and made the long climb up to my room. I set the notebook carefully in the middle of my bed and proceeded to eat the chips, feeling impatient, but knowing I didn't want to get greasy fingerprints on the pages. And, if I were being honest, I was also procrastinating a little. I didn't know what I was going to find when I opened that thing up, and a part of me wasn't sure if I was going to be ready to see what was inside.

When I'd finished with the chips and washed my hands, I grasped the apple tightly and settled myself on the bed. *Maybe I shouldn't be eating while I do this,* I thought, reasoning that there were bound to be more gory visions that could turn my stomach. So, reluctantly, I set the apple aside, rubbed my palms against the bedspread, and reached forward to flip open the cover.

It was reassuringly normal. Boring, even. Austin had organized everything, noting the date and time he'd had each vision. Sadly, this fastidiousness hadn't extended to his grammar.

female kid, he'd written on the first entry, which was dated January 27th, three years earlier. she's lying in bed, face is all bruised like someone beat the crap out of her, she's not moving, then she's coughing but I can't hear anything so I don't know for sure but it look's like it, her eyes stay open really wide but she stop's moving and then she just disappear's

I flipped to the next entry. He'd limited them to one per page, no matter how short they were. It made for a lot of blank space in the notebook.

male old guy, look's like Thor or something, he's being hung with this thick rope around his neck, he's got his hands tied behind him and he's sort of hanging in the air and his legs are

So the visions weren't quite as bad as I'd been expecting.
Certainly not as bad as what I'd seen myself. I grabbed the
apple and took a bite, chewing thoughtfully as I flipped to
the next page. Had Austin and I even seen the same things?
Maybe Kemp was wrong about these visions being Austin's
past lives. If that were the case, why was *I* seeing them? But
if they were ghosts, why were we seeing a different set? And
how did it all tie back to the house?

I raised an eyebrow as I kept chewing. Turning the apple
to get at another bite, I moved on to the next entry.

I dropped the apple on the bed and leaned forward to
read the entry again. My heart was pounding. *It can't be the
same,* I thought, though I wasn't sure why. Maybe I didn't
want it to be true. Because if it was . . . was I going to go

crazy like Austin? Would I end up sleeping on the floor of my parents' bedroom, self-medicating with pot and doing weird things like splashing around in creeks in the middle of the night? I didn't have a sibling who could be there to witness it. I could fall in, be swept away, and nobody would ever know what had happened to me.

My fingers shook as I turned the page to the next entry. It didn't strike me as familiar, but it was still pretty awful, with a little girl who'd burned to death. He saw her go up in flames, her skin blistering and her clothes charring. He thought maybe she'd had oil splashed on her or something, the way the fire had engulfed her so ferociously. Burning oil would've been my first thought, too. Or maybe it would be, when that vision finally came to pass. And, as soon as I started to read the next entry, I knew, with a lead-heavy certainty, that it would.

young guy, like my age, he's running and reaching up for some metal handle, it's like in those movies from the 30's when people tried to jump on trains, he catch's the handle, but he can't hold on, so he fall's and then his body's like ripped in half by the train's wheels and he's looking over at his legs and his mouth is wide like he's screaming but there's so much blood coming out that he dies pretty quick

My hands shook so much as I fumbled for my phone that I felt like I'd just come in from making a snowman without wearing gloves. Fingertips numb, I made the call.

"Yeah?"

"It's the same," I said, and my voice shook so hard that it sounded like I was crying, even though I wasn't.

"What's the same?" Kemp asked, his voice growing a bit

louder, as if he were holding his phone really close to his mouth. "Which one?"

"I don't know!" I wailed. "Probably all of them. I don't think . . . I don't think I can do this. I've only had a few, but they're in here."

"All of them?"

"I don't know!" I shouted.

"Calm down, Ivy. Where are you?"

"At home."

"Do you want me to come over?"

I opened my mouth to say "no," but clamped my lips together instead. I didn't really want him to have to come over to our house, which probably held a lot of uncomfortable memories. But I wanted to be alone even less. I had no idea when my parents would be getting home, and this wasn't something I would be able to talk to them about, anyway. At last, I nodded. Then, when I realized Kemp couldn't see me, I uttered a feeble, "Yes."

"I'm on my way," he said, and hung up. I sat there, clutching my phone and staring at the open notebook, not ready to look at any more of the entries by myself. I didn't move until I heard the doorbell ring almost ten minutes later. Then I scrambled off the bed and thundered down the stairs.

"I'm coming!" I shouted, just in case he thought the wait was too long and he assumed I'd gone out. My socks skidded on the first floor as I made a sharp turn to run for the front of the house. When I pulled open the door, Kemp took one look at my face and shook his head.

"Shit, Ivy. You look—"

"Terrible. I know."

"No, you look scared." He stepped into the foyer, glanced at my shoes sitting to the left, and kicked off his own. I pushed the door closed and threw my arms around him from behind, as if to anchor myself. He laughed at first, but as I squeezed a little tighter, trying to still the tremble in my arms, he probably started to understand how awful I was feeling. Gently, he pried my hands away and turned around before gathering me into a proper hug. I took a deep breath and, even though my nose was pressed against the shoulder of his jacket, I didn't detect even a whiff of pot smoke. So much for that rumour. He was telling the truth about that, at least.

"I'm sorry," I said, pulling away. "You didn't have to come all the way over here. I should've been able to handle it by myself."

"Austin couldn't," he said. "Don't be so hard on yourself." His gaze flitted around before returning to fix itself on my face. "The place looks different."

"Is that a good thing?"

"Yeah. Yeah, it is."

"Do you want to see the rest, or would that be too weird?"

"Actually, it might be a good thing. Especially if I'm going to be spending time here."

I didn't bother to correct that assumption. He was probably right. So I led him back toward the kitchen, listening to our socks whisper on the floor.

"Do you want anything?" I asked. "I think there's some pop in the fridge."

"No, thanks. I'm good." He peered around the room, then looked down at the floor. "Did you change the tiles?"

"It was like this when we moved in. Didn't your parents do it?"

He shrugged. "Maybe. I know they did some work on the house when they finally decided to sell it."

"What took them so long?" I asked as I led him over to the stairs. He reached out and slid his hand over the handrail, almost reverently.

"Mom wasn't sure if she really wanted to sell. Dad just wanted to get out of here. So they compromised. We rented another place for a while, and Dad tried to get Mom to let go of the house."

"For three years?"

He let out a short laugh. "She can be stubborn." We reached the second floor, and he leaned sideways to see through the open door to Mom and Dad's room. "Huh."

"Was that your room?"

He shook his head. "Nope. Austin got the bigger one. I was stuck in there." He pointed down the hall toward the office; the door was closed. "Using it for storage?"

"No. It's my parents' office."

"Can I see it?"

When I turned the knob and pushed open the door, he let out a chuckle. With the new desks and two chairs and a couple of filing cabinets in there, the space looked pretty crowded . . . and small. "How did you even fit a bed in here?" I asked.

"It fit. There just wasn't room for much else."

I pulled the door closed and led him toward the third-floor stairs. If he was bothered by being in his old house again, he wasn't showing it. As we began to climb, he moved so we were side by side, even though the staircase was pretty narrow.

"It's not as bad as I thought it would be," he said, at which I whipped my head toward him.

"Excuse me?"

He shook his head quickly. "I didn't mean it like that. It's nice. It just feels totally different with your stuff in it. I barely recognize the place."

"Oh."

"I think *all* the floors have been redone. I don't remember the wood being this light. And they were pretty scratched up before."

I let him muse about the floors as I stepped onto the landing and led him into my room. The notebook was still open on the bed, along with my dropped phone and the apple (which had gone pretty brown where I'd gnawed it). I walked inside, not realizing he wasn't right behind me until I turned around to look.

"Are you okay?" I asked. He nodded, staring at the floor at the foot of my bed. I almost wondered if there was a puddle of blood there, or something else that would've shown that so many ghosts kept reliving their deaths in that spot. But, when I looked, the floor was bare.

"Yeah, I'm fine. Is it . . . okay?"

"Is what okay?"

"If I come in."

"Why wouldn't it be?"

"If your parents come home and find me in their daughter's bedroom, am I going to have to jump out the window?"

I snorted and shook my head. "My parents trust me." I sat

on the edge of the bed. "I haven't given them many reasons not to."

"Yeah, but would they trust me? They don't know me."

"I'm sure they know *of* you. They're realtors, and they knew this place used to belong to your family."

He grimaced. "Is it too weird that I'm here?"

"No." I shook my head and stood up, and was about to hold out my hand to beckon him closer to the bed. But I stopped myself at the last moment. Instead, I picked up the notebook. "I really should read this, but . . . I'm too afraid."

"Why?" he asked, taking another step into the room. The floor let out a creak and he stopped.

"What if there's something in here I can't handle and I . . ."

"Lose it?"

"Basically."

He shook his head. "Have you ever lost your mind from reading something scary before?"

"No. But I might lose my mind from one of these visions."

"That's why you should read them all. Then you'll be prepared."

"But what if Austin didn't . . . What if there are others? Ones that he didn't get?" Clutching the open notebook to my chest, I shook my head. "What if this is just starting, and I—"

"That's all there was," he said, tilting his chin toward the notebook. I frowned and released it a little until I could see the pages.

"What? Really?"

"Yeah. He had these visions or dreams or whatever they were. But he only had them for like a month or so."

"And then what?"

He shrugged. "And then he was a freaked-out mess. He probably thought they were going to come back."

"Did he tell you that?"

"He didn't tell me anything," he said, then sighed deeply. "I only found out what was going on because I found the notebook. But if you look at the dates . . . There's plenty of space for other entries after those, right? I think that, if he'd had more visions, he would've written them down. So they probably stopped."

"But why?"

"Maybe he didn't have any more past lives."

"If that's what they were." I stepped back until my legs hit the bed. Then I sat down and set the notebook on my lap. Kemp stood still, curling his toes against the floorboards. "Maybe there's some sort of weird mould in this house that's making us hallucinate," I said.

"Then why were you and Austin the only ones it affected?"

I shook my head. "Why would *his* past lives be affecting *me?*"

He stared at the floor, frowning, before he looked back up at me. "Maybe it has nothing to do with you."

I scoffed. "I kind of think it does."

"No, I mean . . ." He shook his head, looking lost. I gently patted the bed beside me. He raised his eyebrows, but when I didn't say anything, he came and sat. "I just meant," he said, lowering his voice to almost a whisper, "that maybe it's just a location thing. If Austin's trying to communicate . . ."

"By showing me his past lives? What's the point?"

"I don't know. But *my* point is that it could just be that you're convenient."

"Convenient?" I echoed.

"Yeah. If his spirit is tied to the house, he can't exactly come haunt me with this shit, can he? But you're here."

"Why isn't he haunting my parents?" I asked. "If their room was his before, wouldn't that be the logical choice?"

"Would they be open to something like this?"

I bit my lip. Mom, maybe. If presented with enough evidence. But I was fairly certain that, even if Austin were to appear in front of Dad and say, "Look, Mr. Ross, let me show you my past lives in a series of gory, traumatizing visions," my father would simply write the whole thing off as a bad dream or the result of too much spicy food before bed.

"I take it that's a 'no,'" Kemp said. "So you see my point." He reached for the notebook, and I let him take it. "Which one have you gotten to?"

"The one where the guy gets cut in half."

"You didn't read any more?"

"God, no!"

He nodded and flipped to the page in question. "I always figured this was one of those guys who rode the rails during the Depression. This kind of thing had to have happened quite a bit."

I shuddered and looked away as he flipped to the next page. "If there's anything else like that," I said, "I don't want to hear it."

"If I remember right, that was the worst one."

"How come none of these lives ever ended peacefully? Don't most people simply die in their bed?"

"Probably."

"So why are violent deaths so over-represented here?"

"Mm," he said, distracted as he read the next entry. I turned my head away so I wouldn't accidentally see anything. "I figured this one was probably someone who got trampled by a horse. Maybe got run over by a carriage."

I hated to ask, but I couldn't help myself. "What happened?"

He turned the notebook toward me so I could read Austin's grammatical mess.

female kid, look's like a doll, she's fucking excited about something, look's like someone call's to her or something, because she look's back toward me, and then the stupid kid run's forward, and something kind of punch's her into the ground and break's her bones, there's blood all over her dress, something round (a wheel?) crush's her skull, but I blinked and sort of missed that part, she must've died instantly because she just blinked out

"Holy crap," I said.

"Familiar?"

"Yeah. It was one of the first."

He pulled the notebook away, licked his thumb, and turned the page. I watched him as he read the next entry, his dark eyes scanning his dead brother's words.

"If this is too weird," I said, "we don't have to—"

"It's fine," he said. "I've already read this thing a few times. It's not like it's going to shock me now. I'm just checking to make sure there's nothing in here that's going to freak *you* out too badly." He turned to the next page. "What other deaths did you see that you haven't come across in here yet?"

"Well, the first one," I said, drawing my shoulders up toward my ears. "There was this guy, almost naked."

He let out a short laugh. "You'll have to narrow it down, unfortunately. I seem to remember a few naked guys in here."

"Really?" I asked, my voice dripping with so much dismay that his next laugh was a little more hearty. With a shake of his head, he flipped through a few more pages.

"I'm going to need details."

"He wasn't that old. A bit younger than us, maybe. And he wasn't totally naked. He was wearing a loincloth or something."

"Ah. I know which one you mean." He flicked through the notebook, then paused for a moment to read something on the page. "Young kid, bare ass, he's laying on the ground and I don't think he can breathe, maybe he got stung or bit by something because there's this bulge on his neck with dots of blood in the middle, he's probably poisoned, looks like a shit way to die, he can't breathe and his eyeballs are nearly popping out of his head—'"

I didn't know if that was the end of it or not because I snatched the notebook out of a startled Kemp's hands and flung it across the room, out the door, and into the hallway. Unfortunately, the layout of the third floor being what it was, the book also sailed over the railing and disappeared down the stairwell. I heard a gentle, muffled thump as it landed.

"What?" he asked, his hands in the air as if they were still holding the notebook. "What's wrong?"

"That's *worse*," I said, my voice practically a growl. "What's the matter with you?"

He blinked his thick eyelashes at me as he tried to put

together the pieces. I saw the moment when he got it. "Oh, my god, Ivy. I'm sorry. I didn't mean to—"

"Is that why your brother showed me that one first? To get my attention? Because he knew how Jade died?"

"How would he know how Jade died?"

"They're both dead. Don't they have some sort of . . . connection?"

He shook his head. "I don't think it's like a club. They didn't know each other in life. Why would Austin have even paid attention to what was happening to—" He broke off as I stood.

"Did the weed help?"

He frowned up at me.

"Did it help?" I asked again. "Was that what stopped the visions, or . . ."

"I don't think so. Not based on the timeline that I'm aware of."

I let out a strangled groan and pressed my palms against my forehead. When I pulled them away a moment later, my bangs stuck to my sweaty hands. "What am I supposed to do, then? Just let your stupid brother fuck up my mind until I go completely insane?"

"He's not doing it on purpose, Ivy."

"How do you know? You don't even know *why* he's doing it."

"Maybe it's not in his control. Maybe—"

"Stop. Just stop." Shaking my head, I stormed from the room and leaned over the railing. The notebook had landed all the way down on the second floor, and the way it was lying propped against the bottom step made me think that it had probably slid part of the way down.

"Get back," Kemp said, grabbing my arm and pulling me

back so suddenly I let out a yelp. I wrenched away and looked up, only to notice his ashen expression.

"What's wrong with you?" I shouted.

"Don't."

"Don't what?"

He groaned and rubbed his hands over his face before sliding his fingers back through his hair. Then he moved past me and thumped down the stairs. When he reached the bottom, he scooped up the notebook. I hurried after him.

"Kemp, wait! I haven't read—"

"Here," he said when I caught up with him. He pushed the notebook into my hands. "Read it. Get what you need out of it."

"I'll give it back to you tomorrow."

He shook his head and started down the stairs to the main floor. "Take your time. I don't need it."

"Are you leaving?"

He didn't answer. I followed miserably until he got to the front door, replaying everything I'd done, everything I'd shouted at him. He reached down for his shoes, but instead of putting them on, he picked them up and started back toward the kitchen. I frowned in confusion.

"Where are you going?"

"Bring your shoes."

I snatched them up and ran after him. As soon as we were standing on the small patio outside the kitchen door, we slipped our shoes on. The air was still warm, but there was a definite bite of autumn in it. Dad had mowed the crispy lawn once since we'd moved in, and it hadn't needed it again. Most of the grass—save for a few green tufts that had been nourished by the brief rain—looked dead.

I clutched the notebook tightly in one hand as Kemp led me down the hill toward the back of the property. I'd yet to venture down there, toward the trees. The slope grew a little steeper the farther we got from the house, and soon enough I could hear the sound of trickling water. The fences on either side stopped, and before us stood the third side of the wooden obstruction. Placed within was a solid gate. Kemp undid the latch and swung it open, and we stepped through into what seemed like another world.

The creek ran, sparkling, over the stones in its bed. The afternoon sun cut through the trees that surrounded us, that lined both sides of the water. I watched as a leaf rode the gentle rapids downstream, then stepped forward a little so I could see in either direction. When I looked down, I could tell that the water was only a few inches deep, and it certainly wasn't rushing with any sort of force. I turned back to Kemp, who was standing with his hands shoved in his pockets, staring at the far side of the creek. I followed his gaze to the steep, root-gnarled bank that rose up toward a hill studded with trees.

"You're wondering how he died in that," he said. "Aren't you?"

"This is Smokefish Creek?" I asked, frowning at the trickling water. "It doesn't look like much."

"And it's not. Not at this time of year, anyway, and not here." He took a step forward and pulled out one hand so he could point downstream. "It gets dicey down that way, and during runoff season . . ."

"What was he doing?" I asked, my voice almost a whisper. But the creek wasn't so loud that it drowned me out.

"Trying to kill himself."

"In four inches of water?"

"In March," he said. "I think he was aiming for hypothermia. He didn't realize I'd followed him out here, and when he did, he was pissed."

"Because you tried to save him?"

He let out a harsh laugh. "I didn't try to save him, Ivy." Shaking his head, he jammed his hand back into his pocket so hard that I was surprised he didn't rip it.

"Oh. But . . . you were just a kid. You can't blame yourself for his—"

"Yes, I can." He looked down at the ground and, spying a rock, bent to pick it up. Then he hurled it at the opposite bank so hard that I took a step back in alarm. "Sometimes we're blameless. Like you were with your sister. But other times . . ." He picked up another rock. This one landed downstream, sending up a splash. "Other times, we deserve every bit of guilt we're feeling." The third rock hit a tree with a knocking sound. He turned to me as he brushed off his hands. "It should've been me."

My eyes widened. "You should've died?"

"Maybe. But I meant that I'm the one who should be dealing with Austin's shit right now. Not you. The last thing you need, on top of everything else, is my asshole of a brother driving you literally insane."

"But why do you deserve it?" I asked, and my mind instantly flashed back to our conversation on the lawn after our wipeout when he'd mentioned the three rumours, only one of which was true. *No, I thought. He wouldn't have done anything like that. He* couldn't *have done anything like that.*

But how did I really know? I'd known Kemp for a week. Sure, we'd gone on a date and shared a face plant during cross-country, but . . . I barely knew the guy. Maybe I should've been paying more attention to those rumours and less attention to my own stubborn optimism.

"Did you kill your brother?" I asked, hoping that the bold ridiculousness of the question would finally make him admit that he was just being dramatic. He took a deep breath and tilted his head back a little, his eyes narrowing.

"If I did?"

I shook my head. "Stop with the bullshit, Kemp. You're not the type of person who would—"

"How do you know?" he asked, echoing my own question of just moments earlier. "You don't know me, Ivy. You don't know what went on. So don't pretend you do."

"I wasn't."

"Austin's probably trapped, tied to that house, and he's pissed. So now he's taking it out on you because he can't take it out on me. I'm the one who deserves it. I'm the one who . . ."

"The one who what?" I whispered. He stared at me for a moment, then turned and walked back toward the open gate without a word. I ran after him, reaching him just as he was about to swing the gate closed again. "The one who what?" I repeated.

"Maybe you should talk about your visions with someone else. I'm sorry. It was probably a mistake for me to come here. It's . . . messing with my head." He slammed the gate closed behind us and latched it before storming up the hill. I stayed where I was, hugging the notebook to my chest, as I watched him grow smaller and smaller. He didn't go back through the house, but went out through the side gate.

"Asshole," I said, even though he couldn't possibly have heard me. I made my way back to the house, slipped in through the kitchen door, and put my shoes in the front foyer before heading back up to my room. The apple on my bed looked disgusting, so I moved it aside to the dresser. Then I lay down on my bed and opened up the notebook, bracing myself to read the next horrible vision.

12

Ice Cream and Boys

THAT NIGHT, I HELD MY PHONE AS I SAT IN BED AND WAITED for the inevitable. It came at precisely 11:21.

I saw a man dressed in an old-fashioned outfit, like from the late 1700s. His expression was dour. He was around Dad's age, or maybe a little older. And he was talking to someone, shooting sharp words over his shoulder. I frowned as I watched. Austin's visions had seemed to be a little more complete than mine. I remembered this one from the notebook, so I wasn't surprised when the man went and took his position, standing ramrod straight, his right hand raised as if he were holding a pistol. Except I couldn't see it. Austin had referred to this episode as a duel, so he must've been able to see the gun. I saw nothing except the man count out a number of paces, his feet sliding across my floor as if he were walking against the tide on one of those moving walkways. He turned, raised his arm, and crooked his finger. The shot from his opponent's pistol tipped his head back, just as his left eye seemed to explode. The vision immediately vanished.

I checked my phone, only to see that a minute had passed. Exactly a minute. Whether there was a significance to that or not, I didn't know. It may just have been Austin's way of showing me the last, most spectacular moments of all those lives.

Kemp had been right about one thing, though: Reading about the visions beforehand helped. The death didn't come as much of a shock, especially when I knew Austin's interpretation of the event. I had to rely on that somewhat, since I couldn't see as much as he'd seen. Had I watched that last one without knowing what was going on, I might not have figured out it was a duel.

I grabbed a pen and a pad of sticky notes, then scribbled my own observations. I recorded the date, the time (which was probably unnecessary; all the visions seemed to happen at 11:21), and anything else I'd noticed that Austin hadn't. Then I peeled the note from the stack and affixed it to the corresponding page in the notebook. I spent the evening doing that with all the other visions I'd experienced. There were five so far, including that of Mr. Dueller. That left twenty-one more to get through.

And then . . . What would happen when I got through them all? By that point, would I be reduced to a terrified toddler? Would I have to sleep on my parents' bedroom floor? Would I be spending my days in a haze of pot smoke, trying to relax enough to make it through another day?

Eventually, would I end up in the creek myself?

Thursday was unbearably awkward. Kemp didn't talk to me at all during PE, and when I slid onto my stool for Art, he ignored me. His drawing had turned out nicely, and it looked nearly done. Mine, on the other hand, was a miserable mess. I spent the class adding random dots, trying to get my creative juices flowing, but it was like I had a block against doing that particular project. Eventually—because I was running out of time—I just started doodling a bunch of random objects, trying to trace them out with dotted lines. An apple. A leaf. A train with a curly puff of steam coming from its smokestack. I just couldn't be bothered, and I didn't care. There were more important things to worry about . . . not least of which was the guy sitting beside me.

But I didn't even have a chance to talk to him because, as soon as the bell chimed, he swept his paper off the table and strode to the front of the room. I gathered up my things a little more slowly, then headed to the cafeteria for lunch.

Friday was much the same, except for the fact that we had to turn in our pointillist pieces, and I could tell that Ms. London wasn't impressed with mine. Her nose wrinkled a little bit—probably unconsciously—and she must've wondered what an absolute dud like me was even doing in her class. At that stage, the only kids who were still taking Art were ones who wanted to pursue it after high school. I had no idea what I wanted to do . . . but I was fairly certain it wouldn't involve anything that required creativity and the skilled use of a pencil.

When I got home, I did my homework so I could relax for the rest of the weekend (yeah, right), and by the time I was done, Mom and Dad were home. As we all sat down to a dinner of pizza, green salad, and ice cream, they chatted amicably with each other about their day, even though I knew for a fact they'd spent much of it together, showing a couple of houses on the other side of town.

"You're looking a little better," Mom said, just as I was tucking into my bowl of vanilla-caramel crunch. I pushed up my glasses (I was still wearing the old ones, which were annoying me with their propensity to slip) and shook my head.

"So I looked awful before? Thanks a lot."

"You did have a bruised nose," Dad pointed out.

Mom smiled. "I just meant you look less tired. Things are settling down? You're getting used to school?"

"I guess."

"Have you made any friends?"

I shrugged and shovelled in a huge bite so I wouldn't have to answer right away. The cold made my teeth ache. "Yeah," I said when I'd managed to swallow some of the creamy lump. "Rissa and Eunice. I eat lunch with them every day."

"You should have them over sometime. If you want."

"Maybe," I said, though I wasn't sure if that was something I'd ever want to do. Rissa would probably figure out that our house had used to belong to Kemp's family, and she'd most likely tell Eunice, and . . . well, I didn't know how the girl would react to that. I had a sudden vision of her prowling through the rooms, snapping pictures with her phone like she was in some historical site. My parents' office would probably get the most attention.

"What about boys?" Dad asked. "Anyone we should know about?"

"Dad. Seriously?" Stabbing at the remainder of my ice cream, I shook my head.

"She's not going to be bringing any of them over if you're just going to scare them away," Mom said.

"When have I ever scared away my daughters' boyfriends?"

"I don't have a boyfriend," I said before the conversation could go any further. "Okay?"

Mom and Dad exchanged a look. I sighed.

"What?"

Mom shook her head. "It's just that . . . Jade had Stefan. We thought you might have someone by now, too."

My mouth dropped open a little. "You actually *want* me to have a boyfriend?"

"I want you to enjoy your teenage years, Ivy. Go to parties and school dances. Have some fun. Experiment."

"Not too much," Dad said.

"No. Not too much. I know you're a smart kid, and you wouldn't do anything stupid. I just don't want to see you miss out because you're trying so hard to be good."

"I'm not *trying* to be," I said sulkily, scraping at the dregs of cream in my bowl. "Maybe that's just the way I am."

"Sometimes you don't seem very happy."

"Why?" I asked, dropping the spoon into the bowl with a clatter. "Because I'm not stealing your car and going for joyrides? Because I'm not drinking and having sex in the back of my boyfriend's truck?" *Because I'm not Jade?* I almost added, but I'd probably said too much already. Not that they were oblivious. They knew Jade and Stefan had been pretty serious. And they would've had to have been ridiculously unaware not to have known what the two of them were doing, especially when she had come home smelling like hand sanitizer and stumbling into the walls.

"Those things wouldn't make you happy," Mom said, her

voice soft. "That's not who *you* are." She reached for my empty bowl, then stacked it with the other two. "You need to find what makes Ivy happy."

A good night's sleep, I thought. *Friends who don't secretly despise me because I talked with a guy. Having said guy actually talk to me again.* Those were the things that would've made me happy. Unfortunately, there wasn't much I could do about any of them.

"Do you want to watch a movie?" Dad asked. "We haven't done that in a while."

"I've got homework."

Mom frowned as she straightened up from the dishwasher. "More? How much are they giving you?"

"It's grade twelve. There's a ton of homework."

She nodded as I slipped out of the kitchen. I tried to ignore Dad's disappointed expression and failed miserably. And then I felt guilty all the way up the many stairs to my room. It wasn't like they had another kid they could turn to for family movie night. Not anymore.

I closed the door and sat cross-legged on my bed, my laptop in front of me. I stuck on a pair of headphones before I started up a movie. There were still a few hours to go before I had the nightly breathless visit from whichever past persona it was going to be. The night before, it had been a young man who'd been running (in place, it had seemed to me, but he'd obviously been running from something) and looking back over his shoulder. That mysterious something seemed to slam into him from behind, and he tumbled head over heels, his mouth gaping, as cuts and wounds appeared all over his body. His hair flew wildly about his head, as though he was in zero gravity, but judging by the way he was dressed, I was pretty sure he wasn't an astronaut. It had taken a few minutes of searching before I'd finally found the entry I thought was the match. Austin had thought it was a tsunami, so I suspected he'd actually seen the water.

The movie was over by nine, so I watched another, which took me almost to eleven o'clock. At that point, I got up, stretched, and headed for the bathroom. After brushing and flossing and whatnot, I went back to my room, plugged in my laptop to charge, and crawled into bed. I stayed sitting up, glancing at the clock on my phone. As the terrible minute grew closer and closer, I found myself actually holding my breath, and then having to remind myself not to. Whatever this thing was, it would be doing enough breath-holding for me.

But as the clock flipped over to 11:22 and nothing had happened, I began to grow annoyed. It seemed that Austin's past lives took weekends off. Not that I was complaining about having a break, but I would've much rather had those breaks during the week when I had to get up and go to school every day.

"You're dead," I whispered into the stained-glass glow of my room. "Why do you even need a schedule?"

There was no answer, of course. So I turned off the lamp, pulled the covers up around my neck, and closed my eyes. If I only got two nights a week free from the ghosts of the past, I was going to make the most of them.

13

The Last Vision

BY THE END OF THE SECOND WEEK IN OCTOBER, I'D MADE IT through all of the entries in Austin's notebook. I'd watched people be hanged, drowned, and stretched just beyond their limits on a rack. I'd seen a baby tossed down a well and a little boy break his neck after being thrown from a horse. One night, I'd watched a woman simply evaporate in a flash of white; Austin had written "Hiroshima or Nagasaki?" on that page, and I had no reason to doubt him. Not all of the deaths had been sudden, though, and in some ways, those were the worst. Like the young man whose face was still smeared with dirt from battle, who'd had both of his legs amputated. His eyes were glassy and his breathing was quick, and it didn't take a genius to figure out he was suffering from some sort of infection. There was also the young man who'd been burned from head to toe, though neither Austin nor I knew how. All we saw was his last minute of life in a body that could no longer sustain it.

But, when I flipped through the notebook after Thursday night's vision (which involved a not-too-bright soldier loading a cannon and then leaning down to examine it; I never would've known what had happened, had it not been for

Austin's notes), I realized I'd witnessed every one that was in the book. My brightly coloured sticky notes were plastered on every page, an unnecessary complement to Austin's already-detailed descriptions. I closed the notebook and stuck it in my bag so I could give it back to Kemp the next day.

He wasn't in PE, though, and when I stepped into Art, he wasn't there, either. I slid onto my stool at the table that suddenly felt way too big for one person and frowned at the spot where he should've been.

Though we hadn't spoken in weeks, other than a few grunted words here and there to pass a paintbrush or borrow an eraser, I still felt his absence. With a glance up at the front of the room to see what Ms. London was doing (she was facing the empty whiteboard, and I could see her elbows sticking out on either side of her body, as if she had her hands pressed together in front of her), I pulled my phone out of my bag and quickly sent him a text.

Where are you?

I waited, tapping my toes against the rung of my stool. After a few seconds, I got a notification that he'd seen the message. So he was still alive, at least. I wasn't sure why I would've thought otherwise. But after nearly a minute of waiting, there was still no response.

I'm done with the notebook. You can have it back.

keep it

There was a really long pause. And then:

I let out a long sigh, which drew the attention of the kids at the table in front of me. I quickly stashed my phone in my bag and pretended to be interested in what Ms. London had started to say, even though all I could think about at that moment was Kemp.

———

I TOOK A LITTLE DETOUR ON THE WAY HOME, HEADING FOR a local coffee shop where I ordered a caramel latte with whipped cream. *To celebrate the end*, I told myself. I'd made it through all of Austin's visions—or past lives, or whatever it was they were—and I hadn't lost my mind. I was a little tired, for sure, but having the notebook had really helped.

As I sipped my coffee on the way home, I breathed deeply and admired the view around me. The leaves had started to change and the air smelled like autumn. Thanksgiving had come and gone, with about as much fanfare as there usually was in our family (which was to say, not much), but I was already starting to think about Christmas and all the baking Mom would be doing in the run-up to it.

Or would she? I wondered. This would be our first Christmas without Jade. The holiday was a potential minefield of memories, and I wasn't sure how any of us were going to react.

I'd almost finished my coffee when I stepped in the front door. After kicking off my shoes, I headed upstairs, then shed my bag and jacket, leaving them on the chair by the window. I paused there for a moment, gazing out at the slowly changing leaves. The sight reminded me of Kemp's pointillism assignment, which I knew he'd gotten a really good grade on, even though he hadn't said a word to me about it. Still holding my coffee cup, I fumbled in my bag and found my phone. Then I sat down on my bed, set the cup on the nightstand, and tried again.

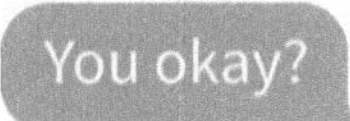

There was a long pause, long enough for me to take another sip of my drink. Finally, a message appeared on the screen:

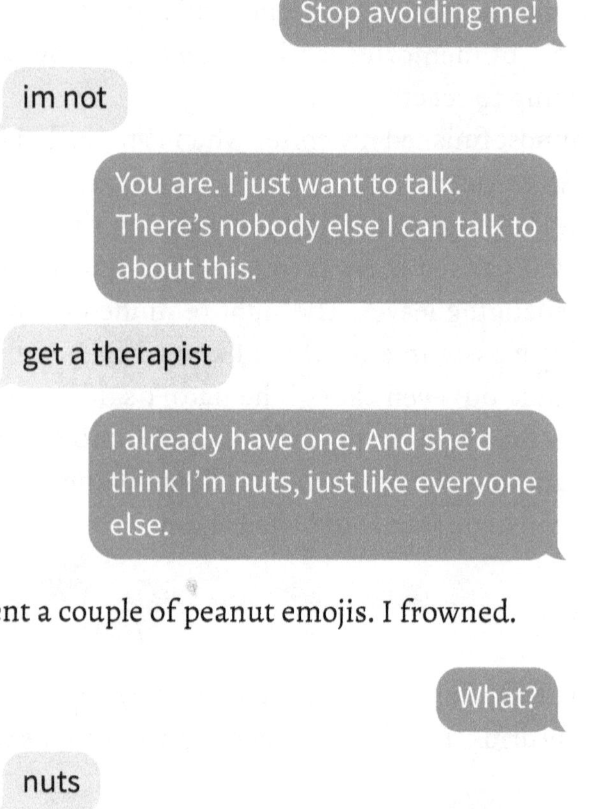

He sent a sleepy face. I sighed and tapped my thumbs against the screen.

He sent a couple of peanut emojis. I frowned.

I began to smile a little. Maybe our friendship wasn't a lost cause, after all.

I sent the barfing emoji and waited. The next message was a face laughing so hard it was crying.

A nose emoji appeared. I was about to write it off as a slip of his fingers when I realized he was making a pun.

Don't OD.

mom wont let that happen

I began to type again, to let him know I'd see him on Monday, when another message popped up.

u ok

I nodded and sent back the thumbs-up sign. The conversation seemingly over, I plugged my phone in to charge and grabbed my nearly empty coffee cup. The remaining drops were kind of cold. I sprawled on my bed as I tipped the last of the sweet liquid into my mouth, feeling—for the first time in a while—that maybe things were going to be okay after all.

IT WAS THE FAMILIAR, UNWELCOME SENSATION THAT WOKE me, and I sat up in the darkness, pulling the neck of my pyjamas away from my throat. In my half-asleep state, it took a few seconds for me to realize what was going on, and when I did, I felt my face flush in anger. *This was supposed to be over!* I thought. *There aren't any more deaths to see!*

But when I looked over at the spot on the floor, I was surprised to see it was empty. There weren't any ghosts in their death throes. No horrible visions of death and terror to haunt my dreams. All I saw was the pale light from outside streaming in through my window, illuminating the completely empty patch of hardwood.

Despite the fact that I still couldn't breathe, I scrambled out of bed and fell to my knees beside the spot. But getting closer couldn't help me see what wasn't there. I closed my eyes for a moment as I waited for the paralysis in my lungs to end. When it did so a few seconds later, I took in a deep, relieved breath.

"*Now* it's over," I whispered, knowing (somehow, without any good reason) that this was the case. I pressed my hand over the spot where so many ghosts had lain, almost expecting to find that it was warm or tingly. But it felt just like a wooden floor on the third storey of an old house in the middle of October: cold, hard, and lifeless.

14

Austin

ON SATURDAY NIGHT, AS I SAT STARING AT THE BOY LYING on my bedroom floor, I realized I was in uncharted territory. I could breathe, for one thing. He'd been there for over five minutes, for another. *So much for your schedule, Austin,* I thought as I squeezed my phone in my hands. I debated turning on the lamp, but was afraid that would just scare him away. It wasn't that I particularly *wanted* a ghost lying curled up on my floor. But I did want proof, and for that, I needed him to stay put. Carefully, quietly, so I wouldn't rustle my covers too much, I leaned over and aimed my phone at him, centring his face on the screen. I took the picture, wincing as the flash went off in the darkened room. As my eyes readjusted to the darkness, I saw him lying there still. He hadn't moved. When I looked at the screen, though, all I saw was a rather boring picture of my floor.

I put down the phone, turned on the lamp, and got out of bed. Creeping closer, I stared down at his sleeping form. He wasn't wearing a hospital gown like I'd been expecting. Instead, he was dressed in a t-shirt and flannel pants, and he was curled up on his side. *On the floor of his parents' bedroom*, I thought, crouching down beside him. Did he even realize they weren't here anymore? Did he realize I was?

"Austin," I whispered, so quietly I could barely hear my own voice. A part of me was afraid he would actually respond. *And do what?* I wondered. *Shout, "Boo!" and knock my lamp off the nightstand?* He'd never done anything like that, or anything at all, really, other than show me death after death, played out in grisly detail. Even then, it might not have been on purpose. "Austin," I whispered again, a little louder. He slowly opened his eyes. I froze, my heart hammering in my throat. For a moment, he seemed to stare straight through me, as if *I* were the ghost. But then, with a deliberateness that made my skin crawl, he turned his head and looked directly into my eyes.

I wasn't sure whether to run or to scream (though that would've just brought Dad upstairs for another lecture about the non-existence of ghosts, which—given the circumstances—would've been pretty annoying). I decided to stay put and stay quiet, so I settled myself on the floor and wrapped my arms around my knees. Austin watched, and I could tell he saw me, that he wasn't just staring at something that had only existed during his life.

"What are you doing here?" he asked. His voice was strange, almost echoing. It seemed more like the memory of a voice rather than anything that was in the room at that moment.

"This is my room," I said, then immediately regretted my words. How many movies had I seen about ghosts? It seemed like the number-one rule was: Don't make them angry. And what better way to make a ghost angry than by challenging its perception of reality?

"Sorry." He pushed himself up to a sitting position and looked around. His uneven eyebrows twitched into a frown. "I can't . . . I can't really see it."

"See what?"

"Where's Kemp?"

"At home."

"Not here."

"No. Not here."

"I didn't think so." He let out a long sigh and rubbed his hands over his hair in a mannerism that reminded me a lot of his younger brother. They didn't look that much alike, really. Austin's nearly black hair was buzzed short and formed a thick, dark cap for his scalp. He lacked Kemp's heavy eyebrows that almost met in the middle, but the one that his brother had shaved off was in the process of growing back; it looked pretty stubbly. Instead of the rich brown eyes that Kemp had, Austin's were dark blue with a golden ring around the pupil. When he suddenly reached out toward me, I noticed the scars that laced up the inside of his wrist. They didn't look like the kind you'd expect from an actual suicide attempt; rather, it looked like he'd been trying to cause himself pain. I scuttled back, and he stopped moving, leaving his hand hanging in the air.

"Can we touch?" he asked, his voice hesitant, as if he didn't really want to know the answer. I shook my head.

"I don't think so."

"Because I'm dead?"

I blinked. "You know you're dead?"

"If I'm not, I'm in a shitload of trouble. I'm in some girl's room in the middle of the night, and I have no idea how I got here." He frowned and dropped his hand. "Who are you?"

"Ivy."

"Did I know you . . . before?"

"No."

"I didn't think so."

"Why are you here, then?" I asked. "Why me? Why not . . ."

"Why not Kemp?"

I nodded. "What's going on? Why did you show me all those deaths?"

He sighed, the sound echoing around us. "I don't know. I'm not sure what's going on. It *should* be Kemp, but . . ."

"Why should it be Kemp?"

He scratched at the top of his head and stood up. I used the bed to help push myself to my feet; I didn't trust my shaking legs to do it on their own.

"Austin, why should it be Kemp? Do you have a message for him?"

He snorted, in almost the same way his brother did, and shook his head with a wry smile. "I'm not *that* kind of ghost." Wiggling his fingers in the air, he took a menacing step toward me. "I have a message for youuu . . ."

"Why are you a ghost at all?" I asked, standing my ground, even though all I wanted to do was throw my arms forward and wave him away like an annoying puff of smoke. "Doesn't that imply unfinished business?"

"Everyone has unfinished business. That's the nature of life. And death."

"But not everyone ends up as a ghost . . . do they?"

He shrugged.

"That's not very helpful."

"*Sorry*," he said, though his tone of voice suggested he was anything but.

"So what's your unfinished business?" I asked. "And why does it involve traumatizing me?"

He suddenly looked apologetic. He took another step forward, but when I stumbled back, knocking into the nightstand, he stopped. I reached behind me for the lamp. I didn't know what I would be able to do with it, since it would probably go right through him if I tried to hit him with it, but I felt like I at least needed to be prepared.

"I saw all the deaths," I said. "That should've been the end of it. Why are you still here?"

He tilted his head and smiled a little. "You're Kemp's friend?"

"You'd have to ask him about that," I said. "He's barely talked to me for the last month."

"Why not?"

"He's your brother. You tell me. I don't know him well enough to understand his weirdness yet."

"He's a good kid."

"Aside from the eyebrow-shaving?"

"Yeah." He reached up and rubbed the stubbly tract of skin. "It served me right. I let him smoke that shit."

"He doesn't do that anymore."

"He's a good kid," he said again. He dropped his hand to his side and looked down at himself. "Better than me. He always has been."

My sweaty fingers felt slippery on the lamp base. I finally

let go and rubbed my hand over my pyjamas. "Is that what you came here to say? I'll pass on the message, if you like."

Austin frowned at me for a moment, then shook his head. "I don't know."

"You don't know what?"

"I don't know if that's the message. I don't know if there *is* a message."

"How can you not know?"

"I'm dizzy." He pressed his right hand to his forehead and closed his eyes. "Shit. What is this?"

"How should I know? You're the one who— Austin?" My voice seemed to echo in the room. The spot where he'd stood just moments before was empty. My breaths sounded loud in the quiet space. I stepped forward, into the patch of pale light that was coming in the window, but I felt nothing. Even though I was occupying the same space a ghost had just moments before, I didn't feel anything weird. There was no heat, no cold, no tingle. My hair didn't stand up. My skin didn't crawl. Austin simply wasn't there. He *had* been, but then he'd disappeared, removing himself from my reality entirely.

I crawled back into bed, turned off the lamp, and checked the time. Then, with a groan, I pulled the covers over my head and curled up into a ball.

15
An Accident

When Austin appeared again on Sunday night, curled up on the floor in his pyjamas, I left him there and tried to go back to sleep. I had no idea when he actually disappeared, but when I woke up at around three and checked, he was gone. I went down to the kitchen, got myself a glass of water, and settled myself in front of the TV to watch the quality programming that graced the airwaves in the early hours of the morning. I fell asleep, only to wake at the sound of the toaster launching bagels into the air. I dragged myself to the kitchen, exchanged my empty water glass for a full coffee cup (while Mom frowned at me the whole time), and took it upstairs with me when I went to get ready for school.

The morning air was cold, and it helped to wake me up a little as I walked. Though I was still feeling a bit sluggish during my first class, by the time PE came around, I felt almost normal. Kemp gave me a little wave as I jogged onto the field, then turned away to cough into his elbow. Even from where I stood, I could hear the rattling mucus.

"Should you even be here?" I asked.

"It's just a cough. I'm over the worst of it." He hawked and spat onto the grass.

"Hayes!" Ms. Kelski barked. "That's disgusting. People have to use this field."

"It's real grass," he pointed out.

"Still."

"What do you want me to do with it? Save it in my pocket?"

"Swallow it, Hayes. And if you keep giving me lip, you're doing an extra lap in warm-up."

"But I'm sick!" He coughed again, dramatically. A couple of the guys standing near him started to laugh.

"If you're well enough to give me a hard time, you're well enough to get going." She blew her whistle. "Warm up!" she shouted. "Two laps. Then grab a piece of equipment and start practicing."

Kemp actually gave her a salute. He seemed to be in a better mood than he had been in weeks. As he caught my eye on the way to the track that ran around the edge of the field, he grinned. I didn't bother trying to keep up with him, but just settled into a comfortable jog with a few of the other girls. I could see Ms. Kelski setting up the equipment in a few different stations, far enough apart that we wouldn't endanger each other with what were, essentially, weapons: javelins, shot-puts, discuses. As I huffed my way around the last turn, I headed for the shot-put station, only to realize before I got there that it was the most popular, and therefore full. I'd never had any luck with the javelin (it always landed flat on the grass), and the discus kind of scared me (my aim was terrible, and I was always afraid I was going to embed the thing in the side of someone's head). Vowing to be extra careful, I hurried over to the discus station where I could see Kemp testing the weight of one in his hand, but before I could get there, Ms. Kelski shouted.

"Ross! Javelin."

I sighed heavily and changed course. A few guys were already playing with the long spears, using them like fighting staves. Hunter was waving his around, making noises like a light sabre. I rolled my eyes and got in line. There weren't enough for all of us, so I was going to have to wait my turn.

While I did, I watched the others take theirs. Brianne was amazing with the shot-put; she hurled that thing like it was nothing more than a softball. It surprised me, given the lanky look of her. She seemed more like she should be running marathons, not throwing heavy balls around. My gaze drifted over to the discuses. Nobody was allowed to do any sort of spinning moves; that was too dangerous. Instead, each student wound up by swinging their arm back and forth, then let the discus fly. Kemp's throw was actually pretty impressive, landing close to the edge of the field.

"Your turn," Hunter said, handing me a javelin. I stepped forward. My hands felt sweaty. I rubbed the right one against my shorts before grasping the metal shaft. On either side of us, a few students were in the field, jogging to collect the shot-puts and discuses that littered it. I waited, bracing the end of the javelin on the tip of my shoe.

"What are you waiting for?" Hunter asked.

"I don't want to impale anyone."

He snorted. "I doubt you could."

"Let's not test that theory," Ms. Kelski said, obviously overhearing our conversation. As the last few people ran back to the throwing line, I lifted the javelin, glanced behind me, and took a few steps back.

Then I ran, feeling the muscles in my arm tighten as I prepared to throw. Suddenly, Austin was right there, standing in front of me in his stupid pyjamas, less than ten feet away. Before my mind could remember that he wasn't solid, my body had already started to react. It tried to abort. I turned to the side as my hand released the shaft, and in that horrible moment I registered Kemp darting back onto the field to retrieve the last discus. I knew it was going to be bad even before the javelin met its mark.

I watched in disbelief, willing my throw to have been as weak as Hunter had said it would be. Unfortunately, I was stronger than he'd given me credit for. The point of the javelin buried itself in the side of Kemp's calf. He staggered, seeming to reverse course as if to get away from the offending shaft of metal, and fell back on the grass. The whole class seemed to gasp as one.

"No!" I screamed, pressing my hands over my ears and bending double. I screwed my eyes shut as I fell to my knees. I couldn't look. I was pretty sure I'd just killed him—if the stabbing hadn't done it, the blood loss certainly would—and I couldn't bear to see that.

It wasn't until someone tugged on my arm, freeing my left ear, that sound flooded back into my world. I blinked and pulled away.

"I'm sorry!" I wailed. "I didn't mean to!"

"I know." It was Ms. Kelski. I looked up, into her concerned face. "Are you all right?" she asked.

I just stared at her. *Why the hell are you asking me?* I thought. *I'm not the one who just got stabbed with a . . .* My gaze drifted over to where Kemp was lying on the ground. He was still alive, apparently, because I could see his chest moving as he talked with the boys standing over him. As he . . . laughed. I looked at Ms. Kelski in disbelief. She nodded, her eyebrows raised, and helped me to my feet. When I was standing and stable enough, she hurried back to Kemp, stepping over the javelin that was still sticking out of his leg and crouching down beside his head. I looked around at the other students, expecting to see them staring back with accusatory glares. But most of them were just watching Kemp. I walked a little closer, feeling like my innards were made of jelly.

"Careful," Ms. Kelski said as she saw me get close. "Don't touch the javelin."

I hadn't been going to. I didn't even want to look at it. I stepped around to his other side and stood there, staring down at him. He raised his hand to shade his eyes from the sun and squinted at me.

"Nice one," he said.

"I didn't mean to."

"You sure it's not payback for the basketball?"

I fell to my knees at his side and grabbed his free hand. I didn't care who saw. He smiled a little and gave my hand a squeeze before trying to sit up. Ms. Kelski shoved his shoulder back to the ground.

"Come on! I don't even get to see it? It's not every day someone gets pierced by a javelin."

"Thank goodness," she said. "The school's lawyers would be rich."

My heart galloped into my throat. "Are you going to sue me?"

Kemp burst out laughing and squeezed my hand again. "No, Ivy, I'm not going to sue you."

"He's as much to blame," Ms. Kelski said. "Darting back out there like that." She shook her head. "If that had hit your thigh or your abdomen . . ."

"Or his junk," one of the boys muttered behind me. A few of them laughed.

"Ha, ha," Kemp said. "Shut up, or I'll give you a Prince Albert with this thing once they pull it out of me."

Ms. Kelski's eyes went wide and half the class erupted in nervous laughter. Kemp blew out a breath and stared up into the sky. As I noticed the tension on his brow, I realized how much pain he was in. Pain that I had caused.

I chewed on my lip and held his hand until the firefighters showed up, and then everyone was shooed off the field. Ms. Kelski stayed with him. I wanted to, and Kemp might've been okay with that, but I had to get out of the way and, once I did, I was herded back to the school—along with the rest of the class—by a couple of the other PE teachers who'd heard about the incident.

I changed out of my gym strip in a daze, my mind still on the field. How were they going to get him into the ambulance? If they didn't want to remove the javelin right there, they'd need to move him . . . but short of cutting the thing, I didn't know how they were going to do that.

Ms. London didn't comment on Kemp's absence, which

was just as well, because I didn't want to have to tell her that I'd stabbed him with a piece of track-and-field equipment. I figured she would find out, anyway, as the story spread. Sure enough, as soon as I walked into the cafeteria, Josh shouted at me as I went to sit down beside Rissa.

"Hey, Ivy! I heard you killed Hayes in PE!"

Eunice's head snapped up and the colour sort of drained from her face. Rissa began to shake her head.

"Oh, my god," she said, a laugh of disbelief just on the edge of her voice. "What the hell is that about?" When I didn't answer, she turned back around and called out to Josh. "What happened?"

"She stabbed him with a javelin. Firefighters had to cut it to make him fit in the ambulance!"

I slammed my elbows on the table and threw my head into my hands.

"Is he all right?" Rissa asked.

"No idea," Josh said.

"Jeez, Ivy. I knew you two were having problems, but—"

"Problems?" Frowning, I lifted my head to look at her. "What do you mean?"

"Mattie said you don't even talk to each other in Art anymore. She said it's pretty chilly back there." She cracked open her can of energy drink and took a sip. "Did you have a fight or something?"

"Does it matter?" I asked. "I stabbed him with a javelin. He'll probably never want to speak to me again."

Eunice suddenly got up and ran for the door, leaving her barely touched lunch behind. Rissa frowned as she watched her go.

"I didn't mean to," I said. "It was an accident. I *suck* at PE."

"Yeah, you do. Honestly. I'm surprised the two of you have survived as long as you have. Basketballs to the face, road rash, stabbings . . ."

"Just in the leg."

"Yeah, I figured it was something like that. If it were really serious, Josh wouldn't be joking about it."

"Well, somebody better let Eunice know before she thinks her soulmate died."

She laughed and shook her head. "If there is such a thing, I doubt she's his. You might be, though." She peeled open a packet of ketchup and squirted it into a corner of her cardboard bowl.

"I think we'd be the opposite of soulmates," I said. "I doubt soulmate interactions are supposed to be so violent."

"All those incidents were accidents, weren't they?"

"Yeah."

She shrugged and popped a fry into her mouth. "I don't think you can rule anything out, then. You've obviously got some kind of . . . I don't know. Some kind of magnetism thing going." She wiggled her fingertips together, then dove back into her fries. I realized I hadn't even bothered to get my lunch from my locker. *Did I bring one?* I wondered. I couldn't remember. Not that I was hungry. I was too worried to be hungry.

I pulled out my phone and checked the local news stories, fearing I would see something about how a local high school student had died in a freak PE accident. But, of course, there was nothing. Even if he had died, his parents would have to be notified, and only then would some sort of article appear . . .

"Is he answering?" Rissa asked. I looked up with a frown. "What?"

"You're not calling him?"

I shook my head. "His phone's probably in the locker room. He wouldn't have had it on him."

"Too bad."

"Yeah." I dialled him, just in case, but of course it went straight to voicemail. So I sent a text message.

And then I stuffed the phone back in my bag. The only thing I could do now was wait.

"WERE YOU *TRYING* TO KILL HIM?" I HISSED AT AUSTIN AS soon as the boy appeared on my bedroom floor that night. I'd been waiting, sitting in the chair so I wouldn't fall asleep and miss him. He sat up, looking around for a moment before he spied me.

"What?" he asked, somewhat sleepily.

"When you appeared right in front of me on the field. I was holding a javelin, you asshole. What were you trying to do?"

He rubbed the sleep from his eyes, then dropped his hand with a little smirk.

"It's not funny!" My voice very nearly came out in a shout. I took a few deep breaths, trying to calm down, but that was easier said than done. All I wanted to do was throttle the ghost sitting in front of me. Or stab *him* with a javelin and see how he liked it.

"He's fine, Ivy."

"That's beside the point. What the hell were you doing?"

"Are you on speaking terms again?"

I just stared. And then I lunged toward him and took a swing at his head. My fist went right through it. He scowled up at me.

"You think that's going to work?"

"I could've killed him!"

"I doubt it. You're not that strong." He stood up. Like his brother, he was a good head taller than me, so it was a little intimidating when he stepped forward. "He's fine."

"How do you know? You haven't been to the hospital. Aren't you tied to this house?"

"Not exactly."

I frowned, then remembered the reason I was angry in the first place. "You're tied to *me*, aren't you?"

"Looks like it."

"Why?"

"No idea. Maybe because you're connected to Kemp."

I shook my head. "Yeah, well, I might not be for long. I don't even know if he's still alive."

"He is."

"How do you know, if you're tied to me?"

"Believe me. I'd know if he were dead. He's probably still in the hospital, nursing his wounds and waiting to hear from you."

Sighing, I went to sit on the edge of my bed. "I doubt that."

"Did he tell you to get lost or something?"

"No, he held my hand. But he probably thought he was dying. When the adrenaline wears off, he's going to be pretty pissed that I almost killed him."

He rolled his eyes. "You didn't almost kill him."

"I'm not an idiot, Austin. Deaths can happen after a non-fatal injury, too. Don't you remember that Civil War soldier who lost his legs?"

"Don't you remember that you live in the twenty-first century with antibiotics?"

"They don't always work."

He shook his head in exasperation. "What the hell does he see in you?"

"I honestly have no idea. But whatever it was, I'm sure it doesn't matter now."

With another roll of his eyes, he waved his hand in my general direction. "Get out your phone. Call him."

"I already did. He hasn't answered. He probably doesn't have his phone."

"Call my mom."

"How am I supposed to do that? I don't have her number."

"I do."

I waited, my eyebrows raised in anticipation. But he didn't tell me. All that happened was that his expression slowly changed, deepening into a puzzled frown.

"I don't remember," he said quietly. "I *should* remember, but . . ."

"You probably don't remember because it's not important. Not for someone like you."

"Someone dead, you mean?"

"The dead don't use phones, do they? When they want to communicate, they just appear in the middle of someone's bedroom floor, or stand in front of a javelin thrower so some innocent kid gets stabbed."

"You threw it, not me."

"Don't pin this whole thing on me," I whispered loudly, my voice a grating hiss. "If you hadn't jumped in front of me, none of this would've happened."

"Would you be on hand-holding terms with Kemp right now?"

"Like I said, he was just scared. He's sure as hell not going to speak to me after this."

Austin's lips turned up on one side. "Yeah?"

"Yeah."

"We'll see," he said.

16
What Happened

THE FIRST THING I DID WHEN I WOKE UP THE NEXT MORNING was check my phone for messages. But the text I'd sent the day before was unanswered and unseen. My hands shook as I did another search through the news, trying to tell myself that he probably just didn't have his phone back yet. There was still nothing about any javelin stabbings, so I put my phone in my bag and got ready for school.

It wasn't until just before my first class that my phone buzzed. I pulled it out, my heart pounding, and saw the two ridiculously small words that caused an oversized amount of relief:

> not dead

I nearly cried. Instead, I hurried to class and slid into my seat so I could have a couple of minutes to chat. But he didn't seem to be in a very chatty mood, because I didn't get a response to my first question (*Are you okay?*) until the teacher started talking, and I didn't even have time to glance at my phone before I stuffed it back in my bag.

When the class was over, I pulled out my phone and hurried through the hallways, trying not to smack into anyone while I attempted to type. I already seemed to have a reputation for being dangerous in PE. I didn't need that to extend to my walking.

The last message he'd sent was just a thumbs-up emoji. I quickly tapped out my message:

> I'm so sorry. I need to tell you what happened.

He didn't answer. Frowning, I plowed my way through the crush of students until I reached my next class. Then I kept my phone on my lap, out of view, waiting for his response. Finally, I got the notification that he'd read it . . . just in time for the teacher to start talking. I let out an audible groan before I could stop myself.

"I'm sorry, Miss Ross. Is my class that boring?"

I looked up to find Mr. Wall staring at me. One of the guys behind me snorted, though he tried to turn it into a cough. Mr. Wall had about as much sense of humour as a piece of cabbage; I doubted he even knew how to laugh. Shaking my head, I slid my hands over my phone to try to hide it. But he could obviously see what was going on under my desk.

"Turn it off and put it in your bag, please."

I did as he said, and quickly, too, not wanting to give him any excuse to punish me . . . or anyone else. I didn't particularly want to be the reason we got an extra helping of homework.

The third of that morning's classes was English and, luckily for me, the teacher was late. I slid into my seat and pulled out my phone again. This time, there were two messages from Kemp.

> lunch

And then, as if he'd thought better of it:

> no wait after school my house

I quickly typed in my response:

> Are you sure?

This time, he answered right away:

> yeah mom will pick us up

> What happened to your car?

> nothing cant drive a standard
> with one leg

I sent a frowny face and left it at that.

He wasn't in the cafeteria at lunch, but everybody else—seemingly everybody who'd heard about the incident—was. So I had to hear a number of weird congratulatory comments, mostly from guys.

"Is Kemp not that popular?" I asked Rissa while Eunice was busy feeding her change into the drink machine on the other side of the cafeteria.

"What?"

"Why does it seem like I did all these guys a favour by stabbing him?"

She shook her head with a smile. "They're *guys*. It's like some weird badge-of-honour thing. He's cool for getting stabbed. You're cool for doing it."

"That's messed up."

"Yeah, well, it's a high school. These places aren't exactly known for high levels of logic and sanity, are they?" She poked at her fries with a shrug. "He's pretty popular. I mean, he *was* before his brother died."

"He's not now?"

"I don't know. Not like he was."

"Who is not like he was?" Eunice asked, sliding into her usual seat. Rissa frowned at the bottle she was holding.

"What the hell is that?"

"Orange juice."

"Why?"

"I need to stop having so much sugar."

Rissa flipped a curl over her shoulder. "Whatever."

"Who is not like he was?" Eunice asked again. "Who were you talking about?"

"Who do you think?" Rissa asked. "Ivy just wanted to know if Kemp was popular before Austin died."

"I wasn't here yet," she said.

Rissa rolled her eyes. "Yeah, I know."

I double-checked the cafeteria again, just in case I'd missed him, but he didn't seem to be there. It was with a weird, nervous energy that I finished up my classes for the day.

As I walked out to the pick-up area, I spotted him from

behind, sitting on the wooden barricade that ran along the edge of the sidewalk. A pair of crutches sat propped up beside him. Despite the cool weather, he was wearing shorts. I didn't really understand why until I rounded the barricade and saw the brace on his left leg. He turned at the sound of my footsteps and smiled.

"Hey."

Before I could overthink it, I bent over and gave him a hug. He laughed a little, then awkwardly put his arms around me. "I'm *so* sorry," I whispered, pulling back to look down at his leg. Under the brace, I could see the white bandages that covered what I was sure was a fairly sizeable wound. I sat down beside him, still staring at his leg.

"I'm not. It'll be a great story to tell my grandkids." He cleared his throat and spoke again, this time in a hoarse, wobbly voice. "'Did I ever tell you young'uns 'bout the time Ivy impaled me with a piece o' gym equipment?'"

"I am *never* going to live that down, am I?"

"Aim that spectacularly bad should be celebrated."

"I wasn't aiming for you."

"I know."

"I was trying not to hit Austin."

He blinked slowly, staring straight ahead.

"Sorry," I said. "I forgot the rule."

"Screw the rule," he said quietly. He turned to face me, his eyebrows pulled into a deep frown. "What the hell do you mean?"

I shook my head. "I'm not talking about it here. People already think I'm some sort of homicidal weirdo. I don't need them thinking I'm batshit, too."

He grunted and pulled his phone from his backpack. I watched his thumbs tap the screen, a little miffed that he was going to have a conversation with someone else when I was sitting right there.

"Why weren't you answering?" I asked.

"Huh? When?"

"Today. Is there something wrong with your phone? Your response time was awful."

He turned to me with a look that made me feel like I'd missed something important. "Can *you* text and use a pair of crutches at the same time?"

"Oh. I doubt it."

"I'm not *that* coordinated." He paused, then typed something else. "I'm not coordinated, period."

"You're a pretty good runner."

"I'm human. We're built for running."

"You're okay with a discus."

"I'll be sure to put that on my résumé." He tapped the screen to send the message. In my bag, my phone began to buzz. Frowning, I pulled the device out, staring at Kemp the whole time. He just raised his eyebrows a little and remained silent.

u can tell me now just type it

I glanced at him, then shook my head as I began to type.

It's complicated.

y

"Seriously?" I said with a laugh. "You're *that* lazy? You could at least capitalize it."

He grinned and bent his head back over his phone.

> Y

> That's better. Does your leg hurt?

> what was that about austin

> He appeared on the field.

> when

> PE. Right before I threw the javelin.

> so u thought it would b better to hit a living person than a ghost thanks

"That wasn't it at all," I said. "It was some sort of reflex. I was just trying to avoid the very real-looking person standing in front of me. I didn't know you were going to run out there and throw yourself into the path of my javelin."

He snorted. "That sounds kind of dirty, Ivy."

While I rolled my eyes, he turned back to his phone.

> did he say anything

He chuckled as he put his phone into his backpack. I was kind of surprised that he didn't want to talk some more, but then I saw him start to gather up his crutches. He hopped a little as he got them situated under his arms and nodded his chin toward a black SUV that had just pulled up in the loading zone. He hobbled toward it, crutches clicking.

"Mind getting the door for me?" he asked. I scurried forward and pulled open the passenger door. A middle-aged woman sat in the driver's seat, and it didn't take more than a glance for me to realize she was Kemp's mom. She smiled at me, then frowned in concern as she watched her son struggle into his seat. When all his limbs were safely inside the vehicle, he handed the crutches to me. "They'll fit between the seats."

I got in the back and managed to manoeuvre the crutches into the indicated space where they wouldn't impale any of us in the event of an accident. Then I quickly buckled my seatbelt. His mom glanced at me in the rearview mirror before pulling away from the school.

"Mom, this is Ivy."

"Ivy?" she said, in such a way that I knew he'd told her about me. She probably already knew I was the reason he'd had a metal spear impaled in his leg.

"Hi," I said, which seemed completely inadequate. But I

wasn't about to apologize yet, just in case she *didn't* know I was behind the incident.

"So you're the girl with terrible aim?"

"Mom." Kemp craned his neck to shoot an apologetic look at me. "Sorry."

"I'm really sorry," I said. "I didn't mean to hit him."

"I know," she said. "What did he expect, running out onto the field when people were throwing spears?"

"Javelins, Mom." He shook his head. "You make it sound like we were out hunting."

"That's not an elective," I said.

His mother laughed and glanced at me. Her eyes were brown, like Kemp's, and lined with the same thick eyelashes both her sons had. "Kemp says you're new to the area."

"Sort of," I said, choosing my words carefully. I wasn't sure if Kemp had told her where, exactly, I lived, and I didn't want to dredge up something that needed to stay buried. "We used to live over in Cedar Valley before. We moved just before school started."

"I'm sorry to hear about your sister."

"Thanks. And I . . . was sorry to hear about Austin."

She didn't say anything, and, for a moment, I was afraid I'd done something really wrong. But, when I looked at her eyes in the mirror, I could tell she was just really focused on the road.

"Mrs. Hayes—" I began.

"Nina."

"Are you sure?"

She laughed. "Yes, I'm sure."

"She doesn't even use Hayes," Kemp said.

"Oh. I'm sorry."

"It's all right," she said. She quickly checked her mirrors before pulling into the left-turn lane. "You were about to say something?"

"Yeah. Just that . . . I'm *really* sorry about hitting Kemp with that javelin."

She glanced at her son, who appeared to be sitting innocently in the front seat. Then she turned her eyes up to the mirror and her gaze met mine. "He smashed your glasses and nearly broke your nose with a basketball. Why don't you two call it even?"

THEIR HOUSE WAS A COZY RANCHER WITH A BEAUTIFUL garden out front. At least, I thought it would probably be beautiful when it was in bloom. At that moment, it was kind of drab, the shrubs dormant, the ornamental trees shedding their leaves. As we got out of the SUV and headed for the front door, Nina sighed.

"I *was* going to ask you to rake the leaves this weekend," she said to Kemp.

"Dad can do it." He paused by the front door as she fumbled with the key in the lock.

"He *can*. Whether he'll want to or not is up for debate."

Kemp snorted. "What's to debate? If it involves fresh air, he's going to avoid it like the plague."

His mom frowned at him as she got the door open. He hobbled into the house, glancing back at me over his shoulder as if he wanted me to follow. I did, stepping into the unfamiliar space. Other people's houses always smelled weird, and this one was no exception. But it wasn't a *bad* kind of weird; in fact, it sort of made me relax. I felt the tension start to fall away from my muscles as I followed Kemp into the kitchen, where he leaned his crutches against the peninsula and hopped over to the fridge. The house wasn't new—though it certainly wasn't as old as ours—but the kitchen had been redone recently. The fridge looked like something out of a sci-fi movie, with some sort of screen in the door.

"Is that a smart fridge?"

Nina snorted as she walked in after us and tossed her keys on the corner of the counter next to an ancient-looking cordless landline. "Hardly."

"Mom calls it Moron."

"Not officially. I'm not about to start naming the appliances." She sorted through a stack of mail, then set it down next to the phone. "But it is pretty stupid. It keeps autocorrecting my shopping lists."

Kemp grinned as he pulled a plastic container out of the fridge and handed it to me. I lifted it up to see through the transparent bottom and spied a few slices of pizza. "That okay?" he asked me.

"Looks good."

He closed the fridge and hopped back over to his crutches. "We'll be downstairs, Mom. Have fun with Moron."

"Fun. Yes." She waved her hand and shooed him out of the kitchen. He laughed, leaning heavily on his crutches as he made his way down the hall.

"Should I tell Ivy about the time the fridge told you to buy penises?" he called back over his shoulder.

I nearly choked. "What?"

"She wanted a pack of ballpoint pens," he said, letting go of one crutch to push open a door. "See? Our fridge is a moron. Why would anyone have penises on their shopping list?"

I held the chilled plastic container as I followed him—very slowly—down a set of carpeted stairs. At the bottom was a finished basement, a cozy space that looked like the perfect hangout for a couple of teenage boys. *One teenage boy*, I reminded myself . . . though it was easy to forget. The room had plenty of reminders of Austin, from the photographs that stretched from infancy to almost adulthood, to the framed rugby jersey that hung on the wall. (Based on what I knew about Kemp's level of coordination, I was able to deduce that it was *not* his.) I paused in front of a wall covered in myriad small frames, peering at the pictures. It was easy to tell which little boy was which, since they looked so different.

"Check out the one in the middle," Kemp said after a quick glance back at me. "The black frame."

"There are lots of black ones."

"The one with the naked mole rat."

I peered closer and finally spied the one he meant. "Oh. Was that after Austin shaved your head?"

"No," he said, flopping onto the overstuffed beige couch that took up much of the space. "That was after Mom dragged me to the barber and got him to finish the job."

The poor kid looked like he'd just been through a few rounds of chemo. The fact that he was pretty skinny didn't help.

"I did get a ton of candy that year," he said, arranging his crutches so they were out of the way, then scooting over so he was stretched out on the piece of couch that was more like a lounge. "I think people felt sorry for me."

After a quick scan of the other photos, I wandered over to the couch and set the pizza container down beside him. He grabbed it and opened it up, then held it out to me. I quickly took off my bag, shrugged out of my jacket, and sat down beside him before reaching for a slice.

"No meat?" I asked. He shook his head. "Vegetarian?"

"Nope. But Mom is. So we pretty much eat that way at home." He sighed and sank back into the cushions as he took a bite. "I'm exhausted. Crutches must use way more energy or something."

"So what's the prognosis?" I asked, trying to keep my voice light. I took a bite of cold pizza, getting a whole mouthful of green peppers as I did.

"The doctors *think* they can save the leg," he said, picking off a couple of olive slices and tossing them back into the container. I gaped at him, my slice wavering in the air in front of my face. He chuckled. "I'm just joking."

"Don't joke about that."

"Sorry. You didn't hit anything vital. I'm going to be sore for a while, but I'll be okay."

"Good." I leaned back on the cushions and took another bite.

"Want to see my stitches?"

"I do not."

He laughed. "Squeamish?"

"No. Normal. I certainly wouldn't have been trying to look at a javelin sticking out of *my* leg."

"Why not? That was pretty cool."

"You're weird."

"Hey! I'm not the one seeing ghosts." He took a bite, casually, but I knew he was dying to ask about Austin.

"That wasn't the first time I saw him," I said, at which he turned his head toward me, slowly, the movement like something out of a horror movie.

"What? When were you going to tell me?"

"When was I supposed to tell you? I mean . . . I was going to, but then I stabbed you in the leg and things got weird."

"Weren't they already?"

"I guess."

He scarfed down the last of his slice and rubbed his hands on his shorts before turning to face me. "Okay. What, exactly, did you see?"

Instead of answering, I went for my bag. Holding the piece of pizza between my teeth, I fumbled inside until I found the notebook. I tossed it on the couch between us, then released the pizza from my mouth.

"You didn't have to bring it back yet."

"I'm done with it. We got through all the visions. Lives. Deaths. Whatever." I tore off another bite of cold pizza and chewed. "I made notes."

"I see that," he said. He was already flipping through the notebook, pausing to examine the brightly coloured sticky notes that I'd affixed to the pages.

"Thursday night should've been the last one. I was going to give the notebook back to you on Friday, but you weren't there. And then, on Friday night . . ."

He frowned and flipped to the last page. There wasn't

any of Austin's writing there. Instead, the page was covered in four sticky notes with my hastily jotted observations. He read what I'd written, his eyebrows drawing together.

"I didn't want to actually write in the book. But I thought that last one—lack of one—should be in there, too."

He looked up at me and shook his head a little. "You watched all of these? All of . . ."

I nodded.

"Are you okay?"

"I think so. Having the notebook helped. Nothing really came as a shock. Except for the last one . . . but that was more surprising than terrifying."

He closed the notebook and leaned forward to set it on the coffee table. "You said Austin appeared on the field."

"Yeah." I shook my head and popped the last bit of crust into my mouth. "I don't get that. There was a pattern, before."

"What pattern?"

"I only ever saw him at night. At a specific time. And he took weekends off. Or something."

He let out a short laugh of disbelief. "What?"

"The visions only came five nights a week. Sunday through Thursday. I always had Friday and Saturday nights off . . . until that last one. Which I don't get. Why didn't I see his actual death? He was in the hospital, right?"

"Yeah." He blew out a breath. "For a week. But his brain was wrecked, so the doctors pulled life support and let him die." With a frown, he reached for the last piece of pizza in the container. "Want to split it?"

"No. I'm good. You go ahead."

He took a big bite and chewed, seemingly in thought. "He always did like weekends."

"Yeah, well, it wasn't exactly convenient for me. I would've rather had some weekdays off. I didn't sleep well after those visions."

"Who would?" He picked off some more olives. I raised my eyebrows. "What? I'm not a fan. So . . . after you saw the last vision—"

"Non-vision."

"Whatever. After that, he showed up on the field?"

"No. He's been showing up every night since that last one. Curled up on my bedroom floor in his pyjamas."

He blinked. "Mom and Dad's bedroom floor."

"Exactly."

"Have you talked to him?"

"Oh, yeah. We've talked." I sighed and folded my arms as I slumped back into the cushions. "I know he was your brother, but . . ."

"He could be an ass," he said. "You can say it."

"What does he want? I thought he had some sort of message. I thought that's why he was showing me all his past lives. Past deaths. Whatever. But when I asked him, he was kind of cagey. It was like him being there was perfectly normal. Like he didn't need a reason."

"Maybe there is no reason."

"So I just have to put up with a seventeen-year-old ghost in my room for the rest of my life? I don't even want to change my clothes in there now. Who knows if he's watching?"

He suddenly snorted, then coughed. That turned into a

bit of a fit, and he turned his head away to cough into his elbow. "Sorry," he said when he'd managed to compose himself. "But you don't need to worry about that."

"Why shouldn't I worry about some horny teenage boy getting off on watching me undress?"

He raised his eyebrows. "Because he was gay?"

"Oh." I frowned. "I don't know if that makes it any better. He's still watching."

"Is he? Can you see him?"

I shook my head. "Not until later. He just appears on my floor, in the same position every time. Then we can communicate."

He picked at the remaining bit of crust in his hand, looking thoughtful. "Maybe that's the only time he can see you."

"We don't know that."

"Why don't you ask him?"

I snorted. "Yeah, right. 'Hey, Austin! Are you watching me undress?'"

"Why not?"

"Would he answer truthfully?"

"I don't know." He shook his head. "Maybe. What reason would he have to lie now?"

"Now?"

He tossed his crust into the container and moved it to the table so there was nothing between us anymore. I wasn't sure if he expected me to move closer or what. I stayed where I was, staring at the brace on his leg. He wiggled his toes. "Sure you don't want to see my stitches?"

"Very."

He grunted with laughter and sat up a little straighter so

he could reach over the side of the couch. When he pulled back, he had a remote in his hand. He pointed it at the rather large TV on the wall across from us and turned it on.

"Want to watch a movie? Or we could play a game or something."

"I usually do my homework after school."

He raised his eyebrows. "Well, aren't you responsible?"

"When do you do yours?"

"Usually in the middle of the night."

"Why?"

"Can't sleep."

I chewed on my lip for a moment. "Does Austin visit you, too?"

"I wish. That would at least be a good reason for my sleeplessness." He shook his head. "It's just good, old-fashioned insomnia. I've had it for years." He muted the sound on the TV as he began to flick through the channels. "Yes, three years," he said before I could ask.

"Nights are hard sometimes."

"Hell, yeah." His voice was soft. "All of it is. Sometimes it seems like it'll never get any easier."

"Did your parents send you for counselling, too?"

He nodded. "I still see someone every month or so. You?"

"I talked to someone at first. But . . . I felt like it was making things worse. So eventually I refused to go."

"Why was it making things worse?" he asked gently. I shrugged and tightened my grip on myself. I suddenly felt like I might break apart. Or burst into tears. And I really didn't want to do either. I could just see Kemp's mom having to call my parents to come and pick me up because

I'd turned into a puddle of gooey emotion on the middle of her basement floor. He set the remote on his lap and held out his arm. "Come here."

"Why?"

"Because if that's not the face of a person who needs a hug, I don't know what is."

So I slid a little closer and tucked myself in under his arm. He felt so warm; it was a balm against the chill that seemed to be radiating from somewhere deep within me. Both of his arms encircled me, and he gave me a gentle squeeze.

"Better?" he asked.

"I felt guilty," I said, then went on before he could ask me to elaborate. "And talking about her was just making it worse. It didn't feel healthy, dredging all that stuff up, but everyone said I needed to cry."

"You didn't?"

"Not really."

He sighed. "I didn't, either. I wonder what that says about us."

"I'm sure my therapist would have some thoughts."

"Mine, too." He rubbed his thumb absently against my shoulder. "Maybe it's guilt. Maybe we don't cry because we feel like we don't deserve to."

I craned my neck until I could see his face. "Why would *you* feel guilty?"

He bit his lip and looked away. I instantly regretted asking.

"Sorry."

"He was never the same after the car accident. He changed, and I didn't know what to do about it."

"How is that your fault?"

"He was picking me up from hockey practice. Me. The shittiest athlete in the world."

"Kemp."

"If it hadn't been for me, we wouldn't have been in that car. We wouldn't have crashed, he wouldn't have gotten messed up."

"You don't know that."

"Well, when you're thirteen and you live with that thought for long enough, it starts to become part of you. There's logic to it, so it's really hard to convince yourself that you weren't to blame. Stuff happens, but . . . the justifications and the guilt . . . I think it's just something people do to make sense of that stuff. We need to blame something."

"You don't blame your brother?"

He shook his head. "He hit a patch of black ice. Could've happened to anyone."

We sat in silence for a few minutes as the TV flickered on the wall. He'd landed on some news channel, which was at that very moment displaying a nighttime accident scene, all flashing lights and darkness. He noticed, quickly letting go of me so he could reach for the remote.

"Shit." Clicking the TV off, he sighed. "Do you feel like there are reminders everywhere?"

"Not really," I said. "You saw our house."

When he didn't say anything, I turned to look at him.

"No photos?" I prompted.

He shook his head. "I didn't notice."

"There's not much to remind me of her. Especially not after we moved."

"Yeah. I get that. Dad wanted to get away from that house. And the creek. Especially the creek." He shuddered.

"You okay?"

"Yeah. I just don't like being reminded of that place."

"Is that why you got so weird last month? Why did you take me down there if it was going to—"

"That's not where he died," he said. "I thought I'd be able to handle it."

I frowned. "That's not Smokefish Creek? I thought you said—"

"It is. But he went in downstream. Where the water runs faster. In the spring, it's almost strong enough to sweep you away." His voice had taken on this weird, flat tone that reminded me of his brother's. Coming out of a living person, it made my skin crawl. I grabbed his arm and pulled it back around me. He got the idea and gave me a little squeeze before pulling back so he could look at me. His gaze slipped to my lips, then back up again. I leaned forward in answer.

Annoyingly, the first thought I had when our lips touched was that Eunice was not going to be happy. *So what?* I thought. *I don't owe her anything, and if she's too afraid to even approach Kemp, why should I sit back and wait for something that might never happen?* He slid his fingers into my hair, holding me closer. I could taste the pizza on his lips as I kissed him again, and I turned my body and slid my hand up over the slight roughness of his jaw, hungry for more. He seemed a little surprised when I straddled his legs and held his face, and I could feel him smiling under my embraces. He moved his hands to my waist and then slid them lower, pulling me against him.

"Before you get too excited," he said, his words barely managing to escape past my desperate kisses, "Mom's still upstairs. And she's got *really* good hearing."

I pulled back, staring deep into his eyes as I rubbed my thumb over his plump lower lip. "Then we'll just have to make out quietly," I whispered before I leaned down and prevented him from saying anything else.

A Weird Conversation

By the time Dad came to pick me up, I felt flushed and giddy, and I wasn't quite sure if I'd be able to stand up. I wanted to do more but had to content myself with kissing and the feel of Kemp's hands sliding up under my shirt. He looked exhausted, so instead of making him accompany me to the door, I gave him one last kiss, then grabbed my stuff and ran up the stairs alone. When I caught a glimpse of myself in the car's side mirror, I noticed that my hair was kind of dishevelled. But it was windy out, so Dad probably assumed that was the cause of the mess.

We hadn't gotten any homework done, of course, so after dinner I retired to my room and tried my best to do it, but all I could think about was what we'd done that afternoon and how much I wanted to do it again. That distraction made the work take twice as long, and by the time I was done, it was after eleven. I threw all my books back in my bag, plugged my laptop in to charge, and retreated to the bathroom, taking my pyjamas with me. That had become my habit ever since Austin had shown up. After my conversation with Kemp that afternoon, though, I wasn't sure if it was even necessary.

When I hopped into bed, I reached for my phone. The screen was a bit blurry, but I didn't bother with my glasses. I could see well enough to type.

You still awake?

The answer came back almost immediately, as if he'd been waiting for the message.

of course

Just wanted to say goodnight.

austin there yet

Nope, I typed, though I'd spoken just a moment too soon. The ghost appeared on my floor, curled up on his side as usual, apparently asleep.

Wait. He's here.

send me a pic

I can't. I tried taking one before but it didn't work.

try again

I did, but of course all the flash did was wake Austin up. He frowned, not even bothering to get up off the floor.

"What are you doing?"

"What does it look like?" I asked.

"And how's that working out?"

"That's what I tried to tell him," I said, holding up the phone. He scrambled into a sitting position.

"Kemp?"

When I nodded, he stood up and practically ran toward me. His footsteps made no sound, and I knew, logically, that if he tried to touch me, his hand would go right through my body. But I still drew back, cowering.

"Can I talk to him?" he asked, his eyes shining with hope. I pulled my phone toward my chest. The new-message alert sounded, but I didn't bother to look.

"Why can't you talk to him yourself?"

"No idea," he said. "I can't even see him. But even if I could, they left and . . ."

"They moved."

"Yeah, Ivy, I know."

"How am I supposed to know what you know and don't know?" I snapped. "I don't know the rules for . . . whatever this is."

"I'm still learning them myself." He peered at the phone in my hand just as it let out a second alert, and crouched down beside the bed. "Please, let me talk to him."

"How? If you can't touch anything, then—"

"You can give him the message. Tell him I'm here. Tell him I'm not angry. Tell him I forgive him."

"Forgive him? For what?"

"He'll know what I mean."

Warily, keeping my gaze fixed on him to make sure he didn't make any sudden moves, I pulled my phone away from my chest just as another alert sounded.

ivy, the first message read, *did u*

r u there, asked the second.

ivy whats going on, demanded the third. *if u need help send me a sign*

I glanced at Austin before turning back to the screen.

> Your brother's here. He has a message for you.

> what

> He says he's not angry. He forgives you.

There was a long pause. Kemp had gotten the message, but he wasn't responding. I looked at Austin.

"Maybe he *doesn't* know what you mean."

"He does."

"Care to share?"

He shook his head. "That'll be up to him to tell you. If he wants to."

"Why? What's so—"

> tell him if he doesnt leave u alone im gonna kick his ass

> Why? What's wrong?

> what did he tell u

Nothing. He said you should tell me.

There was another long pause. And then:

tell him to go to hell

Kemp!

tell him to go away ivy im serious

I turned my gaze to the ghost who was crouched there, waiting patiently. Shaking my head, I turned the screen toward him so he could see the exchange. "What the hell is going on here?" I asked. Austin's expression went from puzzled to angry before finally settling on sad. He sighed and stood up, then laced his fingers behind his head as he turned away.

is he still there

Yes, he's still here. And you're being rude. Do you know what I would give to talk to Jade one more time? What's the matter with you?

He didn't answer. I looked at Austin, who was pacing . . . if you could call it that. He didn't have a lot of room to work with. He probably could've walked through the bed, but maybe that was uncomfortable or something.

"Austin," I said, keeping my voice low, "are you here all the time?"

He raised his eyebrows and stopped moving. "All the time?" he repeated.

"Are you here, watching me even when I can't see you? Or are you . . . somewhere else?"

"I don't know," he said, and the puzzlement on his face made me believe him immediately. "I don't *think* I'm here. At least, I don't remember being here. I only remember . . ."

"What?" I whispered.

"This. Being here. In your room. Or near you. Like that day on the school field." He rubbed his palms over his forehead. "I mean, I must be *somewhere* when I'm not near you. But I don't remember. I don't know if I *try* to show up, or . . ."

"It's okay," I said, because I could see he was getting a little upset. He dropped his hands to his sides and looked at me with eyes so sad that I felt like crying in sympathy.

"I'm scared," he said. "I don't know what's happening to me. I don't even know if I'm alone. I think I am, but . . . I don't remember." He took a step forward. "All I know is that, when I'm with you, I'm not alone. So . . . please don't send me away, Ivy."

"Would you go if I asked you to? *Could* you?"

"I don't know," he whispered. "I don't know."

I set the phone down and got out of bed. My instinct was to reach out and hold him, but I could imagine how that would go: empty swipes through the air, my skin crawling, and his despair growing. Instead, I reached out and held my hand toward him. He stared at it for a moment, then looked into my eyes. Hesitantly, he raised his hand and aimed his fingertips at my own. I think we could both tell we weren't actually touching each other. But it looked like we were.

"Can you feel that?" I asked.

"No. But I feel . . . you." He dropped his hand. "I don't want to be stuck here, Ivy. I never meant to haunt you. I'm sorry."

"We'll figure it out," I said.

"What if we can't?"

"Then I guess I'm going to have a roommate for the foreseeable future."

His lips twitched in a wavering smile. "I'll try not to get in your way. You can ignore me. Just step over me if . . ." He shook his head and looked down at the floor. "Or step through me. Whatever."

My phone suddenly buzzed, causing me to jump. I reached for it, only to see Kemp's ID on the screen. I held it to my ear.

"Hello?"

"What's going on, Ivy? Are you all right?"

"Yeah. I'm fine. Austin and I are just working out some logistics."

"Huh?"

"He can crash on my floor if he keeps quiet and lets me sleep."

"Did you tell him what I said?"

"I showed him. Why were you so rude?"

"Don't listen to him, okay?" He lowered his voice as if he were afraid Austin would hear. I didn't know if he could, so I pressed the phone a little more tightly against my ear. "He was messed up before he died, Ivy. I wouldn't trust anything that comes out of his mouth."

I glanced over at Austin, who was waiting patiently, his eyebrows slightly raised. The desperation in Kemp's voice made me curious, but I was hesitant to ask about the mentions of anger and forgiveness that had elicited such a strong reaction. "I'll talk to you tomorrow, okay?"

"Remember what I said."

"I will."

He mumbled something that I didn't catch and hung up. I turned back to Austin, who let out a sigh.

"He feels guilty," he said.

"Yeah."

"'Cause he . . . um . . ." His face seemed to pale a little, as if he'd just been hit by a wave of nausea. With a bemused nod, he abandoned the thought and looked down at his spot on the floor. Folding himself onto it, he reached up and clasped his hands over his head. "Okay. Ivy . . ."

"What's wrong?"

"I don't know. Something's happening. I . . . feel like I'm falling."

"You can't fall," I said. "You're already on the"—his body vanished—"floor. Austin?" Shuffling closer to the spot, I wiggled my toes across the smooth wood. It felt like it always did. The visit was over, and I was once again left alone with nothing but the ghost of a ghost for company.

18

Halloween

Kemp had ditched the crutches by Halloween, which was good because they certainly wouldn't have gone with the zombie costume he'd put together. He played up the slight limp he still had, and actually made the music teacher scream when the poor guy rounded the corner and ran into a rotting corpse, which of course made all the students in the vicinity laugh. But by lunchtime, Kemp was missing, and I'd heard through the grapevine that he'd been sent to the principal's office for his costume being too graphic.

When he flopped onto the bench beside Eunice in the cafeteria, though, he was still impressively gory, and she leaned away from him more than she usually did.

"If you think I'm kissing that mouth," I said, "you're sadly mistaken."

"What?" He pulled the fake, rotted teeth from his own and stuck them in his pocket. "Better?"

"Not really," I said. There was still a massive sore on his right cheek and a fake eyeball dangling from a bundle of plastic nerves. His hair looked so filthy that I wondered if he'd avoided bathing for a week in preparation (though he'd looked just fine the day before, so I knew that wasn't it). He pulled off his backpack and dropped it on the bench beside him with a moaning growl in Eunice's direction. She just stared at him with wide eyes. Rissa laughed. She was dressed as a fairy, and there was so much glitter in her hair that I had a feeling we'd be hearing her complain about it for the next few months.

"I thought they made you tone down your costume," she said.

"They did." He pointed to his chin. "I had some blood capsules. Made it look like I'd just had a fresh kill."

"*That* was the part they objected to?" I asked. "Not the dangling eyeball or the missing arm?"

He shrugged. It looked like he had his left arm bound at his side somehow. There was a bloody stump hanging from his shredded sleeve.

"Good thing we don't have PE today," I muttered, watching as he struggled with the zipper on his backpack. He looked up at Eunice, but she was edging slowly away from him. If she went another few inches, she was going to end up on the floor. "I'll help," I said, standing up and rounding the table so I could do so. I pulled out the container, which appeared to hold some sort of pasta, and set in on the table in front of him. As soon as I was sitting in my seat again, I noticed him staring at me. "Stop it."

"Stop what?"

"Looking at me. It's freaking me out."

He reached up and flicked the eyeball. It bounced against his cheek. Rissa snorted and turned back to her fries.

"Guess I'll be eating these without ketchup today."

"A little help?" Kemp said, pointing at his lunch. I slid the spork out of its compartment in the lid, then took the lid off. It wasn't exactly something that could be done with one hand.

"I'm not feeding you as well," I said.

"Not feeding a zombie is a dangerous thing to do."

"Yeah, if they eat brains. You're eating pasta."

"You sure about that?" he asked, shovelling in a huge sporkful with a creepy slurp. Rissa flicked a fry in his direction. He plucked it out of his lap and ate it. "Thanks."

"I thought you guys were going to dress up together," Rissa said, eyeing my utterly normal attire. Normal for me, anyway. For the few people who'd cheekily asked what I was supposed to be, my answer had been, "Sixties schoolgirl." That had shut them up pretty quickly.

"I couldn't manage *that* on my own," I said, waving my hand at Kemp. "Besides, I don't really want to pretend to be dead."

"I'm not quite dead."

"You look pretty close to it."

"You're going to dress up for the party, though, right?" Rissa asked.

"What party?"

"Norris's party."

"Who?"

"Ethan Norris," Kemp said, his mouth full of sauce-coated pasta. "He's had one every year since we were too old to trick-or-treat."

"Do you usually go?"

He shook his head, forgetting, perhaps, about his eyeball.

It swung crazily until he dropped his spork and grabbed it. Rissa started to laugh.

"We have a different tradition," he said, letting go of the now-stationary eye.

"What's that?" I asked.

"Dress up and hand out candy."

I snorted. "You're not doing it like that, I hope."

"Why not?"

"You'll traumatize the poor little kids."

"Mom handles the little ones. I don't take over until later, when it's just greedy teenagers. Besides, I kind of have a reputation. People know where to go if they want to be scared . . . and where to avoid if they don't."

"Nice."

"We give out awesome treats. If you can't get close to me, you don't get one."

"I remember that alien thing you dressed up as a couple years ago," Rissa said. "I swear, Ms. Vye almost wet her pants."

"It wasn't *that* bad," he said.

"You had gills. And something living in those gills." She turned to me with a grin. "You should've seen his eyes. Solid red. And all this makeup to make it look like they were bleeding."

"Just contacts," he said. "And I wasn't an alien. I was a human who was slowly being taken over by an alien parasite colony."

I grimaced. "Gross."

Eunice had just been sitting there the whole time, looking rather shaken. The extent of her costume appeared to be a headband with fuzzy white bunny ears and a pink nose drawn on the tip of her own with what looked like lipstick.

"That was before you were here," Rissa said.

"What was?" she asked, her voice almost a whisper.

"The alien costume."

"It wasn't—" He broke off with a sigh. "Never mind." He peered at me over his half-eaten lunch. "You sure you don't want to come over and help? I've got enough stuff to do your makeup, too."

"Why can't you use your artistic powers for good instead of evil?" I asked, which only made him smile. He spooned in another mouthful and reached up to flick at his dangling eyeball. I just rolled my eyes.

"Hayes! Nice." Josh held out his fist as he passed. Kemp bumped it with his own knuckles, still clutching the spork. "Heard you got busted."

"Yeah."

"Me, too."

I peered at Josh, but I didn't see any gore. In fact, he didn't have a scratch on him. I didn't know why he would, since he appeared to be a cowboy.

"For what?" Rissa asked. He gestured to the empty gun holsters at his hips.

"Zero tolerance. You coming to Norris's party?" he asked. Kemp stabbed at his pasta.

"Nope."

"Scaring the kiddies?"

"Yep."

Josh slapped his hand on Kemp's shoulder, which, for

some reason, sent up a cloud of dust; the cowboy waved it away, laughing, and headed over to his usual table.

"Is this party a big deal or something?" I asked. Eunice nodded. Rissa shrugged. Kemp just kept eating.

"It's big," Rissa said. "It usually gets a few hundred kids."

"I'm sure his parents appreciate that."

"They're not home."

I raised my eyebrows. She nodded.

"Yeah, I know. Not too bright. Their house hasn't burned down yet, though."

"Are you going?" I asked.

"Probably. Eunice wants to, so . . ."

"You should come," Eunice said to me.

"I don't know. It doesn't really sound like my kind of thing."

"She's probably spending the evening with Kemp," Rissa said. "Aren't you?"

"I hadn't really planned on doing anything."

"Really?" Kemp asked, his grimy eyebrows rising in surprise. "I thought you were coming over."

"That was before I knew you were going to give half the neighbourhood PTSD."

He rolled his visible eye. "Nobody's getting PTSD. Like I said, the people around our place know what they're getting. If they can't handle it, they stay away."

"Still."

"It's usually over by nine, anyway. We can do something after that."

"I already told you, I'm not kissing that mouth."

He grinned as he slipped the rotten plastic teeth over his real ones and lunged across the table at me. The fake eyeball hit my cheek as his lips pressed against mine. The slight floral scent of the makeup belied the gruesomeness of it; I couldn't see anything that close, anyway. He pulled back and, as his gaze dropped to my mouth, he smiled. Rissa burst out laughing as he sat down.

"What?" I asked. She reached over and rubbed her thumb against my chin.

"You look like you've just eaten a hippie."

"Zombie schoolgirl," Kemp said, his words partially distorted by his fake teeth. He put his dirty spork back in its compartment and tossed the empty container and lid into his backpack. "Pretty hot, if you ask me."

"Hold still and bite down hard," Kemp said, which just made me give him a look. He paused, the fake blood capsule pinched between his fingers as he held it between us. "That sounded kind of dirty, didn't it?"

"Just a little." I took the capsule from his impossibly grimy fingers—I wasn't letting them get anywhere near my mouth—and placed it carefully between my teeth.

"Keep your lips open and try not to swallow too much."

I bit down hard, then bent my head forward as the sticky liquid gushed out. It actually tasted like cherries, so it wasn't too bad. As I looked up at him, he grinned.

"Perfect. Now do you see why I told you to wear something old?"

"Yeah." I looked down at the red dribbles all over the front of the ratty sweatshirt. It was one I often wore for bed, and it was getting a little threadbare. After Halloween, it would be going straight into the garbage. "Am I zombified enough yet?" I asked, regarding the dirt ground into my jeans and the smudges on my exposed skin. Kemp's suggestion that I crawl around in his mom's garden had been met with a snort . . . but I had to admit, it had done the job. He grabbed my hand and pulled me toward the bathroom, just as the doorbell rang again. I could hear the door open, and then there was a rustle of costumes as a chorus of little voices shouted, "Trick or treat!"

"Well?" he asked. "What do you think?"

I peered at the flap of fake skin that was hanging from my cheek. With the red-covered chin and messy hair and dirt rubbed onto every bit of skin that hadn't been bloodied, I had to admit that it was fairly impressive. I smiled a little, startling myself with my bloody teeth. "Is that permanent?"

"Nope. It'll only last a few minutes. I'll give you another cap when the blood starts to wear off."

"When I've swallowed it all, you mean."

"It's food grade. You're fine." He reached for a small case on the counter that looked like the one Jade had had for her contacts. "I'm going to need you to help me with the rest of my costume, because once this goes in, I won't be able to see much." He pulled a white contact from the case with one finger and peeled back his eyelids so he could insert it in his left eye, covering up his rich brown iris.

"Um . . . shouldn't you wash your hands before doing that?"

"Too late now."

"Aren't those things dangerous?"

He frowned, which looked really weird, given the state of his eyes: one was dangling, the other was clouded over. "You know Dad's an optometrist, right? Believe me, I've heard all the warnings. He makes me get these things fitted properly." With another blink, he turned to me.

"Can you see anything?"

"Yeah. I see you. Details are pretty fuzzy, though. That's why I didn't wear it to school. Kind of hard to read through a zombie cornea."

"Where *is* your dad?" I asked. "Hiding out? My dad's not a fan of Halloween, either."

He reached for the long-sleeved plaid shirt that had the fake arm already attached to the sleeve. As he pulled it on over his t-shirt and settled the stump on his shoulder, he shrugged. "He's probably handing out candy."

"He is?"

Kemp froze and stared at me with his cloudy eye. "Yeah . . ." he said, drawing out the word. "At his place."

"Isn't this—" I started to say, then broke off, feeling utterly stupid. "They're divorced?"

"Yeah." His lips quirked. "You hadn't noticed?"

"I just assumed . . . I'm sorry. Your mom talked about your dad raking leaves and stuff, so I thought . . ."

"He still comes over and does yard work sometimes. We do it together." He pulled the shirt closed, tugging at the placket. "Would you mind helping me with the buttons? Try to offset them. Zombies wouldn't dress perfectly."

"Wouldn't you have gotten dressed before you turned into a zombie?"

He chuckled. "Good point. I guess nobody's eaten *your*

brains yet." He waited until I'd fastened the buttons before wedging his arm behind him. Then he reached for his fake teeth, slipped them in, and stumbled toward me with a groan.

"Get back," I said, trying not to laugh. I held my hands out to stop his advance, but he just staggered against them.

"Ghaaah . . ."

"You're disgusting."

He suddenly straightened up in a very unzombielike way and pulled something from his pocket. I wasn't sure what it was until a moment later, when he reached up to his mouth and a cascade of blood followed, dripping over his chin and down the front of his shirt.

"You're going to use those all up before you even have a chance to scare anyone."

"Taste . . . good . . ." he growled, and sort of flailed out of the bathroom. We emerged into the hallway just as Nina was coming out of the kitchen. She jumped, putting her hand on her chest with a nervous laugh.

"I miss the days when you used to dress up as a super-hero," she said, looking over Kemp's costume. "If you got blood on my floor, please clean it up before it stains."

He sighed and straightened up. "Way to ruin the illusion, Mom."

She shook her head and pointed to the bowl of treats sitting by the door. It still looked about half full. "The kids are getting bigger. Time to scare them."

"What time is it?" I asked. My phone was in my bag in Kemp's room. Nina glanced at the delicate watch on her wrist.

"Around eight-thirty. The little ones should be in bed."

"They *should* be," Kemp said, shuffling to the window beside the door and pulling the curtain aside to take a peek.

"I'll leave you to it, then. I'm going to get some reading done before bed."

"What if we run out of treats?"

"Then turn off the light and bring in the pumpkin. But I doubt you will." She retreated to her room. Kemp turned to me with a rotten, lopsided grin.

"Ready?"

"I guess. But if I make anyone cry, I'm done."

"You're not going to make anyone cry." He reached down and grabbed a couple of treats from the bowl. They were the sort of thing most kids craved: full-sized chocolate bars, not those tiny little things that were barely a mouthful. He handed one to me, but I knew even before I read the ingredients that I wouldn't be eating it.

"No, thanks," I said, tossing it back into the bowl. He frowned as he pulled out his fake teeth and stashed them in his pocket. He had to use his real ones to peel open the wrapper.

"You don't like those?" he asked around a mouthful of peanuts and caramel.

"It's not that I don't like them. My body doesn't like them." I stood on my toes and peered out the little window in their front door. "I'm allergic to peanuts."

Kemp sort of choked, and when I looked over at him, he took a step back. "I'm sorry! Are you—"

"It's fine," I said.

"You should've told me!" he almost shouted. "What if I'd kissed you?"

"I'm not *that* allergic," I said. "I just got a little swollen from eating peanut butter once."

He swallowed what was in his mouth, though it looked like he was trying to swallow a mouthful of sawdust. "What if it's more than that?"

"I've got an EpiPen in my bag. I've never had to use it, though." I took a step toward him, but he drew back, his cloudy eye wide. "Kemp, it's fine. I promise. You've probably eaten peanut butter and breathed on me before. Relax."

But he was shaking. I grabbed his arm—even though he tried to pull away—and marched him down the hall to his room. My bag was still sitting on his bed. I reached inside and rummaged around until I found the injector, then pulled it out to show him.

"See? If anything were to happen, I've got this. I've *always* got it with me. I'm always prepared."

"Are you sure?" He looked down at the half-eaten chocolate bar that was still in his hand, then held it away from me as if it were a blowtorch and he didn't want me to get burned.

"Yes. I'm sure." I tossed the injector back into my bag and reached around him for a hug. He stopped breathing. "If you're going to be weird about this . . ."

"If anything happened to you, I wouldn't be able to forgive myself."

"Nothing's going to happen," I said, just as the doorbell rang. I pulled back and looked up at him. Despite the makeup, I could see that he was a bit pale. His lips were, anyway, at least where they weren't covered in cherry-flavoured fake blood. "Come on. It's time to scare people."

He didn't look so sure. His grimy brow creased in a deep frown. I finally had to take the initiative and march back out to the front door. Luckily, it was a group of young teenage boys, and some of their costumes were just as gory as ours. I dropped the chocolate bars into bags and pillowcases, and the group grew smaller and smaller until at last it was just a couple of kids waiting for their treats. It was then that I heard a groan behind me. I dropped a treat into one bag, just as the kid turned and bolted. The other one didn't even bother to stick around. He leaped off the porch and sprinted after his friend. I turned around, the last treat still in my hand, and saw Kemp limping toward the door. He really was a gruesome sight, especially with a fresh capsule of blood dripping from his chin. He came to a stop beside me and frowned out into the darkness.

"Aw. It's no fun when they run away before you can scare them."

"You," I said, "are weird."

He smiled, all rotten teeth and blood.

"That is just about the unsexiest thing ever."

"No . . . sex . . ." he moaned. "Penis . . . fell . . . off . . ." But he couldn't keep that up without laughing. It burst out of him so suddenly that his fake teeth went flying into the treat bowl. Then we were both laughing. I quickly closed the door so as not to ruin the illusion; laughing zombies weren't exactly scary.

WE TOOK THE TREAT BOWL OUT TO THE PORCH AND SAT ON the bench for a while. Actually, we sprawled rather than sat, and Kemp would lurch up and shuffle toward the trick-or-treaters every time they approached the house. I was afraid he was going to get himself punched, or that someone would panic and swing their treat bag at his head. But the kids who came to that house seemed to know what to expect. After those first two that had run, the rest appeared to be braver. A few even complimented us on our costumes, though that was only met with a few inarticulate grunts. Since they had to get past Kemp to get to the second zombie who was handing out the treats, a lot of them got an up-close look at his costume.

"That's awesome," one boy said. He was dressed as a pirate, complete with a plastic hook for a hand. He was too young to have a beard, so it'd been drawn on instead. "How'd you get your eye like that?"

Kemp tilted his head and let out a growl that sort of sounded like a garbled answer. The kid looked nervously at me.

"What's his problem?"

It took a moment for me to decide whether to answer his question or go full-on zombie myself. I lurched up from the bench, treat in hand, and stumbled toward them. The kid started to back away. Kemp reached out and grabbed his arm.

"Dayton, let's go!" another kid shouted from the street. "Don't want Hemp Haze turning you into one of them."

Kemp's head snapped toward him, and his eyeball went swinging. The pirate pried at his fingers, trying to get him to release his grip. I gave up the pretence and jogged over to them, then shoved the chocolate bar in the pirate's face.

"Here. Take it. Kemp, let go."

"Yeah," the pirate said. He wrenched hard and finally managed to free himself. "Asshole."

I held the treat out, but the pirate didn't seem to care. Glaring, he adjusted the plastic hook and shook his head.

"Don't take anything from them!" the other boy shouted. "It's probably poisoned. Everyone knows Hemp Haze is a murderer."

Kemp didn't move. He didn't even look like he was breathing. I gently slipped my hand into his and started to pull him back toward the porch.

"They're idiots high on sugar," I said, tugging him back to the bench. He was still staring at the boys as they made their way to the next house. I couldn't tell how much he was seeing, but I could definitely see the emotions etched on his face. The anger. The hurt. "Forget it," I said. "They don't know anything."

"People think I killed him."

"But you didn't."

He flopped back on the bench and turned his head away. His lips trembled as though he were about to cry, but of course he didn't. He held the emotion in, through some act of sheer will, and stared blankly out at the October night.

WE STAYED OUT THERE LONG AFTER THE LAST TRICK-OR-treaters had come and gone. I was freezing, and all I wanted to do was cuddle, but Kemp was in a weird mood. He'd sprawled there on the bench, barely moving, except for once when a last group of kids (if you could call them that) had approached the house, and he'd staggered into the front yard, a mess of growls and snarls and moans. The kids had laughed and avoided the house altogether, and Kemp had limped back to resume his position on the bench.

Eventually, I couldn't take the cold any longer, so I blew out the candle in the pumpkin and took it inside, along with the almost-empty bowl of treats. Then I retrieved the sad zombie from the porch and dragged him into the house.

When I checked the time on my phone, it was almost eleven. There were a couple of messages that I hadn't seen, including one from Dad asking if I needed a ride home. I glanced at Kemp, who was standing in the middle of his room, swaying slightly.

"Are you okay?"

"Yeah." He pulled out the fake teeth and cast them on the dresser, then reached up and started to peel away the chewed-up eye socket from which the fake eyeball hung. When it was off, he blinked, peering at me with a mismatched set of eyes.

"I never got a picture," I said.

"Don't care." He unbuttoned his shirt and pulled it off, freeing his left arm.

"Kemp." I put my hand on his face, realizing a moment too late that the makeup was still sticky. I pulled away and wiped my hand on my pants. "Why are you listening to that idiot? You know it's not true. *I* know it's not true."

He balled up the shirt with the stump still inside it and tossed it into the corner of his room. Then he flopped onto his bed.

"You're going to make your sheets filthy."

"So I'll wash them." He groaned and pressed his palms over his eyes. "This whole night has been shit."

"No, it hasn't," I said. "It was kind of fun watching you chase those poor kids off the front lawn."

He dropped his hands to his sides so hard they bounced. "I nearly killed you with a chocolate bar. And then that little shit had to go and remind—"

"So don't listen to little shits," I said. "And you didn't nearly kill me. In case you haven't noticed, I'm fine." I sat down on the edge of his bed, even though my jeans were covered in garden soil; his sheets already needed to be washed.

"Are you fine?" he asked, turning to face me with his mismatched eyes. "Really fine?"

I shrugged. A part of me was annoyed that he could see it. That I wasn't fine. Not really. "I just don't like being reminded of what happened to Jade. There's nothing I can do about it now except feel guilty."

"There was nothing you could have done."

"Except be there," I said. "If I had been, I would've had my EpiPen with me. And we could've used it for her."

"You didn't know you'd need to."

I shook my head. "I don't want to talk about it. You should understand that better than anyone."

He reached out and took my hand. I watched his grimy thumb rub my equally grubby skin for a few seconds. At last, he sighed. "Sometimes I do want to talk about it," he said. "Just not with random asshole kids."

"You can talk to me, if you want."

He blew out a breath and stared up at the ceiling. "Austin wouldn't have been down at the creek that night if it wasn't for me. If . . . all that stuff hadn't happened . . ." He shook his head on the pillow. "I wish I could talk to him."

"I thought you didn't want to."

"I don't. But . . . I do."

"Be careful what you wish for."

He turned to me with a frown. "Do you think he's going to show up tonight? I mean, if you're not in your room, will he?"

"I don't know. I've never been anywhere else when he showed up before. Except that time on the field."

"You think he'll come here?"

I shrugged. "Maybe. I don't really understand his schedule. It's mostly regular, but there are some aberrations."

"Like the field."

"Yeah. That was the only time I saw him during the day. Every other time, it's been later. Eleven twenty-one."

"Eleven twenty-one," he repeated.

"Yeah. Is there some significance to that? It wasn't Austin's time of death or something, was it?"

He shook his head, then turned it away from me. I lay down beside him.

"Did *anything* happen at that time?"

He chewed on his lip. His chin was still covered in fake blood, and when he took a deep breath, I noticed he'd gnawed most of the cherry goo off his lips. "The creek. I think that's when he went into the creek."

I didn't say anything.

"But that doesn't explain that morning on the field," he went on, his voice hesitant.

"Maybe the time doesn't really mean anything. Maybe he's just trying to break through. There's something he needs to tell you."

"There's nothing he needs to tell me. I already know what happened."

"Well, there must be something. He certainly wouldn't need to be telling *me*. I didn't even know him when he was alive."

We puzzled over it silently. At least, I did. I couldn't tell what Kemp was thinking. He scratched at the remnants of makeup around his eye and stared at the ceiling. I didn't move. The thought that I might actually get a weeknight without a visit from his brother's ghost was a tantalizing prospect. If he showed up on my bedroom floor—and that was a big *if*—what would happen when he didn't see me there? Or would he even show up there at all?

After a stretch of awkward silence, I held up my phone and checked the time. 11:20. My heart jumped into my throat . . . just as the numbers changed and I heard a familiar, echoing voice.

"Where the hell are you?"

I sat up, only to see Austin standing there in his pyjamas. Right in the middle of his brother's bedroom, though I doubted either of them knew it. He peered at me, and then frowned as he shook his head.

"What happened to you? Are you all right?"

"Of course I'm all right. It's Halloween. It's just makeup."

"What?" Kemp mumbled. I looked at him, only to find him staring at me with a perplexed expression.

"Where are you?" Austin asked again. I turned back to him and climbed off the bed.

"Where does it look like?"

"No idea. I can't see anything except you. But . . ." He looked down at the floor around him, though I didn't think he could actually see it. "The layout is different, isn't it?"

"I'm in Kemp's room."

At the sound of his name, Kemp leaped off the bed. "Ivy? What's—"

"He's here," I said.

"In my room? Why can't I see him?"

"I don't know."

"What are you talking about?" Austin asked, and I realized that both brothers were only hearing my side of each conversation . . . which had to be confusing. I took a step back so I could see them at the same time. Though they were both seventeen—one moving through the age with natural fluidity, the other frozen forever—they didn't look a lot alike. Their height, though, was similar, which left me looking up as I turned my gaze back and forth between them.

"Kemp's here," I said. "And Austin's here. But you obviously can't hear each other. You can only hear me."

"Great," Kemp muttered.

"How did I get here?" Austin asked.

I shrugged. "How should I know? You're the ghost."

"Tell him to leave," Kemp said. I turned to him in disbelief.

"I thought you wanted to talk to him!"

"Yeah. Later. By myself. I have some things to say to him that I don't want you to hear."

I sighed and turned to Austin. "He wants to yell at you, I think."

"For what? Dying?"

"What's he saying?" Kemp asked. I shook my head and held up my hands.

"I'm not doing this," I said, then looked at Austin. "If you want to talk to him, you need to find a way to do it yourself."

"I thought that's what this was!"

"Other than me," I said. "He won't use me as a go-between. There's stuff he doesn't want to say in front of me."

His frown deepened. "Is that so?"

"Ask him if he can hear me when I talk to him," Kemp said.

"He can't," I snapped. "I'm the fucking astral telephone."

"The what?" Austin asked, then started to laugh.

"It's not funny," I said. I stepped forward and poked my finger toward his chest. "And this isn't fair to me. I've put up with this crap for almost two months now. If there's something you need to say, say it. Otherwise—"

"Don't," Kemp said, his voice suddenly panicked. I turned to him with a frown.

"Don't what?"

"If you scare him away . . ."

"You just told me to tell him to leave! Besides, I don't think I *can*," I said, turning back to Austin. "Can I?"

"Can you what?"

"Scare you away."

He shook his head. "I'm not scared."

"Is there any way to get you to leave?"

"Maybe."

"Do tell."

He began to pace a little, stopping just as he started to move through the dresser. As he moved back out into the room, he shook his head. "We need to figure out why I'm here in the first place."

"Unfinished business."

"Obviously. But what does that mean? That could be anything."

I looked over at Kemp, who was standing there, his shoulders raised slightly in an expectant shrug. "It probably has something to do with your brother," I said.

"Duh."

I whirled back to glare at the ghost. "If you're so smart, why don't you—"

"I'm not sure," he said slowly, "but I think all of this might have something to do with karma."

"Karma? You mean . . . it's to do with past lives?"

"It might be."

"Isn't karma something you have to deal with in life? What could you possibly be able to do in death?"

"I don't know. Maybe . . ." He rubbed both hands over his short-cropped hair. "Maybe it isn't so much action as knowledge. Maybe there's something one of us needs to know. Or maybe . . ."

"*Maybe?*" I said, suddenly suspicious. I was getting the feeling that Austin knew more than he was letting on. That his uncertainty was little more than a charade. As if he'd figured out what I was thinking, he dropped his hands and took a step toward me.

"Fine. *Probably.*"

"You know exactly what's going on here, don't you?"

"Not exactly. But . . . I have an idea."

"Care to share?"

"I don't think . . . I don't think I can."

"Why not?"

"I think it's up to him."

"What is?"

"I can't tell you."

I threw up my hands in frustration. Kemp shook his head, frowning.

"What's going on?" he whispered.

"Your brother's playing mind games with me."

"I told you not to believe anything he said."

"I'm not playing games," Austin said. "He needs to tell you—" He winced and threw his hands up to cradle his head. "Oh, shit. Not—" He vanished before he could get another word out. I let out a breath and took a step forward.

"Ivy?" Kemp whispered.

"He's gone." I turned to the pale, half-zombified boy standing beside me. He ran his fingers through his filthy hair and shook his head.

"What did he say?"

"What does it matter? You said I wasn't supposed to listen."

He grabbed my upper arms and leaned down to look at me. The remnants of his makeup still made him look pretty damn creepy, and I had to struggle to maintain eye contact. "Ivy, what did he say?"

I chewed on my lip for a moment before taking a deep breath. "He said there's something you need to tell me."

"What?"

"How should I know?"

He let go and turned to flop, face first, onto his bed. I sighed and sat down a little more gracefully beside him.

"He's a messed-up ghost," I said. "You did warn me. I'm not taking him seriously."

"Good," he mumbled into the mattress.

"Are you supposed to tell me you love me or something?"

He let out a little groan and rolled onto his back, then caught my hand and pulled me toward him. I went, somewhat reluctantly, trying to swipe my thumb at my phone.

"I need to call Dad for a ride home."

"Stay."

"I'm not staying," I said. He pulled the phone from my hand and slipped it under his pillow. "Kemp—"

"Stay," he said again.

"I'm not kissing you when you look like that."

"So close your eyes." He caught the hem of my sweatshirt and slid his hand up underneath.

"Your mom's in the next room, isn't she?"

"She probably fell asleep hours ago."

"You said she has excellent hearing."

"Not when she's asleep."

I chewed on my lip, tasting the cherry-flavoured residue. Kemp suddenly got up and left the room. I dove for his pillow as soon as he was gone and retrieved my phone. There was another message, this time from Mom. I was just formulating an answer when Kemp walked back into his room. His eyes looked normal again, and he'd hastily rid himself of much of the makeup, though I could still see a few smears.

"I can give you a ride home," he said, looking sheepish.

His hands—still dirty—were half shoved in his pockets. "If you want."

"What do *you* want?" I asked. He closed the door, careful not to make too much noise, and padded over to the bed in his bare feet. As he pulled the condom from his pocket, he raised his eyebrows. I could see his hand shaking.

"Oh."

"If this isn't . . . We can do it some other time, if this . . . Have you ever . . . ?"

"Would you mind finishing a sentence?"

He sighed and shook his head. "Never mind. I ate peanuts a few hours ago, so—"

I snorted and stood up. "I'm not *that* allergic. Besides, you'll be using protection."

His eyes widened a little. "You're sure?"

In response, I bent over my phone and sent Mom a quick message telling her that we were watching a movie, and that Kemp would bring me home when we were done. *Don't wait up,* I added.

19

The Train

We didn't bother trying to hide our relationship at all after that. Walking through the hallways at school was done with our fingers intertwined. The seating arrangement at lunch had to be changed so we could sit side by side, our thighs pressed close. He drove me home from school every day, even though it was in the opposite direction from his house. On the days his mom worked late, we'd go to his house, lock ourselves in his room, and explore each other's bodies with the curiosity of two kids who didn't know what the hell they were doing, but who were enjoying every minute of it. I suspected Kemp wasn't exactly experienced himself, but I didn't mind. We were having plenty of fun learning together.

After Halloween, I stopped talking to Austin. I found that, if I didn't interact with him, he'd just lie there on the floor, as still as a corpse, until he disappeared a few minutes later. That was just fine, as far as I was concerned. I was a bit annoyed to still have a ghost in my room, but it wasn't like he was causing any problems. He was just *there*.

As Christmas approached, the weather grew colder. On

the Friday afternoon at the start of the holiday break, Kemp and I sat opposite each other in the banquette, our sock feet twining as we sipped at mugs of hot chocolate and nibbled on store-bought cookies. The only baking Mom had done had promptly disappeared, and I had a feeling her clients had reaped the benefits. From the kitchen, we could look out and see the winter-sparse woods that lined the creek. I hadn't been down there again, and I had no desire to.

"Do you have any homework?" he asked.

I shook my head. "Not really. Just some reading for English. But that's hardly homework. You?"

"Yeah. Bio and Earth Science."

"You want to do it now? Then it's out of the way."

He shook his head and sipped at his drink. "I'll do it later. It's just grade-eleven shit, anyway."

I frowned. "I feel like I'm corrupting you."

"How so?"

"Plying a vulnerable young student with food and drink and the promise of sex when he should be doing his homework."

He snorted into his mug. "I'm older than you, you realize."

"Could've fooled me."

We exchanged a smile. I slid my toes up his leg and into his lap. At least, I tried to. My legs weren't quite long enough.

Sliding out of the banquette, I picked up my mug and tilted my head. We went up to my room, where we set our mugs on the dresser.

"Are you sure your parents won't be coming home soon?"

"They've got some sort of Christmas-party thing at one of the pubs," I said. "They won't be home for hours."

At that thought, he grinned and proceeded to shed his clothes. I watched quietly, as I often did, enjoying the view before I started to undress myself.

"Are you going to take your socks off?" I asked.

"My feet are cold."

"You look ridiculous."

He lounged on the bed, propping his head up with his hand, and struck a pose. I laughed and folded my arms across my chest.

"Did you bring a condom?"

"Check my pocket."

I pawed through his pile of clothes until I found the item in the back pocket of his jeans. As I slid onto the bed beside him, I held it up between us. "Were you expecting some action in the library or something?"

"Nope." He leaned forward and kissed me, then slipped the condom from my fingers. As he positioned himself on top of me, I ran my fingers over his chest. "Shit, Ivy. Your hands are cold."

"So I better not do this," I said, and he yelped as I moved my hand lower.

"You're so cruel." He kissed me again, first on the lips, then down my neck, his lips moving lower and lower. My heart quickened in anticipation as his hands led the way, caressing my waist, then my hips. I gripped the sheets and turned my head . . . only to see Austin standing less than three feet away.

I jumped and scrambled into a sitting position, accidentally kneeing Kemp in the face.

"Shit, Ivy! What was—"

"Get out!" I shouted.

"But I—"

"Not you. Your pervy brother." I tugged at the blanket that was lying under me as I tried to cover myself up. Kemp looked around the room, trying to see something that—for him—wasn't there.

"He's here?"

"It's like four o'clock in the afternoon!" I shouted. "You can't just start coming around any time you feel like it."

"Has he told you yet?" Austin asked.

"Told me what?"

"He doesn't want you to know. I get that. But . . . you don't know the whole story, Ivy."

"I don't want to."

"None of this will make sense until you do."

"I said, I don't want to." I stood up, holding the blanket around me and fumbling for Kemp's hand so I could pull him to his feet. Austin looked almost frightened for a moment. But then his expression melted into a steely resolve. He walked forward until he was within arm's reach of both me and his brother.

"I'm sorry to have to do this," he said. "Just remember, it's in the past."

"What is?" I asked, just as his hands darted out and plunged into me and Kemp at the same time.

I wasn't in my room anymore. I wasn't *me* anymore. I stood in the clattering boxcar, watching the ground rush past. We were going too fast. I didn't know how I knew that, but I did.

"He ain't gonna make it," a male voice said, blasting a

breath of onions and stale alcohol against the side of my face. I shook my head.

"He ain't," I agreed. My voice was deep. I looked at my hand, which was braced against the edge of the door. It was large and callused, emerging from the end of a worn, blue shirt cuff that rippled in the wind caused by the speed of the train. I leaned forward and peered out, watching the young man pump his arms and legs, thrusting his chest forward as he ran with all his might.

"Forget it, Neil!" the man beside me shouted. "It's goin' too fast!"

Neil gritted his teeth in determination and kept running. The train was going slightly faster than him now, and picking up speed all the time. He kept looking to his left, toward us, as he ran alongside.

"Meet me in Springfield," I said. "I'll wait."

But Neil didn't seem inclined to wait. He veered closer and threw his arms out as he reached for the handle on the door. His fingers closed around it, and his feet left the ground.

"Rex!" he shouted. I crouched down and braced my hand on the door. There was nothing to hold on to, and I knew that as soon as he grabbed me he'd end up pulling me right out of the boxcar, possibly onto the tracks. I adjusted my knees, trying to find a secure position. "Rex!" he screamed. The man beside me shouted, just as I heard a distant shriek rise up over the sound of the train. Daring to poke my head all the way out, I spied the empty handle. All I could see of Neil, growing ever more distant, were his head and shoulders, right beside the tracks.

Before anyone could stop me, I leaped from the boxcar, tumbling into a heap in the bushes. I disentangled myself and started to run, limping back toward the small figure I could see on the ground. The train shrieked past, wheels screeching on the tracks.

He lifted his head and saw me. But I was still so far away. The caboose passed me by, and still I ran, tripping, falling, cursing as I drew nearer and saw the impossible sight with its inevitable conclusion. I stumbled past the crumpled legs and ran the last twenty feet to where the rest of Neil lay, eyes wide like a terrified child. I skidded to a stop on my knees, the blood-soaked gravel cutting into them, staining my pants.

"Neil."

His eyes were already distant. In the second or two it took for me to scoot closer, he went still. There were no more words. No more breaths. I reached down and took his face in my hands.

"Aw, Neil. I'm sorry, kid. I'm sorry." I started to cry as I gathered what was left of his body against me. "I told Ma I'd take care of you."

I fell back, only to find myself in my own room, naked on the floor, cradled in Kemp's arms. I took a deep breath and let out a scream. Judging by the raw sensation in my throat, it wasn't the first one.

"It's okay," Kemp was saying. "It's okay. I've got you. I've got you." He kissed my forehead. "Shh, Ivy."

"What the fuck was that?" I screamed, twisting away from him and lunging at Austin. Predictably, my fists fell on empty air and thumped to the floor. "What's the matter with you? I already saw that. I didn't need to *live* it!"

"Live what?" Kemp asked. He grabbed me and pulled me back, then held me against his warm body. I began to sob, curling against him as if he could save me from the horrors that lurked in my own mind.

No, I thought. *The horrors that Austin put there.*

"What did he do to you?" Kemp asked. "Ivy, what did he do?"

"You need to understand," Austin said. "Do you understand, or do I need to show you more?"

"Get out!" I screamed. "Get out! Get out! Get *out!*" Squeezing my eyes shut, I grasped at Kemp's shoulder. I couldn't seem to get close enough. Or maybe it was just that I couldn't get far enough away from Austin.

"What happened?" Kemp whispered. "Please, talk to me. Let me help."

"You can't," I said miserably.

"What did he do to you?"

"Didn't you feel it?"

He hesitated. "Feel what?"

I pulled back to stare at him with wide eyes. "You didn't feel any of that? You didn't see . . ."

He shook his head slowly.

"But he touched you." I looked over at Austin, who was still there despite my commands. He crouched down and shook his head.

"I can't make him see what he doesn't want to see."

"Then why did you touch him?"

"I needed to make the connection."

"Why?"

"So I could show you."

"What does Kemp have to do with your past lives?" I asked. Austin smiled sadly.

"Haven't you figured it out yet?"

I shuddered and leaned into Kemp's warmth. He was barely breathing, though I knew he was listening, trying to interpret the conversation even though he could only hear half of it. "Stop playing games," I said.

"I'm not. This isn't a game, Ivy. And the sooner you figure it out, the better off you'll be."

"Why?"

"I'm not leaving you alone until you get it. All of it."

I moaned into Kemp's chest. He held me tightly, and I could feel his heart thumping in time with my own.

"Fuck off and leave her alone, Austin," he said.

"He can't hear you," I mumbled.

"I can guess what he said." Austin's voice drew closer for a moment, and I had a feeling he was right next to me. "Think about what I showed you, Ivy."

"I don't want to," I whimpered.

"I know. But that's the only way you're going to understand why this is happening."

I sniffed and wiped my eyes. "Bullshit. You don't even know."

"Yes, I do. I wasn't sure before, but I am now. It's just that every time I get close to telling you about—"

As his voice cut off, I whipped my head around, only to find the room devoid of ghosts. Slowly, I turned back to Kemp, who was looking ashen. He put his hand on my cheek, trying to brush away my tears with his thumb.

"What did he do?" he whispered.

I shook my head. "He showed me one of those deaths again."

"But . . . you were screaming."

"He didn't just show me. He made me live it."

His eyes went wide. "Which one?"

"Man versus train."

Kemp's expression rounded into absolute horror. But something was niggling at my consciousness. I grabbed the blanket from where it sat a few feet away and pulled it around myself, frowning as I tried to work it out.

"Austin said to think about it."

"Yeah, well, then he's a sadist."

"No. I don't think so." I shook my head and tugged the blanket up around my chin. "I didn't see the death from the victim's point of view. I never saw *any* of them from the victim's point of view."

"So? What does that—"

"I saw the whole scene from a bystander's point of view. Not Neil's."

"Neil?"

"The guy who fell under the train and got cut in half."

He frowned. "And the others?"

"The same. I was always watching *them* die." I chewed on my lip for a moment, staring at the floor. "I watched Neil die. As Rex. Austin was showing me. He showed *all* of those notebook deaths to me. But . . . they weren't his deaths. He was just there."

"If those weren't his past lives, then whose were they?" He shook his head with a frown. "Yours?"

I gasped as the answer hit me, as I remembered the way Austin had shoved his hand toward his brother, just as the vision began. *To make the connection.*

"Oh, my god," I whispered. "I think they're yours."

20

Shut Out

THE MALL THREE DAYS BEFORE CHRISTMAS SHOULD'VE BEEN a distraction. But all I could think about was Kemp.

As I sat in the food court, waiting for Eunice and Rissa to finish our shared plate of greasy chow mein, I tapped my thumbs on my phone, sending yet another message in yet another going-nowhere conversation. I wasn't sure what number it was; I'd lost count.

Sighing, I shook my head. Rissa poked my hand with her sticky chopsticks. I pulled away with a glower.

"Gross."

"He's still not answering?"

"He's answering," I said. "He's just being a giant dick."

"Huh. Does he have one?"

"One what?"

"A giant dick," she said, and let out a giggle. Eunice shook her head with a frown.

"Being one and having one have nothing to do with each other," I said. Both girls looked a little surprised. I shoved my phone into my pocket and leaned my forearms on the table. "Of course this had to happen right before Christmas."

"Have you got him a gift yet?" Rissa asked.

"Yeah. Ages ago. I bought him a nice sketchbook and a set of drawing pens online." I shook my head. "It's not that. It's . . ."

"I've never had a boyfriend at Christmas."

"I haven't, either," Eunice said.

I shrugged. It wasn't even that. This would be my first Christmas without Jade. Having Kemp to share the holiday with would've helped take my mind off of what was missing. We could've made new memories so I didn't have to dwell so much on the old ones. But, the way things were going, I kind of doubted I was even going to see him again before school started back up in January.

"It's a good thing I don't have a boyfriend to buy for, though," Rissa went on, "because my shopping list is already ridiculous. I still have to get something for Mom, Grandma, Uncle Ray, Adela, Marc—"

"Me," Eunice said.

"Well, that goes without saying."

"Have you done *any* of your shopping yet?" I asked. She shrugged and stabbed at a piece of carrot on the plate.

"I got Dad's present weeks ago. Only because he was dropping hints like crazy. That was an easy one."

"What do you think Kemp is going to get for you?" Eunice asked. I turned to her in surprise, since she rarely talked to me. Rarer still was her talking about Kemp . . . especially now that he and I were a couple.

"I don't know. Maybe nothing. I don't even know if we're still together."

"Of course you are," Rissa said. "He hasn't broken up with you, has he?"

"Not officially. But he's kind of shutting me out."

She gave up trying to grab the remaining individual noodles on the plate and dropped her chopsticks on the tray. "Did you have a fight?"

"No."

"Did you cheat on him?"

"Who would I have cheated on him with?" I asked, casting a dark look in her direction.

"I don't know." Pushing the tray forward, she made more room for her arms on the table. "Just trying to help you figure it out."

There wasn't really anything to figure out. He'd freaked after finding out that all the horrible visions I'd been seeing were actually his past lives and deaths . . . not his brother's.

The more I thought about it, the more that explanation made sense. But he obviously wasn't taking the revelation very well. I couldn't blame him. When I thought about all the horrors in that notebook and imagined that I had actually gone through all of those painful, terrifying experiences, it made me feel as if a heavy weight were pressing down on me, trying to flatten me into the ground. Seeing what had happened to Neil had been bad enough; but the poor guy had had to endure the pain, too, and that was something my brain didn't even know how to imagine. More than anything, I was grateful that Kemp hadn't had to join me in that vision when Austin had made the connection.

"Maybe he misses his brother," Eunice said, jarring me out of my thoughts. Rissa nodded.

"Yeah. That might be all it is, Ivy. This time of year can be hard when you've lost someone. The first year after my granddad died was really tough. Grandma set a place for him at the table without even thinking, and when she realized what she'd done, she cried in her room for an hour. The turkey got a little dry."

Try losing your twin sister, I wanted to snap. But she meant well. And she didn't know. I was surprised she hadn't found out yet. I didn't think Eunice had, either. Kemp was the only one who knew about Jade, and that was just fine with me because he was probably the only one who really understood.

I looked out past the food court, watching the crowds swirl within the mall itself. With a deep sigh, I turned back to my friends. "We should probably get back out there."

Rissa groaned and dropped her forehead onto her arms. "Do we have to?"

"You shouldn't leave everything to the last minute," Eunice said.

"It's not the last minute. The day after tomorrow at closing time is the last minute." She lifted her head and looked at us sheepishly. "Would you think I'm a terrible friend if I just got you guys gift cards?"

"I love gift cards," I said.

"Yeah, because you're hard to buy for."

I blinked. "Why?"

"Anyone with a well-defined sense of style is hard to buy for."

"Is that a compliment or an insult?"

She smiled and tilted her head. "I'm not sure."

"Well, you won't hear me complaining, in any case," I said. "And I really hope you don't think a gift card equals a bad friendship, based on what I got you."

She stared at me for a moment, her mascara-caked lashes wide. And then she just laughed.

21

(Un)Merry Christmas

KEMP STILL WOULDN'T LET ME IN, AND BY CHRISTMAS morning, I was feeling his absence intensely. I opened presents with Mom and Dad, trying to pretend everything was okay. It actually wasn't as bad as I'd thought it would be, especially since Mom changed up our traditions a little. Instead of cinnamon buns and apple cider we had croissants and hot chocolate. Our artificial tree looked totally different in our new living room, even though I'd decorated it with all of our regular ornaments—including Jade's. When we'd finished decimating the wrapped parcels under the tree, I escaped to my room, taking the still-wrapped sketchbook and pens with me. Then I sat cross-legged on my bed in my pyjamas and sent Kemp another message.

> Merry Xmas!

There was no response. He hadn't sent anything back the day before, either. I knew he was getting the messages, but he was shutting me out.

When I still got nothing, I sent a Christmas tree emoji and started to get dressed. If he wasn't going to answer, I reasoned, then I would just have to go over there. I pulled my sleep-mussed hair back into a ponytail, grabbed the gift, and headed downstairs.

I wasn't about to ask my parents for a ride, so I bundled up against the cold and started out. I passed a few other people (mostly older couples) out for walks, and I marvelled at the everyday ordinariness of the act. It might've been one of the biggest holidays of the year, but people were still going about their lives. I seemed to be the only one, however, who was carrying a present in her mittened hands.

By the time I got to Kemp's house, my lungs were aching from the cold and my fingers were feeling a bit numb, even though they were bundled up. His car and his mom's SUV were both in the driveway, so I figured someone was home. But when I rang the doorbell, nobody answered. I sat on the bench, pulled my phone from my bag, and freed my hands from their mittens.

When I still didn't get a response, I got angry.

Still, nothing. I gritted my teeth and typed again.

"Ivy?"

I looked up to find Nina standing in the open door, frowning as she wrapped her cardigan more tightly around herself. "I just came over to . . ." I began. Grabbing the gift from the bench, I held it up as an explanation for why I was lurking on her front porch on Christmas morning.

"That was kind of you."

"Is he here?"

She tilted her head. "He's out back. The gate should be unlocked."

"Okay."

She pulled her sweater a little tighter. "Did something happen with you two? I haven't seen him like this since . . ."

"I don't know. We need to talk. Figure this out."

"But he won't let you," she guessed. I shrugged. "Go on back," she said, letting go of herself to point toward the right side of the house, past the garage. I gripped the present and stepped off the porch, then glanced back.

"Merry Christmas."

"Merry Christmas to you, Ivy."

I heard the door close as I rounded the side of the house and stepped up to the gate. The latch was a little sticky, and it took my half-frozen fingers a few seconds to fumble it open. As I walked down the steps into the backyard, a feeling of dread grew in the pit of my stomach. I wasn't even sure why. But when I smelled the unmistakable scent, I started to get it.

Kemp sat slumped against the foundation, his hood pulled up over his head, a cloud of pungent smoke wafting around his face. He took another inhale, held it for a moment, and let it escape.

"What the hell are you doing?" I asked. If I surprised him, he didn't show it. He turned his eyes slowly in my direction, then lifted the joint to his lips again.

"What does it look like?" he asked, a cloud of smoke escaping with his words.

"It stinks back here." I waved my hand ineffectually in front of my face. He stared at the inch-long joint in his hand, then held it up in my direction. "Are you serious?" I asked.

"It's how I cope. If you don't like it, you can fuck the hell off."

I stood there, frozen, squeezing the gift in one hand. I could hear the paper crinkle under my fingers. That, along with the sound of him blowing out yet another foul-smelling lungful, was all I could hear in the still morning air. He ignored me as he finished up and slumped back against the wall, folding his arms around himself.

"Does this happen every Christmas?" I asked at last. He turned his heavy-lidded eyes up to meet my gaze.

"What?"

"Holidays are hard for me, too."

"Shit, Ivy. It has nothing to do with that." He started digging around in his pockets. To my dismay, he pulled out another joint, along with a lighter.

"Then what are you coping with?"

He snorted as he stuck the fresh joint in his mouth and lit up. "Are *you* serious?" he asked without taking it out.

"Yes, I'm serious. How am I supposed to know? You stopped talking to me. I thought I knew you, but I come over here and see you getting stoned in your backyard, and I don't know what to think."

"Mom doesn't like it in the house." He took a long drag and then offered it to me again. I took a step back and glared at him. "Suit yourself," he said with a shrug. "But don't judge me for it."

"That's not even legal."

"Neither is murder."

"What?"

He shook his head. "Never mind."

"Just because people said you did something doesn't mean you did."

He rubbed his free hand over his face and sighed. "Would you mind going home, Ivy? This is my last one, and you're kind of ruining it."

I didn't know whether to yell at him or burst into tears. In the end, I did neither. I threw the gift at him. He blocked it with his arms, an impressive reaction for someone as stoned as he appeared to be. It fell to the ground beside him.

"Thanks," he said.

"I don't know what the hell is going on, but I don't need this. It's hard enough dealing with my first Christmas without Jade. You're just making it even more miserable."

He tugged his hood lower and stared at the smoking joint in his fingers.

"You didn't even see it!" I shouted. "You didn't see what happened to Neil. You don't get to act all—"

"Didn't I?" he asked. He inhaled so deeply I was afraid all that smoke might actually make him pass out; closing his eyes, he let it out in a long, slow breath. "You have no idea, Ivy. No fucking idea."

My heart thumped painfully in my chest. "What are you talking about?"

"Do you know what that feels like?" he asked quietly. "Do you know what it feels like when something that heavy, that powerful, just tears you in half? You know what you feel, Ivy? Nothing. At first. And then, before the pain even comes, your brain understands that it's all over, and you're going to die, and there's nothing you can do about it. But you still have a few more seconds of so much agony that . . ." He choked, then opened his eyes as he took another drag. "Never mind. You didn't feel it. So don't you dare stand there and judge me for—"

"Oh, my god." I took a step toward him, but he scrambled to his feet, leaning heavily against the wall for support. "Austin said he made a connection."

"Fucking *bastard*," he said, practically spitting the words. He looked at the joint in his hand and shook his head. "I thought I was done with this shit. I barely sleep as it is, and now, every time I close my eyes, I relive *that*. And all the others."

"The others?"

"Yeah. Austin's Notebook of Fun."

"But why?" I asked. "Why is this happening?"

"Like you said. He made a connection. He dragged me

into it, too. Now I'm dealing with shit that should've been over years ago. Centuries ago." He put the joint to his lips and inhaled. "It's what he wanted all along," he said, the smoke escaping with his bitter words.

"But *why?*" I asked again. "What's the point? What's he trying to show you?"

"Nothing. He's punishing me."

"For what?" I asked, exasperated. "Talk to me, Kemp. I want to understand, but I can't if you won't—"

"Why? You think you can fix this?"

"No. But . . . you don't need to go through this alone."

He snorted. "Of course I do. They're my lives. My deaths." He pushed his hood back and scratched his fingers through his rather greasy hair. "Karma. Like he said."

"What do you mean? You think you're being punished with these memories because of something you did in another life?"

He shrugged and took another drag, but he didn't answer.

"So what did I do to deserve seeing all those horrible things?"

"Least you didn't have to live them," he muttered.

"No, I didn't. And I'm glad. But I'm sad for you, that you're having to go through these events again, and feel all the pain and fear and—"

"I deserve it."

My mouth dropped open. "Why?"

He turned away, scuffed the smoking joint on the bricks, and stuck it back in his pocket. Then he headed for the sliding door that led back into the basement. I crouched down and scooped up the present that was still sitting where it had fallen.

"Kemp? I brought you—"

He slammed the slider shut and locked it. Tears prickled behind my eyes, but even stronger than that sensation was the hot fury that started in my belly and rose up through my throat like a volcano. I drew my arm back and almost threw the gift at the glass. But Nina didn't deserve to have her house damaged. She was probably just as frustrated and upset by Kemp's behaviour as I was. Shaking, I pulled the gift against me and turned away from the door.

Then I walked home, my throat tight and my chest heavy. I tore the tag off the present and dumped it onto the first bus bench I passed, cursing the Hayes brothers and their stupid reincarnational mess that had completely ruined everyone's day.

"Get up," I said, my voice almost a growl as I stood over the ghost curled up on my bedroom floor. Austin stirred, then lifted his head. Seeing my legs right in front of his face, he craned his neck and looked up.

"Ivy?"

"You need to stop."

"Stop what?"

"This. All of this." I waved my hands in a vague indication of everything. He sat up and scratched at his head.

"Visiting you?"

"Messing with Kemp," I said. "And, yeah, while you're at

it, you can leave me alone, too. But I'm not the one who's losing his mind and living up to his nickname again."

Austin scrambled silently to his feet. There were no creaks of the floorboards, no sound of his socks on the smooth wood. I took an automatic step back. "He's smoking weed?"

"Like it's going out of style."

"Shit," he muttered, shaking his head and turning away as he laced his fingers behind it.

"Yeah. So you need to stop it with the hauntings and—"

"I'm not haunting him, Ivy."

"Of course you are. He said—"

"I haven't gone anywhere near him. I can't. I'm still tied to you."

"But you made a connection."

"Only because he was with you at the time." He dropped his hands and shook his head again. "What did he say was happening?"

"He didn't say, exactly. I think he might be dreaming about his past deaths, though."

"It worked."

"Yes, it worked," I snapped. "He saw everything you showed me. No . . . I think he relived it. Why would you do that to him?"

Austin looked a little shaken. "I didn't mean to hurt him. I just wanted . . ."

"What?" I asked, folding my arms across my chest and staring him down, even though a part of me was afraid he might reach out and plunk me in the middle of another death vision. "What do you want, Austin? Whatever it is, you need to do it and go. Before you destroy your brother's life."

"I can't!" he said, his voice almost a wail. With its creepy, echoing tone, it made my skin crawl. "I'm trying, Ivy, but I don't know what else to do."

"Do you even know what you're trying to do?"

"I do now." He shook his head and began pacing. "I wasn't sure, at first. But now I know what this is about."

"Care to enlighten me?"

"I can't. Every time I try, this weird dizziness hits me and I disappear. At least, I think I do. It's disorienting. First I'm here, talking to you, and then—"

"Is it something to do with your karma?"

He stopped his pacing and frowned at me for a moment, then opened his mouth slowly, experimentally, as if he expected something to happen. "Yes." When he didn't disappear, he let out a sigh of relief.

"But you're dead. Isn't karma something you have to deal with when you're alive?"

He shook his head again, gripping the sides of his pyjama pants, as if he needed to hold on to something. "He needs to understand."

"Understand what?"

He clamped his lips tightly together.

"Okay, fine. How can I help?"

"You've already helped," he said. "Because of you, I was able to make a connection. That's a start."

"Well, we're both tired of this. So tell me what will bring us to the *end*, and maybe we can all get on with our lives. Or afterlives."

He squeezed his pants and chewed on his lip, and, for a moment, I caught a glimpse of the family resemblance.

"Do you even know what you need to do?" I asked.

He nodded. "I'm just not sure how to get it done."

With a sigh, I sat on the edge of my bed. "Well, when you figure it out, let me know."

"In the meantime, don't let him do anything stupid."

I gave him a withering look. "I'm not his mom, Austin. Besides, he's made it pretty clear that he doesn't want to have anything to do with me anymore. So, thanks for that."

"I'm sorry."

"Don't be sorry. Just figure out a way to fix this before Kemp does something stupid. Because I won't be able to stop him."

He nodded, looking troubled, and released his grip on the flannel before rubbing his hands over his thighs. I climbed into bed and clicked off the lamp. As my eyes adjusted to the dim light coming in through the window, I could still see him standing there.

"Are you going to be a creepy ghost and watch me sleep?" I asked, snuggling down under the covers and closing my eyes. When he didn't answer, I lifted my head and looked over at where he'd been standing. The space was empty.

22

Dropping Out

WHEN KEMP WASN'T IN PE ON THE FIRST MONDAY BACK IN class, I got an uneasy feeling that he wasn't just out with another cold. As we played basketball in the gym, I found myself wishing for one to the nose, if only because that would mean he was there. But the class passed without incident, and without him. After getting changed, I made my way to Art, feeling the dread grow. I told myself I was being silly, that I would walk in the door and he'd be sitting there at our table, ready to make me look like a terrible artist in comparison. But when I stepped into the room, our table was empty.

I slipped my phone out of my bag as soon as I sat down and proceeded to send him a text. Like all the others I'd sent since Christmas, it went unseen and unanswered. I didn't know if he'd gotten a new phone, or if he just wasn't checking his messages.

Ms. London seemed to have gotten some new tattoos over the holidays, and she was showing them off with a long, sleeveless dress that made me shiver just to look at. The room wasn't exactly warm, and I was chilly in a sweater. But she probably didn't want to cover up those works of art. A swarm of butterflies—I could see at least ten from where I was sitting—fluttered up her right arm and onto her shoulder. The sight made me think of the butterfly effect, and how one little thing could change everything that came after, often in unexpected ways. If Kemp's basketball had never hit me in the face . . . what would I have been thinking about at that moment? Probably the wire-sculpture project that Ms. London was rambling on about. Or maybe my homework for another class. Something boring. Something normal. When I thought back, I realized this mess with Austin had all started on that night, right before my first meeting with Kemp, when I'd seen the boy in the loincloth gasp and die on my bedroom floor. Another version of someone I cared about. Another person I hadn't been able to save.

Of course, I couldn't have saved Kemp from any of those deaths. But it was probably my fault he was having to relive them again now. As I doodled on the paper in front of me, I thought about how Kemp wouldn't be suffering the way he was if we'd never met. Did he regret meeting me in the first place?

"That looks interesting," Ms. London said, and I looked up to find her staring at the piece of paper in front of me, where I was supposed to be sketching a concept for the sculpture. At that moment, though, I didn't have much except a couple of lines tapering toward a point in the distance. When I realized they looked like a pair of train tracks, I quickly flipped the paper over.

"I was just doodling," I mumbled. She smiled and drifted

away. If she'd noticed I was alone at the table, she didn't seem to think it warranted comment. I looked over at the empty spot and imagined Kemp sitting there, his dark head bent over his paper as he sketched out what would no doubt be some fabulous idea for his sculpture.

Don't torture yourself, I thought, and turned away. I tried to focus on the empty page, tried to think of what to put on it. But the only things I could think of—stuff like trees or people or animals—seemed both too basic and way beyond my capabilities. Finally, I just drew a lumpy circle and set my pencil down. Ms. London, seeming to have some sort of radar, glided over and peered at my drawing.

"A cloud?"

"A stone," I said, wondering if I was going to be able to get away with it.

"I see."

"It represents the planet we live on. And the tools our ancestors used."

She nodded, her eyes brightening. I sat up a little straighter.

"It can be used for building shelter. Or grinding corn. So it can be a source of life. But it can also be used as a weapon, so it's a source of death."

"I like the way you think, Ivy. You look beneath the obvious and see the real meaning that's hidden from most people."

For a moment, I kind of felt sorry for trying to deceive this earnest, gullible teacher. But then she leaned closer—so close that I caught a faint whiff of incense—and whispered in my ear. "If this is going to be your project, though, you'd better build me one spectacular rock."

I turned to her in surprise. She smiled enigmatically and walked off, her bare feet smacking on the floor.

When the class let out for lunch, I gathered up my things and made my way to the front of the room where Ms. London was rummaging through a crocheted bag. She pulled out a smaller cloth one that I assumed held her lunch, and slipped her feet into a pair of worn leather boots.

"Yes, Ivy?" she said, even though I hadn't been entirely sure she'd noticed me standing there.

"I . . . just wanted to apologize."

She turned to me and raised her eyebrows, causing the ring in the left one to go for a little ride.

"It's not that I was trying to BS. I'm just not very good at art."

She smiled and shook her head. "Art is subjective, Ivy." She looped the handle of her little cloth bag over one arm before folding both across her chest. "You know that I don't fail anyone who completes my classes. As long as they try, and they do all the assignments, they'll be fine."

"Are you allowed to do that?"

She let out a soft laugh. "How else would I do it? Now, I'm not stupid. I know some students take these classes simply *because* they know they can't fail. But, every once in a while, I get someone like you, who thinks they're taking the class for one reason, without realizing that they're really here for another."

I frowned, not quite sure what she was getting at. "You think that applies to me?"

"You told me at the beginning of the year that you were here to honour your sister. But you have a creative spirit of your own, Ivy. I've seen it in the way you describe your pieces. You might think that you're just trying to bullshit your way out of doing the work, but you're being creative in your own way. You're making art." She shook her head. "And that's all I can ask."

I took a deep breath and let it out slowly. She didn't seem angry, or even particularly annoyed. I think I would've been, if I'd been a teacher. I figured that was probably something I should cross off my list of future career choices.

"Go enjoy your lunch, Ivy," she said as she started to move past me. "I'll see you on Thursday."

I frowned and bit my lip. Surely she'd noticed Kemp's absence. But she hadn't mentioned it. Nor had she told me to pass along the assignment. "Did Kemp drop the class?" I asked. She stopped and turned to me with a frown.

"I thought you were close."

"We kind of . . . broke up over the holidays."

"Oh. I'm sorry." She put her hand on my shoulder, her bracelets clacking. "Yes, he dropped the class." Her sorrowful frown deepened, and I knew what her next words were going to be before she even said them. "From what I was told, he's withdrawn from school completely."

"OH, MY GOD," RISSA SAID, SLIDING ONTO THE BENCH IN THE cafeteria, fries and can in hand. "Who died?"

"What?" Pulling my head up from where it had been hanging over the table, I frowned and pushed my glasses back up into position. Her words swirled in my head, and I had a strange urge to say, "Kemp did. Over and over and over . . ."

She plunked the cardboard bowl on the table and grabbed a ketchup packet from the pile Eunice had dumped between them. "So, what did Kemp get you for Christmas? And why didn't you call me? Were you, like, too busy playing with his giant dick to make time for us?"

"You could've called me," I pointed out, my voice dull. I sounded like a zombie. I felt like one, too. After pulling off my glasses, I put my face down on my arms.

"Are you okay?" Eunice asked. I shook my head.

"Uh-oh. Trouble in paradise." Rissa laughed, and then I heard the click-fizz sound of her energy drink being opened. "Where is he, anyway? He's not over at the other table, either."

I lifted my head and blew out a breath, making my bangs flutter. "He dropped out of school."

Her eyes went wide and she froze, her can halfway to her mouth. "He what?"

"Dropped out," I repeated. "Why do you think he's not here?"

"Why would anyone drop out of school in the middle of grade twelve? He was almost done!"

"He wouldn't have graduated, anyway," I said, sliding my glasses back on. Eunice was looking a little pale. And rather disappointed. She wouldn't have her eye candy for the rest of the year. *Too bad for you*, I thought, my annoyance almost making me say the words out loud.

Rissa continued to frown for a few moments. Then she

set her can down, stood up, and walked over to the table where Josh and the others were sitting. When she returned a minute or so later, her frown was even deeper.

"Do they know anything?" Eunice asked. Rissa shook her head.

"Didn't sound like it. They seemed as surprised as we did."

"He wouldn't have told them," I said. "He won't talk to anyone."

"Why not? What the hell happened?"

There was no way I could tell her. Besides the fact that Kemp might not have wanted me to, there was also the fact that I had no idea if Rissa would even believe me. And there was always the risk that the story could make its way out of our little group and go flying around the school at the speed of gossip. So I just shrugged.

"He's messed up," I said. "You did try to warn me."

"Yeah, but . . . I thought . . ." She shook her head. "He didn't *seem* messed up the last time I saw him."

"He hid it well."

"I'll say." She reached out and patted Eunice's hand. The girl looked absolutely devastated; I wouldn't have been surprised if she'd started crying right then and there. "Forget about him," Rissa said. "There are *plenty* of other guys. You don't need to waste your daydreams on one of the messed-up ones."

"I liked him," Eunice said, her voice a whisper of quiet misery. Her words cut to my core, because I understood exactly what she meant. It wasn't her crush. It was her genuine affection for the guy we'd come to know. At least, the guy we *thought* we'd come to know.

"Yeah, well," Rissa said, "I liked Hunter for most of grade five. Look at how that turned out."

"How did it turn out?" I asked with a frown. She turned to me and raised her eyebrows.

"How do you think? Are we a couple?"

I sighed. "Let's talk about something else."

"Nope." She shook her head, sending her ponytail of blond curls swaying. "When you go through a breakup with a guy like that, you need to talk about it with your friends."

"Why?"

"So you don't convince yourself that you made a mistake and go running back to him."

I narrowed my eyes at her. "Rissa, he broke up with me. Not the other way around."

"All the more reason to convince you that you don't need him. He obviously doesn't need you, so . . ."

I wasn't so sure about that. Something was still going on with Austin, and Kemp was connected. As long as that scenario was still happening, I was stuck in the middle of it. It wasn't over, no matter how much I might've wanted it to be.

23

A Terrible Truth

I HADN'T REALIZED HOW MUCH I'D TAKEN KEMP'S PRESENCE for granted until it wasn't there anymore. It wasn't just that I had to walk home from school every day in the freezing-cold air that sank into my bones and left me shivering for a good hour afterward. It wasn't just that I had nobody to pair up with in PE or whisper with in Art. I felt like I'd lost my best friend, a feeling that wasn't entirely unfamiliar. Having to go through it for the second time in less than a year was almost more than I could bear.

I began hanging out with Rissa and Eunice more, but conversation would inevitably turn to boys—and to Kemp in particular—and neither of them seemed to take the hint that I didn't want to talk about him at all. Whenever they'd start up, I'd shut down, becoming really quiet and focusing on the task at hand. We sent in our applications for university, worked on our homework, and talked about the dresses we were going to wear to grad, even though that was still months away. I tried to go along with it—not least because I loved the idea of being able to go all out with my dress—but in the back of my mind was a niggling sadness. If Austin hadn't ruined everything, I would've gone to the banquet with Kemp. He might not have actually graduated with us, but he still could've joined the celebrations. One afternoon, as I was imagining what he would've looked like in a tux, I let out a huge sigh that made both Rissa and Eunice stop talking and turn in my direction. I had to make up some excuse about how I was fretting over my wire-sculpture rock. They looked at me like I was nuts.

I had just been letting Austin sleep, choosing to let that be the extent of our relationship. But one evening about a week into March, he didn't leave me with much of a choice. He popped into existence right in the middle of our kitchen. I fumbled and dropped the bag of microwave popcorn, and it landed with a soft rustle on the floor.

"You okay?" Dad asked, not even bothering to glance up from his laptop. He had it set up on the island and was bent over in a familiar posture, peering at the screen as he checked his e-mail.

"Yeah," I said, shooting a dirty look at Austin as I bent to pick up the bag. "It's hot. That's all."

"What is?" Austin asked.

I waved him away, not willing to risk saying anything with Dad standing right there. Of course, Austin didn't know that. For all he knew, we were alone.

"I forgot, Dad," I said. "I have to finish something for French class."

He finally glanced up. "*Zut, alors!*"

"Yeah. Whatever."

"You don't want to watch the next movie in our triple feature?"

"I do . . . but I can't. Maybe another time. You and Mom go ahead." I set the bag on the counter and sighed quietly as I made my way to the stairs. Out of the corner of my eye, I saw Austin following, sort of gliding along, even though his legs were moving as if he were actually walking. He disappeared as I started to climb the stairs, only to reappear at my side once I'd shut the door to my room.

"Was your dad there?"

"Yes, my dad was there," I said. "You can't just pop in like that."

He nodded, seeming to dismiss my annoyance. "Maybe I won't have to. I think I know how we can finish this up. But I'll need your help."

I gave him a skeptical look as I padded over to my bed and sat down, cross-legged, on top of the bedspread. "You're sure?"

"No. But it's worth a try." He peered at me for a moment, then sort of leaned down. To my surprise, he looked like he was feeling for the bed. His movements were awkward as he arranged his body in a mirror image of my own. I stared at him, wide-eyed.

"You're sitting on my bed."

"Am I? Cool. I didn't know if that would work. I'm still getting used to—"

"Austin, how do we do this? And what, exactly, do we need to do?"

He nodded once, sighed, and placed his hands on his bent knees. "Kemp needs to tell someone."

"Tell them what?"

"I can't tell you that. If I try . . ." He silently smacked the side of his head and rolled his eyes.

"Yeah. Okay. You get dizzy and disappear. So how am I supposed to get him to tell me something if I don't know what that something is?"

"I think you'll know it when you hear it."

I sighed. "Austin, I'm not going to be able to get him to do anything. He won't even talk to me anymore. All this shit has really messed with his head. He broke up with me on Christmas Day, he's smoking weed again, and he dropped out of school."

"He *what?*" His voice got really loud for a moment, and I was afraid my parents would be able to hear him. "That little shit. How are Mom and Dad taking this?"

"I don't know. Your mom's probably worried."

"Why hasn't Dad kicked his ass?"

"Kind of hard to do when he's not living in the same house."

He blinked. "What?"

"Um . . . they're divorced. Doesn't that usually mean living apart?"

"Divorced?" he repeated. The colour seemed to drain from his face.

"What kind of ghost are you? I thought you were supposed to be able to see what's going on."

"I can't," he said, his voice miserable. "Whatever this place is . . . wherever I am . . . I can't see anything. Except you."

"You still can't see Kemp?" I asked. He shook his head. "Then how did you touch him to make that connection?"

"It looked like you were holding his hand. I just kind of guessed where he was."

I lifted my glasses onto my forehead so I could rub at my

eyes. "So you don't actually know what's been going on with him. You haven't seen it."

"No. Like I said, I can only see you. So you're important, Ivy. You have to be."

"Okay." Settling my glasses back on my face, I leaned forward and stared into his eyes. "What, exactly, do we need to do?"

"I think I need to show you something. Like I did before."

"No." I shook my head. "No way. I'm screwed up enough. I don't want to add PTSD to the list of things I need to deal with."

"What I have to show you isn't like that."

"Does someone die?"

"Yes, but—"

"Nope. Not doing it. You'll have to figure out another way."

"There is no other way!" he shouted, slapping his hands on his knees. That should've made a sound, but it didn't. "Do you think I haven't thought about this? Don't you think I would've found another way if there was one? I don't want to hurt you, and I don't want to hurt him. That's the whole *point*," he said, then reached up to grab his head with both hands. "No, damn it. Not yet. I didn't tell her."

"Who are you talking to?"

He took a deep breath and slowly let go of his head. "Nobody," he said, the word coming out hesitantly, as if he were afraid he wasn't allowed to speak. "Myself, I guess. Or whatever's controlling . . . this."

"If I let you show me whatever it is you need to show me, will you go away?"

"I hope so."

I sighed and leaned forward so he was within touching distance. "Fine. Do it."

He shook his head. "No. I think . . . he needs to be here, too."

I threw up my hands. "Austin, I already told you. We broke up. He won't even speak to me. How am I supposed to get close enough to him for you to—"

"You don't need to be that close to each other," he said. "We just need to go down to the creek."

"Why?"

"What's the date?"

"Um . . ." Leaning over toward the nightstand, I checked my phone. "March ninth."

He raised his eyebrows. I raised mine right back.

"What?" I asked.

"What happened on March ninth?"

"I don't know. Someone celebrated St. Patrick's Day eight days early?"

He gave me a withering look, just as the answer came to me.

"That was when you drowned in the creek." I let out a puff of disbelief. "How could I forget?"

"It didn't have anything to do with you."

"Yeah, but . . ."

"I need you to get him down to the creek, Ivy. Once I show you, maybe he'll—" He stopped talking and gritted his teeth. "Maybe he'll be able to tell you . . . what he needs to tell you."

"Why would getting to the creek help?" I asked, watching the tension in his jaw release a little. Whatever he was fighting, it seemed to be taking a lot out of him.

"Because that's where it started."

"I thought it started with the car accident."

He shook his head with a frown. "Okay . . . then that's where it got locked into this weird limbo thing I've got going on."

"What the hell happened down there?" I whispered. But he just shook his head in silence. "Austin, I don't know how to convince him to come. He won't answer my texts."

"So call him."

"It'll just go to voicemail."

"Let it. Leave a message. Tell him . . ."

"He's not going to come."

"Imply you're suicidal."

"Why? Because my boyfriend broke up with me?"

"Why not?"

I shook my head. "He's never going to believe that. I haven't been moping around. Nobody—especially not him—is going to think I'm *that* depressed."

"You can't always tell just by looking at a person." He leaned forward, his dark blue eyes with their little rings of gold seeming to bore into me. "If he loves you, he'll come."

I snorted. "He doesn't love me. He's made that pretty clear. Besides, you just told me you couldn't see anything other than me. How do you know what he's feeling?"

His expression darkened. "He'd be an idiot to not love you," he said. "You got dragged into this mess because of him, but you never held that against him. You accepted all this weird shit and tried to support him." He tilted his head with the tiniest of smiles. "And you still love him, even after all of that, don't you?"

I shrugged and looked away.

"Like I said. He'd be an idiot to not love you." He leaned forward, so I turned back to face him. "Just call him. Please. Get him to come. Let's deal with this, put it behind us, and move on."

"If I do," I said slowly, "will you do something for me?"

"If I can."

"Will you deliver a message to my sister?"

He shook his head. "I don't know if I can, Ivy. I can't force the living to see me."

"She's not living," I said.

"Oh." He reached out, as if to put his hand on mine, then thought better of it. "I'm sorry."

"Thanks."

"No, I'm really sorry. I don't know if I can. There's nobody else here. At least . . . not as far as I can tell. I'm trapped. And I don't think I'm going to be able to get free until we deal with this shit with Kemp." He chewed on his lip for a moment before finally taking a deep breath. "But, I promise, if I ever get unstuck, I'll try to find her. What did you want to say?"

What *didn't* I want to say? For a moment, I wished I could switch places with Austin. Then I could've been that much closer to Jade, that much closer to telling her myself. But . . . I'd be dead. And despite what Austin wanted me to tell Kemp, that wasn't something I was aiming for.

"I need to think about it," I said.

He nodded. "Okay. Just don't leave it too late. I don't know what's going to happen once we've . . ."

"Yeah. I know." With a sigh, I reached over and plucked my phone from the nightstand. It was just after eleven. "How am I supposed to do this?"

"Just pretend."

Frowning, I dialed Kemp's number. "You should've picked one of the drama students," I muttered. "He's never going to believe me." I listened to the phone ring and expected the familiar voicemail prompt, but, to my surprise, I heard his actual voice.

"Yeah?"

"Kemp?" My voice shook, even though I didn't mean for it to. Austin nodded encouragingly. "I . . . Can you come over?"

"Why?" he asked, sounding suspicious.

"I . . ." Letting out my best fake sob, I began to rock back and forth, hoping it would help get me into character.

"Ivy? What's wrong?"

"You!" I said. "You're what's wrong. How could you do that to me? Were you just using me for sex? Is that it?"

Austin raised his eyebrows and gave me a thumbs-up. He didn't seem to realize how close to the truth my words were. It wasn't too hard to pretend to be upset. Because I was.

"No. Never. Ivy, I—"

"I can't take it. First Jade left me, and then you. It's too much. The people I love keep leaving me, and I—" Breaking off with a sob, I pressed my finger over the microphone so I could talk to Austin. "I don't want him driving if he's impaired," I whispered. "What if he—"

"Where are you?" Kemp asked. His voice sounded a little breathless. I pulled my finger away from the phone and sniffed dramatically.

"At home." Austin shook his head frantically at me. "Out back," I added quickly. "By the creek."

"Shit, Ivy." There was a crash, and then a couple of muffled thumps. "Go inside. I'll be right—"

"I can't!" I wailed. "I'm not doing this anymore. I have nothing to live for. Jade's gone, and now you're gone, and there's nothing. There's nothing." It felt like I was laying it on a little bit thick, but I could hear Kemp's frantic breathing on the other end of the line. "Don't come," I said. "Don't come if you've been smoking. If something happened to you, I—"

"I haven't had anything since yesterday. Don't—"

"I have to go," I said. "I have to go. Jade's waiting. I can't—I can't make her wait any longer." My hand shook as I pulled the phone away from my ear and ended the call. Austin began to clap his hands, a weird silent motion that I understood nevertheless. "This is messed up," I said. "He's going to hate me when he finds out I lied." Slapping the phone down on the nightstand, I sucked in a gasp as a new thought occurred to me, and I whipped my head toward him. "What if he calls my parents?"

"Does he have their numbers?"

"I don't think so. But what if he rings the doorbell?"

"You think he's going to waste time doing that?" He let out an appreciative chuckle. "He thinks you're about to throw yourself into a swollen creek. Believe me, he's going to come straight here, then out back. He knows the way."

"If he crashes his car and dies because he was so frantic to get here, I'll never forgive you."

"I'll never forgive myself." He awkwardly unfolded himself from the bed and stood up, which looked like some weird anti-gravity manoeuvre an astronaut might do. Then he started gliding toward the door. "Better bundle up. If this March is anything like my last, it'll be fucking freezing down there."

Before I got dressed for the cold, I ran downstairs to the living room where my parents were snuggled together on the couch, having just started their movie. Mom glanced up with a smile, her hand rummaging in the popcorn bag.

"Decided to join us after all?"

I shook my head and grasped the handle on the sliding barn door, an architectural feature that we'd always left open until now. "Mind if I close this? I can hear the movie all the way up in my room."

"Oh. I'm sorry, Ivy. We can turn it down."

I shook my head and started to tug on the door. "No. Leave it loud. Get the full cinema experience."

Dad chuckled as I pulled the door all the way across the opening. I raced back upstairs, grabbed a scarf and hat, then went back down for my coat and boots, which were in the foyer. I carried the latter to the back door, waiting to slip them on until I was standing on the mat. Then, with a glance toward the closed barn door—through which I could hear the sound of loud, muffled voices—I quickly disarmed the alarm and slipped outside.

I didn't realize Austin wasn't with me until he suddenly appeared at my side as I hurried down the hill. I only just managed not to let out a yelp.

"Don't *do* that!" I said. My breath came out in clouds. I pulled the zipper on my coat higher, though it didn't make much difference. Dressed in my pyjamas, I was feeling the cold intensely.

"Sorry," he said, gliding ahead of me toward the gate. "Did you bring a flashlight?"

I nodded and pulled out the tiny one I kept in my coat pocket. It was often dark when I walked home from Rissa's house, so I carried a flashlight all the time. Clicking it on, I waved it over the ground in front of us. The bluish light made the grass look silver.

"How long will it take him to get here?" Austin asked as he moved just ahead of me. Before I could answer, he disappeared right through the fence. I fumbled with the latch, then pushed my way through.

"Did you mean to do that?"

"Do what?"

"Walk through the fence."

"Oh. I thought I felt something." He shook his head. I left the gate open and turned to the creek. Unlike the last time I'd been down there with Kemp, the water was rushing, and I could hear it. I waved the beam of light over the rapids, watching the splashes catch the light. Cold seemed to emanate from the creek the way heat did from a fire. I adjusted my feet on the rocky edge and turned to Austin.

"Are you *sure* we need to be here? It's freezing."

"I think so. It's not going to hurt, anyway. Besides, I think this will give us the best chance. You don't want to have to do it twice, do you?"

"We're not going to be able to do it twice. Kemp's never going to trust me again."

"Yes, he will. Once he understands." He started to move downstream, following the path of the water. "Come on."

"Where?"

"We need to find the spot."

I remembered Kemp telling me that Austin had gone in farther downstream where the water was deeper. I shoved one hand in my pocket, leaving the other one to light the way with the flashlight, and wished I had thought to bring my mittens.

The ghost moved easily over the rocks, but I had to be a little more careful stepping on the slippery surfaces, throwing my arms out for balance a few times. In some places, bushes grew so close to the edge that I had to push them out of the way. When I caught up to Austin, he was standing in the creek. Or maybe hovering. In any case, the water didn't seem to view him as an obstacle at all; it flowed straight through him. Despite the angry appearance of the water, it wasn't very deep. Only his feet and ankles were submerged.

"Come here," he said. I laughed.

"Yeah, right."

"We need to be in the right place.

"Austin, it's freezing. I'm not losing my toes over this."

"You won't. I promise."

I shook my head. "Not yet. Wait until Kemp gets here."

Austin's expression darkened, and I took an involuntary step back, my foot slipping on the pebbles. "You said you'd help me."

"And you said you didn't want either of us to get hurt.

Have you forgotten that water like this is pretty dangerous for people like me?”

“People like you?”

“Alive ones.”

He shook his head and moved toward me, just as I heard a shout. I turned and looked, but I couldn’t see anything in the darkness. When I swung my flashlight in that direction, it did little to illuminate the scene.

“Kemp?”

“Ivy! Stop! Come here.”

I turned back to Austin, who raised his eyebrows.

“Is he here?” he asked.

“Yeah.”

“Okay. Brace yourself, Ivy.” And before I could ask him what he was doing or beg him to stop, he reached out toward my head.

I was suddenly in the darkness, holding my phone in front of me, trying to see through the night. My feet—clad in nothing but a pair of worn canvas runners—slipped on the stones as I made my way along the creek. It rushed along at my right, chilling the air that I sucked into my lungs. Among the shadows in front of me, silhouetted against the silver rush, was the object of my search. I started to run.

“Kemp!” I shouted, my voice cracking as I slipped and stumbled, falling to my knees and dropping my phone on the rocks. I grabbed it, not bothering to check if the screen was cracked, and struggled to my feet. He stood in front of me, and even in the darkness I could see that his fists were clenched at his sides.

"Go away!" he screamed. He took a step back, but I rushed forward and grabbed him by the arm.

"What the hell are you doing, you little shit? Get back to the house."

He wrenched away so hard he fell to the ground. But he was back on his feet in a second, staring up at me, fury radiating from every greasy teenage pore. "*You* go away!"

"Kemp—"

"It's my fault!" he shouted. "You're all messed up because of me. It was *my* stupid hockey. It should've been *my* stupid brain damage."

"I don't have brain damage," I said. "I had a concussion. That's all."

He let out a sob. "You're not the same. I heard Mom and Dad. They said you're not. Dad said you haven't been the same since the accident."

"That wasn't your fault, Kemp."

"Yes, it was. And now you're not the same. You don't laugh the same way. You don't get the right jokes. You don't like the same movies, and you're not good at the same games. You sleep on Mom and Dad's floor like a big baby. It's like I killed you, and you came back as something else." He wiped his wrist across his dripping nose. "You're not my brother anymore."

"Kemp, no." I stepped toward him and grabbed his arms. "Look at me."

"If Mom and Dad hadn't had me, you would still be the same. You'd still be you."

"I *am* me. I'm just . . . trying to find my way back. Okay?"

"No, you're not. You keep trying to kill yourself."

"What?"

"You cut your wrists."

I sighed. "I wasn't trying to kill myself."

"Then why?"

With a shake of my head, I glanced sideways at the stream. But before I could say anything, Kemp continued.

"You're just self-medicating and isolating yourself."

I blew out a frustrated breath. "You don't have to listen to *everything* they say."

He wrenched his arms free and gave me a gentle shove in the chest. "Get out of my way."

"Why? So you can drown yourself in the creek? So you can mess up Mom and Dad's life even more?"

"Get out of my way!" he screamed, his shrill voice echoing off the water. I grabbed his arm again, ready to march him back up to our gate, when he suddenly let out another scream, this one of pure, wordless fury. He shoved with both hands, catching me in the shoulders. I let go of him as I staggered back, terrified of pulling him into the stream with me. The water was deeper than it looked, and it fountained up around my knees, soaking my jeans in an instant. The darkness dizzied me, swirling about my head as I stumbled on the rocks and tried to get my bearings. Fixing my gaze on Kemp, I tried to stop the motion of my own body. But I knew, the instant before it happened, that I was going to fall. And as I did, my shoe slipped out from under me, rubber no match for rock. I fell sideways, hearing Kemp's panicked scream just before my ears were submerged. A blinding pain shot through my temple, flashing white, just like in the vision of the Japanese woman. I sucked in a breath to try to scream, only to feel my mouth fill with water. I couldn't move. I was frozen.

I scrambled to my feet in the rushing stream, gasping, and turned to find Austin standing just a few feet away, staring at something beyond my shoulder.

"You weren't trying to kill yourself," I gasped. "He was."

The ghost turned to face me, his expression haunted. I moved closer.

"Austin?"

"I'm so sorry," he said. His voice was different. Deeper. Smoother. It no longer sounded like he was in a hollow metal tube. "I'm so sorry, Ivy. I never meant for this to—" He broke off and closed his eyes. I turned around slowly, suddenly aware that I could no longer feel the chill of the water, or even the pressure of it, as it rushed past my legs. And when I saw what was happening on the edge of the creek, the understanding hit me like my wire-sculpture rock to the head. I glided forward, staring at the impossible sight of my own body, still and pale, as Kemp desperately tried to bring me back. I shook my head, glanced at Austin, and slid onto my knees beside myself.

"Come on, Ivy," Kemp whispered. "I've got you." He blew another breath into my mouth and waited, as if listening. But my body didn't respond. He pulled his phone out of his pocket and quickly dialled, then put it on speakerphone.

"This wasn't supposed to happen," I said, staring at my own body. My *dead* body. I turned to Austin and clenched my fists. "This wasn't supposed to happen! What the hell was the point of that?"

"I . . . I'm sorry."

"Did you do this on purpose?"

He shook his head and bit his lips together, but he didn't say anything.

"Oh, my god, Austin. Did you do this on purpose?"

"I was scared, Ivy. I didn't know if our plan was going to work. But I thought . . . if you almost drowned, and I was here, maybe we—"

"Why would that have worked?" I shouted. "You never saw Jade. You told me you never saw anyone else! You could have condemned me to an eternity of being alone, just because you—"

"You wouldn't have been stuck. You didn't have unfinished business."

"And what was your unfinished business, Austin? Showing me how Kemp killed you?"

"That was an accident. I don't blame him." He shook his head and moved toward me. I stood up, hoping to get away. When he reached out, I felt the impossible, horrifying touch of his fingers on my arm. I took a step back, my eyes wide. "Don't you see, Ivy? He blamed himself . . . but I was the one who'd failed."

"I don't understand."

"All those deaths in the notebook," he said. "We were together. And every time, I . . . I couldn't save him. Even when I was his brother, or his best friend, or his child, or even his parent. I failed him, Ivy. Remember Neil and Rex?"

I nodded, staring at him in a daze. "How could I forget?"

"I could've saved him. I could've reached out of that boxcar and grabbed him."

"You both could've fallen."

"Maybe. Maybe not. But I was too scared to take that risk, and he paid for it. Just like all the other times. Like when I spooked that horse when the little boy was riding it and he was thrown and he broke his neck. Or when I didn't stop that duel and the guy got taken out with a head shot." He looked down at Kemp, who was alternately mumbling into his phone and trying to breathe life back into me. My lips were white. I turned away.

"I didn't want to die," I said, looking up at Austin. "You had no right to do that."

"You agreed."

"I didn't agree to *die*," I snapped. "Great. So I know what Kemp did. What good did it do? You're still here." I held out my arms. "We're *both* still here, you asshole. Now we're *both* stuck."

I settled myself down beside Kemp and watched as he tried and tried. Reaching out, I attempted to run my fingers across his cheek. He paused, and, for a moment, I thought maybe I'd managed to cross the impossible space between us. But he just swiped the back of his hand over the spot, shuddered, and bent down to breathe into my lungs once more.

"I'm sorry, Kemp," I whispered. But he couldn't hear me.

24

Second Chances

I DIDN'T UNDERSTAND, AND I SHOULD'VE BEEN TERRIFIED, but I wasn't. Maybe the lack of actual adrenal glands had something to do with that. I watched, almost numb, as Kemp continued to try to bring me back. He was eerily calm, talking to the dispatcher on the other end of the line and following their instructions to the letter. I didn't try to touch him again, even though I dearly wanted to.

None of this was what I'd been expecting. I could see everything around me: the creek, the shadowy trees, the night sky above, and the two boys. One alive. One dead. Austin was still standing in the water, watching without saying a word. At least, he was probably staring at my body. That was likely all he could see.

Kemp suddenly sat back and put a hand over his face.

"Are you still there?" a tinny voice asked, issuing from the phone. "You need to keep going until help arrives. All right, Kemp?"

He took in a shuddering breath and dropped his hand. His eyes shone, though whether from emotion or from the cold, I couldn't tell. He went back to what he'd been doing, trying to breathe warm air back into my frozen form, just as I heard a shout. He turned his head and shouted back.

"Here!" His voice cracked. "We're down here!"

I rose to my feet, though it felt almost like floating. Upstream, I could see the bouncing beams of flashlights backed by a number of shadows that seemed to blink in the darkness. It took a few more seconds before I realized I was seeing the reflective markings on the firefighters' uniforms.

"Yes," I said, and looked down at Kemp. "They're almost here. You're doing great. Just keep going."

But then I heard another voice and my heart—what was left of it, anyway—started to break. I rushed toward the voice, past the firefighters and their equipment, and tried to put myself between my mother and my lifeless body. Dad was with her, holding her hand, helping her pick her way carefully over the rocks on the bank of the creek. Neither of them were dressed for the weather. I realized that Kemp might not have rung the doorbell, but Mom and Dad certainly would have noticed the commotion going through our yard.

"Mom, stop," I said. But she didn't hear me. She looked straight through me, and when she started craning her neck, I knew she'd caught a glimpse of my body lying there. She let out a little cry and tried to rush forward, but Dad put his arms around her and held her back.

"Ivy!"

"Stay here," Dad said. "Let them do their job."

"No." She struggled against him. "I couldn't be there for Jade. I have to . . ." She twisted around and tried to get Dad to let go. "Vaughan! Stop it!"

"Let them help her, Linley." He pulled her close and

closed his eyes so he wouldn't have to see. I turned back to look. I couldn't even see my body past all the firefighters anymore. Kemp was standing, backing away.

"Shit," Austin said, drawing my attention back to him. "Kemp's going to blame himself for this, too, isn't he?"

"Should've thought of that before you lured me to my death," I snapped.

"You're not dead yet."

I just gaped at him. "How do you know?"

"I don't. But I can see your body, so . . . your spirit must still be connected to it."

"And how do you propose I get back into it?" Shaking my head, I moved closer to the commotion and stared down at my motionless form. The firefighters were still trying to get it to breathe. "Is there even going to be anything to get back into? How long have I gone without breathing?"

"The water's cold," Austin said, his voice small.

"Yeah. That makes it all better." I cast a glance at my parents, who were watching with wide eyes and devastated expressions. Dad looked like he couldn't believe what was happening. Mom looked like she'd already accepted it . . . and was just waiting for the firefighters to give her the news so she could scream. I turned back to Kemp and moved toward him. He was shivering, and when one of the flashlight beams caught his legs, I could see he was soaked from the knees down. Patches of wet stained the front of his shirt and jeans. He clenched the trembling fingers of his free hand into a fist and looked up into the sky. "Kemp?" I whispered. "I'm here. I'm right here."

My body coughed. I felt a strange pull, right in the middle of my chest, and I started to move toward myself, as if drawn by a magnet. My first instinct was to pull back. I didn't know the state of my brain cells, and the last thing I wanted to do to Mom and Dad was burden them with having to care for someone in a vegetative state. I reached out toward Kemp as I passed him, but my fingers went right through his sleeve. He shuddered and looked down.

"Kemp? I'm here. Did you feel that?"

More water gurgled out of my body's mouth with another cough. One of the firefighters rubbed his knuckles against my chest.

"Ivy? Come on. Breathe for us, okay?"

But I didn't. I didn't think I could. I took a step back, fighting against the pull of my own devastated body and turned to Austin. He frowned as he glided toward me.

"What are you doing?" he asked. "You're getting a second chance."

"At what? Life in a bed? Meals through a tube? Diapers?"

"You don't know that."

I shook my head. "No. I . . . can't." With a glance over at Mom and Dad, I let out a sob. "I can't," I whispered. "I'm sorry."

"Ivy . . ."

The pull intensified. I fought it, trying to put as much distance between myself and my body as I could. I wanted to run to Kemp, to throw my arms around him, to anchor myself. But I couldn't reach him. It seemed that, no matter how I tried, I couldn't get any closer. His chin was trembling and his eyes were brimming, but he still didn't cry.

"It's all right, Kemp," I whispered. "It's all right."

"It's not his fault," Austin said, suddenly at my side. I pulled my arms around myself and held on.

"Of course it isn't. It's yours."

"But he doesn't know I had anything to do with this. He'll think it's because of him."

I turned to him in disbelief. "Because that's what you told me to tell him!" The rush of the creek threatened to drown out my hissing whisper. "He thought I was trying to kill myself because he broke up with me. He's not going to think it was some asshole ghost showing me his final moments, pulling me into a hallucination long enough for me to drown."

"I'm sorry."

"You're sick!" I screamed, so suddenly that I kind of shocked myself. My voice neither echoed nor was swallowed by the rushing of the creek. It seemed to hang in the air above us, frozen for all time. "You're fucking sick!" When I brought my fists down on him, they thumped against his shoulders with satisfying force. "You did this. You *killed* me. And now I'll never . . . I'll never . . ."

"Never what?" he asked, infuriatingly calm.

"She'll never get a chance to forgive herself for my death," another voice said. I turned, slowly, feeling like my heart should've been pounding. But there was nothing inside the memory of my chest except for the slight tugging toward my damaged body on the bank. Nothing to jump or lurch as I saw the figure standing just feet away, her arms crossed, her lips twisted in a disapproving frown. Bright blue eyes shone out of the darkness, a darkness almost as bold as her blue-black hair.

"Jade?" I whispered.

"Ivy." She shook her head. "What the hell did you let this asshole do?"

25

Reunion

For months, all I'd wanted to do was hug my sister. Now, when I had the chance at last, something held me back. It wasn't until she unfolded her arms and stepped closer that I finally felt that something release, and I realized it was fear. Embracing Jade meant letting go of life. As I threw my arms around her, I felt the ragged edges of the tear between us begin to mend, our twin spirits healing the rift that had torn between us the moment we'd been separated.

"You're all right?" I gasped as I clung tighter, resting my chin against her shoulder. She gave me a squeeze, the way she'd done when we were younger, so tight that I had used to cough, which had always made her laugh. But I didn't cough this time.

"Of course I'm all right. I always was."

Reluctantly, I pulled back so I could look at her. She looked just like she had the last time I'd seen her, her red roots just starting to show, her eyebrows dark from the pencil she'd used to fill them in, the silver ring in her nose glinting in the dim light. Her falsely blue eyes searched my face for a moment before she finally gave me a regretful smile.

"It wasn't your fault, Ivy. You know that, right?"

I nodded, then shook my head. "I do know it. But I don't feel it."

"That'll come with time. You understand it in your head before you'll understand it in your heart."

"If I'd been there—"

"One dose of epinephrine wouldn't have been enough. We were hours from help. I wouldn't have made it, anyway." She gripped my shoulders and looked straight into my eyes. "I made the choice to go on that trip. It's my responsibility, and mine alone. Not yours."

"But I could've been there," I said, my voice small.

"To watch me die? So you could feel guilty when your injector didn't work?" She shook her head. "No. You didn't need to see that."

"But you were scared. I should've been with you."

Her lips twitched in a little smile. "Okay. You're my twin, and I love you—I'll *always* love you—but twins are allowed to have bonds with other people, too. I wasn't alone. Stefan was there, and he held my hand the whole time."

I blinked, feeling my brow pull into a frown that felt dangerously close to an ugly cry. "You didn't want me there?"

"Of course I did! But you weren't, and there's no way we can go back and change it. We have to accept that. I'm just telling you this so you'll know I had someone there to comfort me. I was scared, but . . . I'm all right now. Okay?" She leaned forward and kissed my cheek. "I'm all right."

I grabbed her and hugged her again, sure that, this time,

I would never let go. I didn't need to. We were both dead. I never had to leave her again.

"Ivy, we need to go."

"Okay," I said, closing my eyes and tightening my grip. "I'm ready."

Against all my expectations, she laughed. I pulled back, only to see her shaking her head with a little smile.

"No, you're not. We're not going *there*."

"Then where are we going?"

She turned and pointed up the slight incline to where we could see the firefighters disappearing into the darkness. When I looked over at the spot where my body had lain, I saw it was empty. Kemp was still standing there, though, staring at the wet rocks and shuddering like an old car that was about to lose some vital part on the road. Gripping my sister's hand, I pulled her toward him.

"Kemp?" I whispered.

"He's cold," Jade observed. "He needs to go someplace warm." She frowned over at Austin, who was just standing there, staring at me. "Before that asshole tries that memory trick again."

"You can see him?" I asked. She nodded.

"I can see everything. Unlike him, I suppose." She detached herself from me and glided over to him. "Hey! Numbnuts! Can you feel this?" She shoved her hand through his head. When he didn't seem to notice, she shrugged and turned back to me. "Too bad."

"Why?"

"Because maybe, if he could see *me*, he'd leave *you* alone."

I turned back to Kemp and opened my mouth, but at that moment he started to move, picking his way back over the rocks in the darkness. His phone hung, forgotten, at his side, illuminating nothing but a small patch on his thigh. Jade grabbed my hand and started to pull me after him.

"I don't want to—" I began, but she cut me off with a shake of her head.

"This isn't over until it's over," she said. "And it's not over."

"Ivy!" Austin shouted. "Where are you going?"

"None of your business!" I shouted back. The next moment, he was beside me. I recoiled with a squeak.

"Tell him to back off," Jade snapped.

"He doesn't listen."

"Who doesn't?" he asked.

"You. Leave me alone. Haven't you fucked everything up enough for one night?"

"But . . . I'm still here. Ivy, I'm still—"

"That's not my problem!" I shouted, pulling Jade to a stop and turning to glare at him. "You don't know what the hell you're doing. You're just guessing. And now you've guessed me into a coma or death or—"

"You're not dead," Jade said.

"Close enough."

"What?" Austin asked, his brow creasing in a frown.

"I wasn't talking to you."

"Who are you talking to?"

"My sister," I said. "The sister who died because I wasn't there."

Jade sighed. "Ivy."

Austin chewed his lip for a moment before finally shaking his head. "Maybe that's why," he said quietly.

"Why what?" I asked.

"Why I picked you. Or . . . why you were picked. Two sets of siblings, two guilty parties."

"No." Jade tugged hard on my hand to get me to start moving again. "You're not the guilty party, Ivy. You only feel like you are."

Just like Kemp, I thought. Except that he *had* pushed Austin into the creek. But I knew he hadn't intended to kill his brother that night. Just himself.

"When he got screwed up after the accident," I said, looking at Austin out of the corner of my eye as Jade continued to pull me back toward the gate, "it wasn't just because he was trying to be like his big brother, was it? He was using the drugs to try to forget."

"Or dull the pain. Yeah." He sighed. "You saw what I showed you, right? He blamed himself from the beginning. For the accident. For the changes he saw in me. He blamed himself so much he thought he didn't deserve to exist anymore. So he tried to end it."

"But . . . when I met him, he didn't seem depressed."

"Can you really tell what's simmering under the surface?"

"Why would he seem less screwed up *after* your death?"

"He was probably trying to hide his pain," Jade said. "He saw what Austin's death did to their parents. And he didn't want to give them any more to worry about." She paused in front of the gate, which had been closed by the last person to have gone through it. Probably Kemp. Turning to me, she shook her head. "He didn't want to hurt them all over again. So he stuffed it all down and tried to pretend everything was all right, even though it wasn't. Maybe he didn't even let himself cry. So he never felt the grief. Only the guilt."

I turned to find Austin staring at me, his eyes wide.

"What?" I asked.

"Who is that?"

I looked at Jade, who was smiling triumphantly up at him. "He can see you?"

"Now he can."

"Why?"

She shrugged. "Maybe I said something he needed to hear." With a tug on my hand, she led me forward. "Boys. Honestly. These two are so tied up in their constipated feelings that they're going to need some sort of emotional enema to sort it all out." She yanked me toward the gate. I closed my eyes just before we passed through. For one strange moment, my skin felt wet. But then the sensation passed, and I opened my eyes to our backyard. Kemp was just disappearing through the gate at the side of the house. "Come on," Jade said, pulling me into a weird gliding run, her hand still clamped tightly over mine. "Let's see if we can catch up to your body."

I WANTED TO GO WITH KEMP, BUT JADE PULLED ME INTO THE ambulance. Austin followed, and the three of us huddled in the corner, trying to stay out of the way of the paramedics. Of course, the space being as small as it was, we had arms and hands and elbows thrust through us, which felt a bit weird. But it was already weird for me. Watching them work on my body, trying to rekindle a spark of life, left me feeling both hopeful and anxious. The strange dullness of my emotions ebbed and flowed, though cutting through it all was something that I could only describe as affection. I kept a tight hold on my sister's hand and tried to ignore the clingy ghost who was attached to my other side. It had to have been disorienting for Austin, not being able to see anything except me and Jade, but I was having a hard time feeling sorry for him.

"What if Kemp does something stupid?" I whispered, hoping Austin wouldn't hear me, but knowing he would; the space was far too small for secrets.

"You don't think he's going to be tailgating this ambulance all the way to the hospital?" Jade asked. I turned to Austin. He nodded.

"He's not *that* stupid, Ivy. He probably won't try to kill himself until after he knows you're dead."

Jade looked like she wanted to smack him. "Not helping."

"I'm just saying."

"Yeah, well, don't." She squeezed my hand. I wanted to be reassured, but all I could think about was the fact that Kemp was upset and behind the wheel of a car, and it was late at night and still technically winter. If he became distracted . . . If he hit a random patch of ice . . . "Ivy, look at me." When I pulled my gaze away from my body and turned to Jade, she squeezed my hand again and gave me a stern look. "He's going to be fine."

"You don't know that."

"Well, if I'm wrong, we'll deal with that then. But, right now, let's operate under the assumption that he will be. Okay?"

"Okay," I whispered, turning so I could rest my chin on her shoulder. I could still hear the paramedics working, helping me breathe, trying to get my body to respond. Even though I could close my eyes, I couldn't close my ears. I desperately wanted to.

When the ambulance reached the hospital, the three of us hung back until the paramedics were safely outside with their gurney and patient. Then we drifted out, clambering awkwardly to the ground. I edged away from Austin, but he stayed close, as if he didn't want to lose sight of us. Before we could follow my body, though, two figures came racing out of the darkness. I watched my parents sprint into the ER, almost too fast; the sliding doors barely had time to open. Jade started to pull me after them, but I hung back, searching the night.

"Ivy, come on."

"Not until he's here."

"I'll wait," Austin said.

"You can't. You can't see him."

"Maybe I can now. I can see her."

I shook my head and pulled my hand out of Jade's grasp. "No. I'm not going anywhere until I know he's safe."

Jade let out a sigh and ran her fingers through her feathery bangs. She looked at Austin, who stared right back and gave a little shrug.

"The living can be stubborn," he said.

"Don't try to bond with me, asshole. You tried to kill my sister."

He cleared his throat and turned away, facing the darkness. But, as I stared past him, relief washed over me with such force that I felt like my knees should've buckled. Kemp walked out of the parking lot into the brighter lights around the ER, his keys jingling as he tried to force them into his pocket. He strode through the doors, and I grabbed Jade's hand as I hurried after him.

Mom and Dad seemed to be arguing with a nurse. Kemp came to a stop in the middle of the chaotic waiting room, looking around as if searching for something. I turned to Jade with a frown.

"Where did I go?"

"I don't know. But you've got to be around here somewhere." She squeezed my hand, then turned to Austin. "You," she said, her voice sharp as if she were addressing a naughty dog, "stay here."

He frowned. "But I—"

"You can't see him, can you?" I asked.

He shook his head. "I don't know if I *can* stay here. I'm tied to you, Ivy, remember?"

"He's right," I said to Jade. She grimaced as she fingered her nose ring.

"What if he just thinks he is?"

"We *know* he is," I said. "How else would I be able to see him?"

She shook her head. "No, I mean, what if he's just assuming you're the only one he's connected to? Maybe he could make a connection with his brother if he really tried."

Austin clenched his jaw. "You think I haven't?"

"I think you think you have. But I also know you and your brother dance around your feelings. Maybe, on some level, you don't *want* to connect with him."

"Of course I want to connect with him!" Austin snapped. "Why wouldn't I?"

I stared over at Kemp, who was still standing there looking

utterly lost. He watched my parents beg the nurse for something, myriad flickers of emotion touching his features. But none of them ever seemed to settle. His mouth opened, and I thought he might've been about to say something, but then he closed it again without having uttered a sound.

"Because you feel guilty," I said, turning to Austin. He raised his eyebrows in surprise.

"About what?"

"All those deaths you showed me."

"I *had* to show you. It was—"

"No." I shook my head. "You don't feel guilty for showing me. You feel guilty for causing them. Or playing a part in them. That's it, isn't it? You can't face him."

Austin was frozen, staring at me with a dumbstruck expression.

"Maybe," Jade said, "you never needed Ivy in the first place. Maybe you had the power to contact your brother all along. But you were afraid that, if he knew, he would blame you. Or hate you."

"No," Austin said, his voice hoarse.

"But why would he need to show Kemp those deaths in the first place?" I whispered to Jade. She glanced at me with a knowing smile.

"Ask him."

Austin shook his head again, then bit his lip and turned away. Jade let out a frustrated groan.

"Fine. Don't tell her. But you do realize that doing that is what's prolonged this mess, right?"

"I don't get it," I said.

She shook her head and shot a dirty look at the back of

Austin's. "He needed to show Kemp so the poor kid wouldn't torture himself with guilt for the rest of his life. This was a balancing of karma."

"Karma?" I asked, looking over at Austin. His shoulders tensed and he looked down at the floor.

"Yeah. All those times he couldn't—or wouldn't—save his sibling, friend, spouse, parent, et cetera . . . whatever Kemp was to him at that time. Each time he had a hand in a death, it made the imbalance worse." She let go of me and walked over to Kemp, then around him, as if he were nothing more than an art installation in a museum. He certainly seemed to be doing his best impression of a statue. "But this time . . . Well, after the car accident—"

"Which was an *accident*," I said. "That doesn't count toward karma, does it?"

"No. But they could both feel it had been a close call. Our martyr here"—she gently tapped Kemp on the elbow; he didn't seem to notice—"figured it was his fault."

"I figured it was *my* fault," Austin muttered without turning around.

"Right. So you started getting those dreams about your brother's previous deaths. The ones you'd had something to do with, anyway. But you didn't know that's what was going on. So you spiralled out of control, dragging your little brother with you, and never bothered to even discuss it with each other. Honestly." She rolled her eyes and walked back over to me. "Then, when Kemp couldn't handle the guilty feelings anymore, he tried to kill himself, and Austin tried to stop him. That alone would've helped balance some of that karma. But then Kemp pushed his brother . . ."

"And Austin died," I said quietly.

"Right. Austin experienced the other side of the equation. The one that's repeated over and over in that notebook."

"You know about the notebook?"

She smirked. "I know a lot of things, Ivy. I have connections."

Austin let out a snort and turned around. "Right."

"You're not trapped here, dumbass. You could be as free as I am. The only reason you have the limitations you do is because *you* put them there."

He looked back and forth between us, then looked over at Kemp. *Really* looked. His face seemed to tense. "But . . ."

"Go and talk to him. Wow." Jade rolled her eyes. "You sure know how to pick them, Ivy."

I frowned as I watched Austin slowly glide over to where his brother was standing. "I didn't pick them," I said. "They picked me."

With a wild grin that brought up all sorts of memories, she shook her head. "Do you really think Kemp's aim is *that* bad?" She mimed dribbling a basketball, then shot it over toward the intake desk.

I just stared at her with wide eyes. Abandoning her imaginary game, she grabbed my hand and pulled me past the desk, into the depths of the emergency room. I looked back over my shoulder, only to see Austin standing in front of Kemp, trying to hold on to the latter's shoulders. If you hadn't known any better, you might have thought they could both see each other, that they both occupied the same plane of existence. I didn't know what Kemp was experiencing—if anything—but at least Austin was giving it a shot.

Breakdown and Breakthrough

THE LITTLE ROOM LOOKED COLD, WHICH MIGHT'VE EXPLAINED why the person in the bed was wrapped up in so many blankets. But I knew that was more likely to do with hypothermia than the temperature of the room.

I apparently couldn't breathe on my own, though I didn't know if that was because of what had happened at the creek or because of something the doctors had given me. But all the tubes and wires and whatnot didn't stop Mom from getting close and staying close. At that moment, she was leaning on the bed, her mouth as close to my ear as she could get it, whispering something into it. The fact that I couldn't hear her freaked me out a little, and made me wonder if I was already dead . . . and just didn't know it.

But my heart was still beating. My body was still going, even if there was nothing within to animate it. I sat against the wall beside Jade as I watched the scene crawl forward through time. The window was behind us, above our heads, but I could tell it was still dark outside. The only light in the room came from the wall lamp beside the bed. The overhead lights had been turned off, presumably to help me sleep. Or to keep me unagitated in my coma.

Jade and I kept our heads together, and I closed my eyes for about the hundredth time, trying to calm myself. Aside from Mom, nobody was saying anything. Even Austin had finally shut up, once he'd come back from talking with Kemp. Or talking *at* him. He now stood in the corner, his arms folded, his expression pained. He'd been like that for hours, it seemed, not moving. That was fine with me.

A gentle squeak of rubber forced me to open my eyes, and I saw Dad reappear in the room, a couple of paper coffee cups in his hands. Instead of walking over to Mom, though, he stepped aside to let someone else into the room. I straightened up a little, but didn't loosen my grip on Jade as I watched.

"Linley," Dad said, holding out one of the cups. Mom gently kissed my cheek before she looked up and back, her gaze travelling past the cup to the guy standing beside Dad.

"Kemp." Her voice was a whisper. I didn't know if that was what did it, if it was the choked sound of her voice or what. Kemp blinked, and two tears slid down his cheeks. He sniffed and hastily wiped them away with the back of his hand.

"I'm sorry," he said. "I'm so sorry. This is my fault."

"No," I said, pulling away from Jade and standing up. Kemp reached down to place his hand over mine. I wasn't sure if he'd succeeded, though; my whole body was encased in blankets.

"It wasn't your fault, sweetheart," Mom said, standing so she could pull him into a hug. "And if you hadn't been there, we would've lost her already."

Kemp shook his head and drew away, staring up across the bed and toward the window. For one tantalizing moment, I thought maybe he'd seen me. But then that moment passed and he turned his attention back to my body.

"Is she going to be all right?"

"Of course," Mom said, with all the blind optimism she could muster. Dad, however, shook his head.

"We don't know," he said gently. "The scans were inconclusive. We'll have to see if she wakes up after they withdraw the sedation."

Kemp backed up a step, his eyes widening ever so slightly. I could imagine what he was thinking, those thoughts probably so similar to the ones he'd had before about his brother. I moved forward until I was standing right beside him, close enough that I had to look up.

"Kemp," I said. "I'm all right. No matter what happens, I want you to know that." I reached up and laid my fingers on his cheek. The dark stubble on his jawline was more apparent than I'd ever seen it. I tried to stroke the shadow, but I couldn't touch him. As he reached up to scratch, I pulled back.

"He thinks he damaged *your* brain, too," Austin said. I whirled on him, just in time to see Jade tip her head back with an annoyed glare.

"If you can't say something helpful—"

"What? It's true." He shook his head. "That doesn't mean he's right this time, either." With a sigh, he dropped his hands to his sides. "He still doesn't get it. I'm going to be stuck here forever, aren't I?"

"God, I hope not," Jade muttered. I turned back to Kemp, who was trembling. It was subtle, and I didn't think my parents noticed. Mom slid away from the side of the bed, reluctantly, and took the coffee cup Dad held out to her.

"It's okay," she said to Kemp. "You can talk to her if you like."

But that looked like the last thing he wanted to do. He stared down at me, and then, instead of reaching out, he turned and walked out of the room. Mom and Dad exchanged a glance, probably wondering whether to go after him or just leave him to process his emotions on his own.

"Where's he going?" Jade asked. But I didn't want to wait for Austin to answer. He might not have known, anyway. I slipped out the door and along the hallway, the tugging sensation in my chest growing as I drew farther away from my body, and caught up to Kemp at the elevators. He jabbed the down button with his thumb, over and over again, as if that would make it come any faster.

"Kemp? What are you doing?"

When the doors opened, he rushed inside and hit the button for the lobby. I followed him, looking back just in time to see Jade and Austin gliding toward us. The doors closed before they reached us, though that didn't stop them; they slid through the solid doors a moment later, Jade's hand clamped tightly around Austin's.

"Where's he going?" Jade asked again. I shook my head.

"No idea." I reached up and tried to touch him, but the resulting scratch was far more violent than the last one, leaving him with a series of pink welts on his cheek. "Kemp, can you feel that? Can you hear me?"

He chewed his lip as he stared up at the floors counting down, until at last we reached the lobby. Then he strode out, digging his keys from his pocket. I hurried to catch up.

"No! Kemp, don't do anything stupid. Please. If I wake up and you're not there . . ."

"Kemp! Stop, you little shit." Austin slid in front of him and held his arms out. "Don't you dare do something—" He shuddered violently as Kemp walked right through him. Then he spun around and started after him. "I'm going to haunt your ass if you don't—"

"You won't be able to haunt him if he's dead," Jade pointed out.

"Kemp, stop," Austin said, his voice growing desperate. "Stop!" But no matter how loud he got, his brother didn't seem to hear him.

We followed Kemp out into the darkness of the parking lot, where he found his car and climbed into the driver's seat. For a moment, I had hope that was all it was. He'd just gone out there to cry, to gather his thoughts. But then he started the car. Without even glancing at the other two ghosts to see if they were going to follow, I plunged myself into the passenger seat. A moment later, Kemp tore out of the parking lot so fast I was surprised my ghostly body stayed put.

"Slow down, buddy," Austin said, and I turned to see him—and Jade—sitting in the back seat. He leaned forward and tried to flick Kemp's ear.

"Stop it!" I said, swatting his hand away. "Are you *trying* to get him to crash?"

"No, I'm trying to get him to realize we're here. That we didn't go anywhere."

Kemp's jaw was clenched tight, and his eyes were bright in the lights of the passing vehicles. He slammed his foot on the accelerator and blew through a yellow light, making me squeak in terror.

"Slow down!" Austin roared. But that only seemed to have the opposite effect. The car went faster. Kemp gripped the wheel, his knuckles white. I started to cry.

"Stop, Kemp! Stop! I'm not dead. But you're going to be if you don't—" The bright lights coming right at me as he blew through a stop sign made me scream. I'd never been so scared in my life—or afterlife—and I braced myself for the impact. But instead of the crunch of metal and the shattering of glass, I heard the squeal of rubber and the blast of a horn.

Kemp began to cry as the car slowed. He pulled off the road, down a quiet side street, and finally slammed on the brakes. The car purred as he sat there, breathing hard, tears pouring down his cheeks. A moment later, he reached forward, turned off the engine, and took a deep breath.

"Shit," Austin whispered. But the end of the word was drowned out by the ragged scream that poured out of Kemp's mouth. It seemed to build up from his toes, growing so loud I was afraid he was going to shatter the windows. He slammed his palms against the steering wheel, again and again and again, which had to hurt. Each scream cut to my core, and I didn't want to listen, though I had little choice. I looked back to see Jade sitting there, her eyes wide, her expression a perfect match for Austin's.

"*No!*" The word was barely intelligible as Kemp forced it out on the power of his scream. He struck the wheel again, then gripped it with both hands and shook it as if he were trying to throttle the life out of the car. A last tired scream worked its way out, followed by a huge, choking sob. He leaned forward and rested his forehead on the wheel, gasping through his tears.

I knew it wasn't all for me. As he sank, sobbing, against the wheel, the tension leaving his body, I understood that this was what had needed to happen. The tears he'd kept bottled up for four long years had finally come out, along with all the grief and anger that had gone with them. Carefully, I reached out and placed my hand on his back. I couldn't feel him, but I hoped that—somehow, in some way—he could feel me. He slumped against the wheel, shaking his head as he continued to cry.

"Everything's going to be all right," I said, my hand making gentle circles on the back of his jacket.

"You don't know that," Austin said. "What if you're already dead?"

Jade punched him in the arm. I turned back to Kemp and leaned closer, draping my arm across his back and resting my chin in the general vicinity of his shoulder.

"Then I'll find a way to talk to him. If an ass like you can do it, then I can, too." I moved my hand to the back of his head, my heart aching as I longed to feel his hair between my fingers. He slowly sat up, took a shuddering breath, and let go of the wheel so he could wipe the tears from his cheeks. Then he reached forward and started the car.

"Where's he going now?" Austin asked.

I shook my head. I didn't know. But wherever it was, it was important, because he drove as slowly and carefully as a nervous grandma all the way there.

"Mom?" Kemp whispered. He stood in the doorway to Nina's room, one hand braced on the frame. Austin snorted.

"You'll have to be louder than that, buddy. You know Mom sleeps like a log."

Kemp crept into the room, his feet almost silent on the carpet. Austin glided after him, but I hung back with Jade, clinging to her hand. We watched as Kemp stood at the foot of his mom's bed for a moment, watching her sleep. He took a breath and opened his mouth, then seemed to change his mind. He sat down on the floor, his back against the wall, and began to cry again. His tears were silent this time. Austin sighed as he crouched down beside his brother.

"You need to tell her, or it's going to eat you alive."

"He doesn't *have* to," I said, although I wasn't sure if that was true. Austin shook his head.

"He wants to. He wouldn't have come here if he didn't. But he's scared."

"Wouldn't you be?" Jade asked, squeezing my hand as she turned to me. "Especially if you believed your parents would blame you?"

I stared at her for a moment, understanding she was talking to me as well. But before I could answer, she went on.

"They won't," she said quietly.

Kemp let out a sob. It didn't seem intentional, but it woke Nina up anyway. We heard the blankets rustling before her shadowy form sat up in bed. Likely ruling out the possibility that there was some crying intruder in her room, she whipped her hand over to turn on the light.

"Kemp?"

He pressed his palms over his forehead as he drew his knees up to his chest. Nina got out of bed and walked quickly toward him.

"Habibi. What's wrong?"

"Everything," Kemp managed to get out. He lowered his hands and looked at his mom. What she saw must've alarmed her because she crouched down and grabbed his face in both hands.

"What did you take?"

"Nothing."

"Your eyes are bloodshot."

He twisted his head away and sniffed hard. Seeming to understand that his red-eyed appearance was due to tears and not drugs, her posture softened. She reached out and ran her hand over his hair.

"What happened?"

Kemp drew in a breath as if he were about to speak. But nothing came out. From where I stood with Jade in the doorway, I could see him begin to shake.

"It's okay," Austin said. "Tell her. It'll be okay. You know her as well as I do; she'll never stop loving you."

Kemp took a few more breaths, the struggle in his mind evident. At last, he closed his eyes and bowed his head.

"It was my fault," he said, his voice hoarse and cracking, his words quick and clipped, as if he wanted to get them all out before he could change his mind. "Austin wasn't trying to kill himself. I was. And when he tried to stop me, I pushed him and he fell and hit his head and drowned, and Mom, I'm so sorry. I'm so sorry. I'm so sorry."

Nina didn't say anything, and for one awful moment I

thought maybe Austin had been wrong about how she'd react. But then she crawled closer and pulled Kemp against her. As he began to sob aloud, she kissed his hair.

"I know, habibi. I know."

"No, you don't!" he wailed. "Did you hear what I said?"

"Yes, I heard you." She pressed her nose into his hair so that her next words were muffled. "Your father and I were so worried about you after the car accident. We knew you were struggling. We knew you blamed yourself. But you wouldn't let anyone help you. You wouldn't admit to your feelings." She kissed him again and held his head against her shoulder. "We were told not to push you. We were supposed to let you speak about your feelings in your own time. But you kept them all in, trying to be strong. You never should have had to bear the burden of those feelings. The accident was not your fault."

"But Austin's death was."

"Shush."

"Mom . . ."

"Thank you for telling me."

He shook his head. "Why don't you hate me?" His voice was a choked cry.

"Were you trying to kill him?"

"No."

"Why would I hate my son who has such a big heart and so much love for his brother that he felt responsible when he thought he'd hurt him?"

Kemp began to sob again, leaning heavily against his mom. As he slumped, Nina adjusted her position, drawing his head down to rest on her lap. Her hands gently stroked his head, smoothing his hair back from his brow, brushing the tears from his cheek.

"Your father and I suspected that's what really happened that night," she said softly. "We knew Austin wasn't suicidal. We also knew that he loved you and would've done anything to protect you. The creek was dangerous, especially in the winter. It's as much to blame as either of you."

"Ivy," he gasped. My name seemed to send him into a new round of grief. Nina rubbed his shoulder, waiting patiently for him to go on. "She's probably not going to make it," he managed to choke out.

"What happened to Ivy?"

"She went into the creek. And all because I . . ." His fists clenched and he screwed his eyes shut. "How can you love me? How can *anyone* love me? All I do is fuck everything up."

Detaching myself from Jade, I moved forward, past Austin, who was still sitting beside his brother. I knelt down so I was right in front of Kemp.

"You didn't fuck it up," I said. "I did. I never should've—"

"If you hadn't," Austin said gently, "he never would've opened up."

"That's right," Jade said. "Now he can start to heal."

I turned back to Kemp, who still had his eyes closed. I watched a tear run over the bridge of his nose and drop onto Nina's pyjamas. Bending close, I reached out and laid my hand on his cheek as best I could.

"When this is all over," I whispered, "you and I are going to have a long talk about what really happened."

"Feel free to make me the villain," Austin said. I let out a humourless grunt of laughter.

"Believe me, I will." I brushed my thumb over Kemp's cheek, watching as the tension started to melt from his features. "Can you feel that?" I whispered. He took a shuddering breath and let out a sigh. Nina's hand was still on his head, providing the comfort I longed to be able to give him. All I could do was be there and hope he could somehow feel my presence.

Austin suddenly stood and backed away. I looked up, alarmed at the abrupt movement. He stared down at himself, raising his hands and turning them back to front.

"What is it?" I asked.

"I don't know." He dropped his hands and turned to Jade. "I feel . . . weird."

"Weird?" she repeated, her dark eyebrows rising toward her bangs.

"Yeah. Like . . . lighter. Bigger."

She rolled her eyes. "You're *supposed* to feel like that, dumbass." Turning to me with a smirk, she shook her head. "I think he's finally done it."

"Done what?" I asked.

"Figured it out. Dropped the limitations he put on himself." She turned back to Austin, who was staring down at his brother and mom in disbelief. "You can see everything now, can't you?"

He nodded, awestruck, as he looked around the room. "Wow . . ."

I turned back to Kemp. Though I was happy for Austin, he wasn't my priority at that moment. "I'm here," I said. "Kemp, do you feel it?"

His left hand released from its fist. Maybe I just wanted to believe he'd done it for me. Maybe I just wanted to believe he could hear me, that he knew I was there. Carefully, I reached down and slipped my ghostly fingers into his hand.

"Can *you* feel it?" Jade asked. I shook my head, feeling like I was going to cry. "Then we need to get you back into that body of yours so you *can*."

I looked up to protest, and noticed that she was standing there alone. Pulling away from Kemp, I sat up in surprise. "Where did Austin go?"

"Oh, he'll be back. Now that he can come and go as he pleases . . ." She tilted her head toward the hallway. "Come on, Ivy."

I turned back to Kemp. "But he needs me," I whispered.

"Yeah. He needs you. Alive." She swept forward, grabbed my arm, and pulled me to my feet. "So do Mom and Dad. So do your friends. And your future kids."

"My kids?"

"If you want them."

I shook my head. "Am I going to be able to do *anything* with that body other than lie in a bed and stare at the walls?"

She raised her eyebrow. "I thought you trusted me more than that, Ivy. Do you really think I'd push you back into a body so damaged that you couldn't live a really great life?"

My chin began to tremble, and Jade's skeptical expression morphed into one of concern.

"What?"

"I *don't* trust you," I said. The sob caught me off guard. I swallowed it back as I shook my head. "How can I? You were my identical twin. We did everything together, from the moment we went down the Fallopian tube."

"Yeah . . . so?"

"You *left* me," I said, my teeth clenched as tightly as my fists. "You died and left me here to pick up all the pieces, to have to live a life so big that it would make up for the one you lost. But I can't. I'm not even going to be able to do justice to my own life." The words kept tumbling out. I couldn't look at Jade anymore. I was too afraid to see her expression. So I stared at the quilt on Nina's bed instead, focusing on a giant spray of burgundy blossoms. "You would've had an amazing life. And I would've been content to live in your shadow. But when you died, you weren't there to cast it anymore, and I was exposed. I'm the useless twin. I suck at sports, I suck at art, and I'm supposed to be going to university in September and I have *no* idea what I even want to study because I . . ."

"You what?" she asked gently. I took a deep breath and finally dared to raise my gaze to hers.

"I was the one who was supposed to die, wasn't I?"

She let out a huge sigh and gave me an eye roll even bigger than the ones she'd reserved for Austin. "No, Ivy. You weren't supposed to die. Neither was I. Sometimes things just happen. Would I have liked to finish up that life as your twin? Yeah. Of course! Maybe we'll have another chance to do that sometime."

"What? In another life, you mean?"

"Well, yeah. Don't tell me you don't believe in reincarnation after all this."

I shook my head and turned my back on her to look down at Kemp, who was lying quietly as his mom continued to stroke his hair. "I don't know how I could believe otherwise."

"Every life is different," Jade said, drawing herself close to my ear. "Maybe you started this one out with your twin. But you're going to have to finish it by yourself. That doesn't mean it can't be a great life." She rested her chin on my shoulder as she wrapped her arms around me. I reached up and placed my hand over one of hers.

"I'm scared," I said.

"Yeah. So what? Everybody is. Nobody knows how anything is going to work out, really. The trick is to channel that fear and use it to make your life the best it can be."

I pulled away and turned around to face her. Despite the blue-black hair and the coloured contacts and the shiny ring in her nose, I still felt like I was looking in a mirror. I could see my sister's love, and I knew it was a mirror image of what I was sending her way.

"Are you ready?" she asked.

"To start living again?"

She smiled and nodded. I reached out to take her hand, simultaneously glancing back at Kemp. A wave of affection swept over me, so strong I suspected Jade felt it. She squeezed my hand. "You'll see him soon," she said.

"How do you know?"

As she drew me out the door into the hallway, she cast a mischievous glance back at me. "Just a guess. And maybe wishful thinking." She let out a little laugh and threw her arm around my shoulders. "If I were still alive," she whispered in my ear, "you'd have to fight me for him."

Still Here

As I stood looking down at my lifeless body, a flood of emotions washed over me.

First and foremost was anger: mostly at Austin, for haunting me and getting me out to that creek when he hadn't really known what he was trying to accomplish. I'd been used, and I hated it. But some of that anger was reserved for me, too, because I'd let myself be used. I'd lied to Kemp and gone down to that creek of my own free will. It was partly my fault that my body was lying there, so still.

Next came fear, the terror that nothing would ever be the same, that I would have to spend the rest of my life in a bed, unable to communicate, trapped in a prison of flesh. Even if it turned out my body was fine, I would still have to face Kemp and admit I'd done something *really* stupid. And that I'd lied to him. The thought of losing him over that brought me back to anger, and I cursed Austin for everything he'd put us through.

Jade's fingers were laced through my own as she stood beside me, watching Mom and Dad with a soft smile on her face. Our parents looked tired, and they probably were. The sun was up, slanting greyish light through the window, and they were still sitting upright in their chairs, nursing new cups of coffee. I hated to think how many they'd already had.

"I don't know how to do this," I said. "Do you?"

"Get back in there, you mean?" She shrugged and frowned down at the body in the bed. "Not really."

"I could try lying down on myself. Or . . . in myself?"

She laughed softly. "I don't think so. If it were that easy to take over a body, I would've done it to keep you from falling in the creek."

"Maybe it's easier to take over your own body."

"Maybe."

I watched as Mom set aside her cup and put both of her hands around my right one. I pulled the ghostly version out of Jade's grasp and held it up in front of me, frowning.

"Do you feel something?"

"No," I said, though I was willing it with all my might. "Maybe I'm not even connected to my body anymore."

"I think you are."

"Why?"

"Because you'd know it if you weren't."

I didn't ask her how she knew that. I wasn't sure I wanted to know. My gliding footsteps were silent as I moved around to the other side of the bed. Dad was sitting in a chair there, but it wasn't pulled up right next to the bed, so I had a bit of room. Bending low over my own face, I examined my eyelashes. They were so still; it wasn't like I was sleeping, with my eyeballs moving all about under my eyelids as I dreamed. Though I was still breathing—albeit with the help of a ventilator—the rest of me was as still as ice. It was as if I'd literally been frozen by the creek, and I had yet to thaw.

"There's no rush, is there?" I asked, turning around to face my sister. "Let's go for another walk. Maybe we'll think of a way we can—"

"Ivy." She shook her head. I sighed.

"Yeah. I know."

She walked over and put her arms around me, gathering me into one of her tight hugs. I held her just as ferociously, as if I could fuse myself with her and we'd never have to be apart again. "Maybe you just have to want it," she said quietly, her voice vibrating through me.

"But I don't."

"Don't you? I don't know . . . Hot chocolate, dressing up for Halloween and scaring the neighbours, an awesome attic suite of your very own, university in the fall, grad with a really cute date—"

"He's not going to want to go with me now," I whispered.

"Yes, he will. Like it or not, you guys are connected. And he loves you."

"No, he doesn't."

"What we saw last night? That doesn't happen without love, Ivy. You broke him open so he could start to heal. Even if he doesn't consciously realize it, he knows you helped him." She turned her head so she could kiss my cheek. "Listen," she whispered. "Don't make the same mistakes those boys did. Talk to Mom and Dad. Talk *with* them. Tell them how you're feeling. You might be surprised."

"By what?" I asked.

"Do you think they haven't blamed themselves for what

happened to me? You're all feeling a variation on the same thing. But you're all trying to deal with it by yourselves, each of you locked in your own little puzzle box. It's time to dump out all the contents and start to deal with it. Help each other. Okay?"

"Okay."

"I'm serious. That's my ghost desire."

I let out a short laugh. "Your what?"

"Don't ghosts always want something? Vengeance. To deliver a message. To scare people just for the hell of it." She gave me a squeeze. "This is my desire: I want you and Mom and Dad to open up to each other and start to move past this."

"We won't stop loving you."

She snorted. "I should hope not."

I closed my eyes and rested my head against my sister's. A strange sensation began in my chest, sort of where my heart would've been, had I had one. I sucked in a quick gasp.

"Just go with it," Jade whispered. "It's okay. I've got you."

The bubbling sensation slowly became more solid, turning into something resembling the tug I'd felt the night before when we'd left the hospital. I stayed where I was, with Jade's arms around me, and didn't try to fight it . . . even though I was scared. I tried to imagine myself in the bed, feeling the mattress under my body, the blankets covering it, the pull of the plastic film from the IV, the squeeze of the blood-pressure cuff. I felt my heavy eyelids, the itch of the tape that held the tube in my mouth, and I imagined swallowing . . . but couldn't. I started to gag, and I opened my eyes to find myself staring up at the ceiling. Mom placed her hand on my cheek as she stood up and, as I felt the warmth of her touch, I knew . . .

"It's okay, Ivy. It's okay." She looked up at Dad, who practically ran out of the room. "Relax, all right? It's just a tube to help you breathe."

I knew that, but my body was still rebelling against it, almost automatically. I reached up to try to pull it out, but Mom grabbed my hands and held them down. It was an interminable few seconds before Dad finally returned with a doctor, who released the tape and removed the tube. I coughed and gagged from the irritation in my throat, but when I took a deep breath in, unencumbered and free, it was the best feeling in the world. I started to cry, the relief making me feel like I was never going to stop.

"You're all right," Mom said, smoothing my bangs back from my face. "See, sweetheart? You're all right."

"I'm sorry," I croaked. My voice sounded like I'd gargled with stones from the creek bed. I grabbed for Mom's hand and squeezed it tight. "I'm sorry I almost died."

"But you didn't die," Dad said, pulling his chair up to the other side of the bed and taking my hand as the doctor moved out of the way. "You're still here."

I'm still here, I thought, my bleary eyes searching the room for the last member of the family. But I couldn't see her. *Jade? Are you still here?*

She didn't answer. But as I closed my eyes, anchored by my parents on either side, I could've sworn I felt something whisper against my cheek.

I SWAM IN A HAZE OF DRUGS AND WEARINESS. MY BODY ached. My throat was raw. And, for some reason, I still felt cold. When I curled up on my side to try to conserve warmth, Mom got a nurse to bring me some more blankets. Then I slept fitfully, my dreams a mixture of memories and visions, countless deaths that weren't mine, and one that almost was.

I was sprawled out on my back again, barely able to move thanks to being encased in a tomb of blankets, when I heard the voices. My eyes were closed, my eyelids too heavy to fight. I heard Mom get up and step away, and then—oddly enough—the sound of introductions. Summoning all my strength, I managed to crack my eyelids open. The first person I saw was Nina, her chin resting on Mom's shoulder as they hugged. I dragged my gaze to the side, only to see Kemp standing beside her, staring at me. His hands were shoved deep in his jacket pockets, and his forehead was twitching like he was trying to fight another round of tears. I wanted to tell him he didn't have to hide it, that he could cry if he needed to. But talking was too much work. I let my eyelids slip closed again.

"Do you want to talk to her for a while?" Mom asked.

"I think she's asleep," Kemp said.

"She's been dozing for hours. But she'll be glad you're here."

After I heard their footsteps leave, I didn't hear anything else. In my fuzzy-brained state, I assumed Kemp had left with them. I pulled the blankets up around my chin and turned my head away from the too-bright window.

"Ivy?" The sudden whisper gave me just enough of a jolt

of surprise that I was able to peel my eyelids open. Kemp stood beside the bed, staring down at me. "Hey."

"Hey." I could see him clench his fists in his jacket pockets, his knuckles straining at the fabric. He chewed on his lip for a moment before looking away. I tried to swallow some of the scratchy feeling in my throat and took a deep breath. "I lied," I said.

He frowned and pulled his hands out so he could lean down and brace them on the side of the bed. As I looked up at him, I noticed the pinkness of his eyes and the dusky shadow of stubble on his jaw. His hair was a mess, too. But he was one of my very favourite people, and I was probably going to lose him when he heard what I had to say, so I drank in the sight of him while I could. "About what?" he asked.

"I wasn't trying to kill myself. I only told you that so you'd come."

His eyebrows drew together. "Why did I need to come?"

"Austin thought you did. He thought you needed to tell me what really happened that night." I closed my eyes so I wouldn't have to see him straighten up and walk away. "I'm sorry, Kemp."

He was still there. I could hear him breathing. But I didn't dare open my eyes.

"Did he tell you what I did?" he asked.

"He showed me." I pulled the top blanket up over my face. "If I'd known, I never would've asked you to go down there and relive that," I said, my voice muffled. He didn't say anything. I didn't hear anything at all. The tears started as I realized Jade had been wrong. He was angry . . . and he had every right to be. I couldn't blame him for not wanting to stick around. I scrubbed the blanket into my eyes, then pulled it away, just as a form settled itself down on the bed beside me. I sucked in a little gasp, which made him freeze.

"Am I hurting you?"

"No. But . . ."

He leaned closer and kissed my cheek, then put his arm around me and held me tight. His body was balanced on the edge of the bed, rather precariously. He smelled of morning and winter air and stale cafeteria coffee.

"I'm sorry I lied," I croaked.

"And I'm sorry I didn't tell you the truth." He nuzzled his nose against my cheek. "If I had, none of this would've happened. Would it?"

"You didn't owe me that truth."

"I owed you honesty."

"Why?"

He gave me a little squeeze, and the warmth of his body began to seep into mine. The thaw had finally begun. "Because you should always be honest with the people you love," he whispered, and gave my cheek another kiss before resting his head against my own.

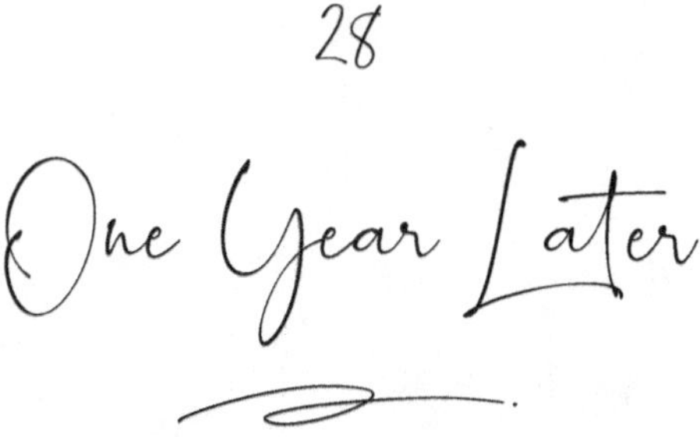

FROM MY PERCH, CURLED UP IN THE NEWLY REUPHOLSTERED chair by my bedroom window, I peered out into the drizzly afternoon. It was almost dark. The sun hid behind the clouds that cocooned the afternoon in a damp chill. My bedroom was a little drafty—especially by the window—but the throw I had wrapped around my shoulders was keeping me nice and warm.

I paused for a moment to tug the throw more tightly around myself. When I was sufficiently swathed, I curled my fingers around the phone and smiled as my thumbs padded over the screen.

Guess what.

what

I got a new boyfriend! This one isn't too lazy to use capital letters or punctuation.

HAHAHA!!!

I couldn't help the giggle that escaped. I bit my lip as I watched the next message appear.

u love the way i text admit it

Never!

He sent an emoji that appeared to be sobbing. I just rolled my eyes.

I do have some news, though.

do tell

Are you trying to text and walk again?

maybe

Be careful. Actually, maybe you should stop for a sec.

y is the news that big

Not really, but you're that oblivious when you're texting. What if you trip over a dog leash and drop your phone in a storm drain?

that was one time

Still.

im fine

Humour me.

There was a pause. A long one.

What are you doing?

sitting

In the rain?

bus shelter tell me now

Okay... Well, remember how I was applying to that interior design program?

yes did u get in

I don't know yet.

u should ur portfolio is great

It's sparse. I might not get in...

u should get in ivy

Well, if I don't, I've decided I'm going to take next year off.

university dropout

High school dropout.

im getting my diploma

After much whining.

He sent a wineglass emoji.

Are you done?

A hysterically laughing yellow face was all I got.

Do you want to hear my news or not?

ur dropping out

That's not the news. Mom got me a summer job.

real estate

No, but close. She knows this woman who runs a home-staging company.

whats that

They make houses look all pretty before they're sold. They take out the owners' crap and then make it look like something out of a magazine.

sounds like ur sort of thing

It'll just be grunt work to start, but I'm told I might get to do a few rooms by myself if I'm any good. So I'll have more for the portfolio.

With a smile, I pulled my gaze away from the phone to stare over at the wall across from the bed. When I'd decided to give my whole room a makeover, that space had been the first one I'd thought of. After getting rid of the massive old dresser (it was still sitting in the garage, Dad's stalled refinishing project), I'd gotten Kemp to paint a whimsical, windswept tree on the wall. It was all in black, a simple silhouette, and reached almost to the ceiling. The branches curved over the sleek new dresser, and I'd hung a dozen carefully curated, black-and-white framed photos in a cluster so that it looked like they were suspended from the branches. There were a couple of old ones of my family—me and Jade and our parents—but the rest were more recent: a group shot of me and my friends in our formalwear for grad; another with just me and Kemp from the same day; a candid shot of me with Rissa and Eunice in our caps and gowns on graduation day; a picture of me and Rissa sitting on the dock near her parents' cabin last summer; one of me and Kemp in matching elf hats and hot-chocolate moustaches at Christmas; and my favourite, the photo of me and Jade that I'd had as my laptop background before she died. That picture, in a rectangular frame, tended to end up askew no matter how many times I tried to straighten it. Dad claimed it was something to do with the settling of the house. I, of course, had another theory.

I realized that the new message alert had sounded a few times. I turned back to find that Kemp had been amusing himself.

This was followed by a string of ghost emojis. With an amused grunt, I bent over my phone.

This was met with a string of various laughing emojis. I smiled, but my heart didn't quite feel it.

I waited while he typed something else. The warmth of the phone was comforting somehow, helping to assuage the loneliness a little. Holding his hand would've been nicer, but I had to take what I could get. At least for the moment.

Taken aback, I blinked. My thumbs hovered over the screen as I tried to think of a response.

i know thats corny but i am u
have changed a lot

I swallowed hard and quickly typed out the only words I could think of.

Is that a good thing?

yeah it is when i met u it was like
u werent sure who to b

I wasn't.

but u r now u know what u want i
dont think u did before

I was flailing.

remember the way u used to bs
the art teacher

Not my finest moments.

u always said u werent an artist
now look at u

My thumbs wavered. I had been about to say that I *still* wasn't an artist. It was so easy to fall back into that, to be that girl who didn't know what she wanted. To be that girl who hid in the shadow of her amazing twin, content to be unnoticed . . . until circumstances forced her out into the light for all the world to see. I was just starting to understand that I *did* have my own talents. Rissa and Eunice had both gushed over my redecorated room. Mom and Dad had said it looked like a professional had done it. Kemp had declared it looked like something out of one of his mom's magazines. There was a part of me that wondered how honest they were being, given that they wouldn't have wanted to hurt my feelings. But the fact that I'd gotten that job with the home-staging company after Mom had shown the owner some photos of my finished room kindled a bit of confidence that felt . . . nice.

I resettled myself in the chair and prepared to type again when a request for a video call popped up. From Kemp. I quickly accepted, only to see his grinning face. He was indoors, though his hair was damp. He appeared to be trudging up the stairs.

"I thought you were sitting in a bus shelter!"

"It's freezing out there. Did you seriously think I was going to stop just to have a chat?"

"You could've tripped."

"I don't think I'm that—" There was a thump and the view hurled in a wide circle before bouncing once. Kemp's chuckle reached me before he could pick up the phone again. "Good thing it's carpeted up here."

"You should be banned from using that thing while in motion."

He shook his head as he stepped into his room and closed

the door. The view steadied a moment later when he put the phone down on the floor, propped up against something. He stretched out in front of it on his stomach and rested his chin on his stacked hands. "Looks dark there," he observed.

"It is. Classic rainy-day afternoon."

"You could turn on a light."

"I'd have to get up. I'm cozy where I am."

He smiled and lifted his hand to brush a few damp strands off his forehead. "I mean it," he said.

"That I should turn on a light?"

He chuckled softly. "That I'm proud of you."

"I'm just doing what I should've done to begin with."

He raised his eyebrows. "Which is . . . ?"

"Come to terms with what happened. Talk about Jade. My parents and I have been talking a lot more. Sometimes, we end up laughing so hard at some of the memories that none of us can breathe. Other times, one of us will start crying, and then we're just this big blubbering mess. But . . . it's good, you know?" Rambling often took over when I started talking about my sister. But Kemp didn't seem to mind. He just lay there and listened, a patient smile on his face.

"Yeah. It helps, right?"

"Some of the memories are fun. You should've seen my parents' faces when I told them how our teetotalling grand-mother got drunk when we were fifteen."

He raised an eyebrow. "Do I want to know?"

"Jade had filled her water bottle with vodka and stuck it in the fridge."

"Whoa. Bold move."

"We all knew not to touch her special bottle. Anyway,

Gran was really particular about her drinks. She always asked for watered-down grape juice. One-third juice, two-thirds water. She didn't like ice in her drinks, but they had to be cold. So, one time, Dad had forgotten to chill the juice or the water. But there was Jade's water bottle sitting there in the fridge . . ."

"Technically, didn't your dad get your grandma drunk?" He raised himself up on his elbows with a frown. "And how did she not notice?"

"No idea. She had three of those cocktails. Maybe she did notice, and she just didn't say anything."

"So what does a drunk grandma look like?"

"Pretty boring, actually. She fell asleep on the couch and had to stay the night because Mom couldn't wake her up to drive her home."

With a chuckle, he shook his head. "Your parents didn't clue in?"

"Nope. Once Jade realized Dad had used her bottle, she poured the rest of the vodka down the drain when he wasn't looking and replaced it with water." I shrugged. "They know now."

"Nice. Ratting out your poor dead sister."

I snorted. "She probably still thinks it's hilarious. Besides . . . what are they going to do about it now? Ground her?"

"I don't know. I'm sure my parents would've liked to ground ghost Austin."

"For what?"

"Turning me on to weed."

"Are you smoking again?"

He gave me a dark look. "Right. You think the cop uncle

I'm staying with would put up with that? Besides, I don't need it. Not now."

"You're different now, too." Adjusting the phone in one hand so I could tug the blanket around my shoulders, I smiled. "I'm proud of you."

"What the hell for? Running half a province away to finish my schooling so I didn't have to face anyone I knew?"

"No. Being brave enough to finish the job."

His eyes widened. "Oh, my god. We're one of *those* couples now, aren't we?"

"What couples?"

"The ones that people can't stand to be around because they're so goddamn *nice* to each other. 'Good job, babe! That was an amazing dinner, babe! Look at that amazing poop! I'm so proud of you.'"

I laughed. "If I ever start praising what you do in the bathroom, you have my permission to break up with me."

"If it's really impressive, I'd like to know."

"Are you done?" I asked, barely able to get the words out because I was afraid I'd laugh again and encourage him. He propped his chin on his fist and grinned.

"Getting tired of me yet?"

"Not quite." I shook my head. "I *am* getting a little tired of this long-distance thing, though. It feels like you've been gone forever."

"I'll be home before you know it. Then we'll spend all our free time together and probably get sick of each other."

"You think?"

He shrugged awkwardly. "I don't know. Probably not. I don't think I'll ever get tired of you."

"What if I attract another ghost and they make you relive another set of deaths?"

"Eh, big deal. Been there, done that."

"Got cut in half by a train."

"Sounds like something that belongs on a t-shirt."

"That would be one gnarly t-shirt," I said. "And you'd constantly be having to explain, and everyone would think you were nuts."

"Aren't we? What happened wasn't exactly . . . normal. Maybe we dreamed the whole thing."

"What? Like some grief-induced fever dream?"

"Maybe."

"That we both shared?"

He shrugged. "Anything's possible. But I don't really care if it was technically real or not. It was real enough to us, right? And the experience brought us closer together." He chewed on his lip for a moment. "Do you wish it hadn't happened?"

"I could've done without the near drowning. But I'm glad I got to see Jade again. And I'm glad you and I got a chance to deal with our issues. So . . . I'm not sorry it happened."

A soft smile played on his lips. "Me, neither."

"They gave us a gift," I said quietly. "If you think about it."

"What gift?"

"Getting on with life. That's what Jade wanted for us. Austin, too. He just didn't go about helping us get there in the most direct way."

"He could be an idiot sometimes."

"Yeah, he could. But his heart was in the right place. He was a good brother. And Jade was a good sister."

Kemp nodded thoughtfully, but he didn't say anything. I

glanced at the clock in the corner of the screen, then peered out the window. Even as we'd talked, it had gotten a lot darker. The streetlights were pretty much the only source of light outside now, bathing the area in a misty glow of highlighted raindrops.

"I should go," I said. "I'm supposed to get dinner in the oven."

"What are you having?"

"Veggie lasagna."

"Can I come over?"

"Can you get here in the next hour?"

He stuck out his lower lip. I laughed.

"I promise I'll make it when you're back."

"Good. I'm so tired of roast beef, I could scream. I could eat about a pound of Mom's falafel right now. Maybe I've turned into a vegetarian from living with her and didn't realize it until I was forced to eat half a cow."

"Technically, I don't think you can call yourself a vegetarian if you're eating roast beef."

"I'm not enjoying it."

"Still."

"Oh, well. A few more months. I just hope my colon can take it." He reached out with one finger and poked at his phone. "Boop."

"Oh, my god," I said. "Don't."

"What? It's cute."

"*You're* cute. That's just weird."

He laughed. "Okay, fine. That'll have to wait until you're home, too."

"Don't you dare."

He wiggled his eyebrows. I just rolled my eyes.

"Talk to you tomorrow?" I asked.

"Of course." He sat up and grabbed his phone. With the awkward angle, I was kind of looking up his nose. But I didn't mind. "I love you, Ivy."

"I love you, too," I said, and quickly ended the call before either of us could say something silly. We were still trying to figure out the whole affection thing . . . with mixed results.

Noticing the low battery, I turned off my phone and plugged it in, then turned on the lamp on the nightstand. The simple fixture gave off a lot more light than the old stained-glass one, but still bathed the room in a warm glow. As I rounded the bed and stepped past the dresser, I happened to glance at the wall and noticed that the picture of me and Jade was off-kilter. Again. I reached up and nudged it back into place with my thumb, then took a moment to look at the rest of the photos. That wall made me happy. Sometimes that happiness was bittersweet, but, more often than not, it was just a calm joy. So focused was I on a selfie with Kemp at the beach that the slight scraping noise caught me off guard. My gaze snapped back to the photo of me and Jade just as the righthand corner of the frame dipped by half an inch.

"I love you, too, Jade," I said. "But I've got an aesthetic going here, and it doesn't include crooked picture frames."

I could almost hear her laughter as I straightened the frame once more before heading down to the kitchen to put the lasagna in the oven.

About the Author

Nissa Harlow wanted to be a writer from the time she was a small child, but it took a while before she finally did anything about it. In the meantime, she worked as a volunteer day-camp counsellor, a movie extra, and a digital-photo editor. She even once worked on a conveyor belt in a chocolate factory (which was as stressful—and delicious—as it sounds). These days, she lives in British Columbia, Canada and writes the types of stories she wants to read.

nissaharlow.com

Two Between Worlds

www.ingramcontent.com/pod-product-compliance
Lightning Source LLC
Chambersburg PA
CBHW051211190726
48288CB00006B/1912